UNDER A SUNBURNT SKY

LILLY MIRREN

black lab press

Epub ISBN: 978-1-922650-10-8

Paperback ISBN: 978-1-922650-13-9

Version 1.0

Published by Black Lab Press 2022

Lilly Mirren has asserted her right to be identified as the author of this Work in accordance with the Copyright, Designs and Patents Act 1988.

Though based on a true story and real people, this is a work fiction and of the author's imagination.

Cover design by Erin D'Ameron Hill.

First published worldwide by Black Lab Press in 2022.

Brisbane, Australia.

www.blacklabpress.com

In 1943, approximately 9.5 million Jews lived in Europe.
This number represented 1.7% of the population of Europe and more
than 60% of the world's entire Jewish population.
Poland's Jewish populace was the largest, with three million within
its borders, the majority of whom resided in the capital of Warsaw.
By 1945, the number of remaining Jews in Europe totalled 3.5 million.
Only 45,000 were left in Poland.

For Janek Kostanski (24.06.1925 - 19.11.2010), who I never met, but who has given me hope that there is yet good in the world.

"We saw ourselves as a Jewish underground whose fate was a tragic one, the first to fight. For our hour had come without any sign of hope or rescue."

— YITZHAK ZUCKERMAN (JEWISH
UNDERGROUND FIGHTER)

I

I love a sunburnt country, a land of sweeping
    plains,
Of ragged mountain ranges, of droughts and
    flooding rains.
I love her far horizons, I love her jewel-sea,
Her beauty and her terror—the wide brown
    land for me!

— DOROTHEA MACKELLAR, 1904

2ND JANUARY 1983

MELBOURNE, AUSTRALIA

The kettle whistles as the water passes its boiling point, and my wife is pouring our *herbata* tea. One of the many everyday habits that bring peace and contentment to our lives. We like our traditions; the routine of the mundane is something too many take for granted.

She sets down the tea tray on the table between us and sits beside me on the small brushed-steel chair with the bird-print cushion. I watch her every move with interest. How did we find each other? How can love last the way it does? These questions will never have an answer other than fate or divine destiny, I suppose. But can we believe in those things now, in spite of all we've been through? Rather, perhaps destiny is proved true because of it.

We sit side by side and sip our tea. She talks about the

garden and the hive of native bees she bought at the market to help pollinate her blooming flowers. I nod and interject with thoughts every now and then, but my mind is elsewhere. I'm poring back through the past. The memories slap into me unbidden, like the flap of gull wings in the air when I'm carrying butcher's paper filled with hot chips across the beach, my feet slipping in the scalding sand.

I close my eyes.

"Jan, you're crying," she says in Polish.

My eyes blink open, and I raise a hand to my wet cheeks.

I want to tell her it's nothing. Not to worry, just a speck in my eye. But she knows. I can't hide these things from her.

Instead, I reach for her hand and squeeze it, unable to speak.

"We don't have to go if you don't want to," she says gently.

I shake my head and swallow down the lump in my throat. "No, I want to." I reply in Polish too. I've never been very good with languages. She's much better than me, so we still use our native tongue when we're alone together.

"It's important, *Doniosły,*" she adds with an encouraging nod.

"I know. I don't think about the past often enough, that's all. Mama doesn't talk about it either. But perhaps she should. Perhaps we all should."

"When it's pushed down so deep, it hits you here," she says, her eyes brimming. *Uderzenie.* She taps her chest softly with two fingertips.

I squeeze her hand again, then reach for my tea and take a sip. "We'll go. It will be good. Good for Mama and the boys. Good for our friends, to help them see."

"They don't know," she agrees. "They don't understand."

"No," I say. And it's all that needs to be said.

They can't possibly understand. They weren't there, with us. They were here, in this distant land, so far away from it all. They think they know, but they don't. They want to understand, but they can't. They still think people are good, like naïve children who've never had to face the truth. They are blind.

Evil lurks in human hearts. One can often find goodness in a heart too. But which heart is which? How can anyone determine which of their friends will turn them in with a kiss on the cheek for a few silver coins, and which will give his life to save them?

I've lived in this place since 1958, and yet I sometimes still feel like an alien. That's what they called us when we first came here all those years ago. We were resident aliens. We couldn't speak the language—we didn't understand anyone around us. The culture was foreign, the people polite and welcoming, but unknowable to us. We were traumatised and exhausted and didn't fit in or feel at home for such a long time. But we were happy all the same. Happy because we were finally free and safe.

We've raised our family here. I've built businesses too, businesses that have thrived and given me the opportunity to get to know the people who live around us in ways I wouldn't have otherwise. We've been protected, loved and happy here. But lately, Poland has been drawing me back in.

My thoughts turn more often these days to the land of my birth, the people I used to know but whom I left behind in the rush and hurry of getting away. People who were so precious to me then, but now are gone. Their voices no more than a whisper in the deep recesses of my mind.

My sons don't understand. This place is all they know. This life of sunshine, freedom and waves, is the only one they've had. They tell me they can't comprehend the things I've done, the places I've been, the horrors I've seen. They don't listen for long when I speak of it. It's too much for them to take in, and I don't blame them. It's too much for any of us, even those who lived it.

For me, the memories are vague. Colourless around the edges, as though they happened to someone else while I watched from a distance. But it was me who stood there on the precipice of humanity's condemnation, a witness to the destruction of the world from the centre of the flames.

There's a photograph hanging on the wall in the living room of a family a world away. My family before we were linked by marriage. The family of my wife's birth. Most of them are gone now, but the image of their faces lingers on in our memories and shine out of the photograph to grab hold of my heart and shake my emotions when I least expect it.

It's not the things I did back then, but the things I didn't do that stumble into my thoughts these days. The things I could've said. Did I say them? It's hard to recall. My former self appears mute when I file back through the events of the past. What words were spoken? Did the friends and family I've lost know how much I loved them? Did I tell them, or was it an agreement between us that we never acknowledged but always knew?

For years, I ran over the memories so infrequently, they've turned soft and malleable. I can transform them into a moving, shifting, abstract thing as easily as swiping a water-colour paintbrush over canvas. But that's not what I want. I want the truth to stick in my mind, to be only what it was. Nothing more or less than that.

They're giving me an award, they say. I don't know how to respond. The things I did were done because there was nothing else that could be done. If I hadn't, it would've changed everything. I wouldn't have married her, there'd be no children occupying every moment of our lives. This home wouldn't exist.

Would we still live back there, in the place that became a

wasteland of rubble and grief? Would we even know each other?

There's sunshine outside. The land is warm and sweet. Prisms of light reflect off fat droplets of rain that squat on bending stems of dark green grass. Flowers dot the backyard with brilliant displays of colour. And we will sit a while longer to stare out over the yard while we sip our tea, chat about life and enjoy the hum of bees and the morning sun on our feet. The sun here is too hot to stay for long—we'll hide in the shadows of the cool house shortly. But for now, I revel in the scent of fresh-mown grass and fallen rain.

I've heard it said that love is hard to find. But for me, discovery was the easy part. Keeping it seems to me to be the most difficult thing. Love creeps up on you and launches itself at you with a shout of joyful victory and you find yourself tumbling downhill at top speed, with love laughing in your ear.

It's the holding on that takes work. And I've held on to her with every fibre of my being and every breath in my lungs for so many years, I can't imagine a life without her. Everything we've been through, so much love and terror all rolled into one broken, beautiful whole. She *is* my heartbeat. There is nothing for me without her.

My eldest says he's looking forward to the ceremony. I know I should be excited to go, but I don't know how to feel, only that there's something gnawing at my insides and a lightheadedness that makes me want to run in the opposite direction. But my wife says that it's time for the world to be reminded of the past. We can't afford for them to forget.

She says it's our duty to expose evil. When I remind her that the worst kind of evil was done by ordinary people, her lips pull tight, and she stares into the distance. She won't talk then, I know. Not for hours. It's the ordinary nature of those capable of the blackest evil that we both find the hardest to reconcile.

Evil lies hidden beneath the surface. It festers and grows when fed with hate. But before the evil manifests like a shark's fin slicing through the ocean's surface, it's impossible to foretell which, good or evil, each heart will choose. Until it's too late.

15TH OCTOBER 1940

WARSAW'S OLD TOWN, POLAND

Janek Kostanski jogged along the cobblestone street and jumped up onto the footpath just as an automobile rattled by. It blew its horn at him as it trundled through a throng of pedestrians and bicyclists outside St. John's Archcathedral.

He slowed to a walk, ducking between a woman pushing a perambulator and a trio of girls wearing matching calf-length dresses and overcoats. The girls giggled at him, and he flashed them a grin. His arms swung freely at his sides, and he dipped his head in greeting at people as he passed.

Two elderly Jewish men crossed his path, deep in conversation, heads bent together and hands gesticulating. White armbands with blue stars flashed stark against their dark clothing. They wore long, black coats over woollen shirts, with *kaszkiet* on their heads, the workers' caps that'd replaced the traditional *yarmulke*. The *yarmulke* was banned when the Germans had invaded Warsaw six months earlier. The distinct headwear changed overnight.

He skirted around them and overheard the words *"Judenrat"* and *"ghetto"* spat from their mouths like poison. Those were words he'd heard more frequently these days, but still didn't mean much to him. He wasn't interested in politics or the musings of adults.

Ever since the Germans invaded Warsaw, people had predicted disaster, but so far, life had carried on. The utter chaos of the German attacks on the city had ended, and the noise and cloying fear that had saturated the atmosphere through a haze of smoke and ash had subsided. He hated to see the fascists parading around the city, but they allowed him to do mostly as he pleased.

There were anti-Jewish posters everywhere now. Nazi propaganda had been accompanied by an uptick in violence against the Jewish citizens of Old Town for months before the invasion, but it'd escalated the moment the *Wehrmacht* marched into the city.

One such poster was pasted to the side of a building across from the cathedral. The poster was white with a picture of a scientist looking into a microscope, alongside a spider with a human face and elongated nose. It read, *"Tuberculosis Syphilis Cancer are curable…It is necessary to finish the biggest curse: The Jew!"* The sight of it sent a shiver down his spine and he pulled his overcoat tighter, then shoved his hands deep into its woollen pockets.

Jan took the stairs to the cathedral two at a time, paused on the threshold to cross himself, and strode inside. Saint John's on *Świętojańska* Street was a large Gothic structure in orange brick with tall, rounded windows on a sharply reaching façade that towered high on either side to a pinnacle. Jan paused in the entry and glanced up. Vertigo swept over him, and he inhaled a sharp breath. He tipped the cap from his head and crumpled it in one hand, then stepped inside.

At fifteen years of age, he'd taken it upon himself to come once per week and light a candle for his father, who'd left them several years before the war in Europe began. Perhaps he'd return one day, if only Jan prayed hard enough. Surely he couldn't mean to stay away forever.

Mama, Jadzia and Danuta didn't speak of him any longer, but Jan missed his father more than he could express. He was gone, Mama had said, and there was nothing more to discuss on the subject. Only where had he gone? And why? Jan hadn't found the answers to his questions. He couldn't help wondering if his father's leaving had something to do with him, though Mama had assured him once that it didn't. Now, he thought about finding his father and asking him all the questions that lingered in the back of his mind daily.

He hurried down the centre aisle beneath the arched dome of the basilica, with its crisscrossed brickwork against the white plaster, and knelt quickly at the altar. He crossed himself again and recited *Our Father*. Several women dressed in black knelt in pews dotted throughout the cathedral. Black shawls covered their heads and they murmured quietly, hands clasped together in front of them.

A man sat on the first pew, staring at his gnarled hands. Two boys giggled from the vestibule, where the table of candles stood. One shushed the other. Jan walked to the vestibule and sent the children a brief smile before taking a match from a jar. He used it to draw the flame of a candle and light one of the others standing upright on the table. He began a prayer for his father, but the words stuck in his throat.

What was the point of praying for a man who'd abandoned them? That was what his sister Jadzia said whenever she discovered where he'd been.

"He left us. He doesn't care about us. I hope we never see him again." She spat the words with fire in her eyes.

But Jan knew she didn't mean it. She missed their father as much as he did. Danuta barely remembered him. Surely when he heard about the invasion of Warsaw, he'd want to find them, to make certain they were okay. Perhaps he'd even want to take them away from here.

The cathedral was promptly filled with the chiming of bells. It was noon, time for him to get back to the market and help Mama. Two priests stood on the other side of the basilica, talking quietly between themselves. They glanced up in surprise as strong hands flung the cathedral doors open and shouts echoed through the building. Jan stopped short of the aisle and shuffled into the vestibule by the candle table again, then peeked around the wall.

German soldiers filed inside. One near the front, dressed in the black uniform of the SS, strode into the cathedral, hands clasped behind his back. He surveyed the room, his gaze fixing on the two priests. He shouted something in German and pointed at the men. Jan knew enough to understand what he'd said — *there they are*. He watched in horror as several *Wermacht* soldiers marched to where the priests stood, questions lingering on their lined faces.

"Can I help you?" asked the elder priest.

The soldiers raised their rifles and shot them both in the head. The priests crumpled to the floor as one of the women seated nearby screamed.

The noise of the gunshots reverberated around the building. The women shrank down behind the pew's timber structure. The soldiers turned at the sound they made and fired into the pews. The man seated in the front began to run. They shot him in the back. The SS officer in charge shouted something else, and the soldiers spun on their heels and headed for the cathedral's inner chamber.

The boys in the vestibule huddled trembling, in a corner of the small room. Jan raised a finger to his lips to quiet them, then beckoned them forward. They crawled to him, stood, shaking, to their feet.

His heart thundering, he studied the exits. He had to get them out of there, but the man in black blocked the door at the entrance and the soldiers had used the exit in the back of the building, the only other door within the cathedral proper. He slipped out of the vestibule and slid along the wall in silence, his eyes wide, heart pounding. The other children followed his lead. He could hear their panting as though it was amplified. His own heart held a steady drumbeat in his ears.

One of the children, a small boy, began to cry. Jan glared at him, nostrils flared, until he stopped. They continued on their way, edging along the wall. The man in black peered through the front doors. A soldier ran inside and handed him a sheet of paper.

"*Entschuldigung, Oberführer* Meisinger..."

Jan had heard of Meisinger. Everyone in Warsaw knew of him, but he'd never seen him in person before. He cut an imposing figure in his black uniform, with jaunty black cap perched on his perfectly smooth brown hair. His eyes were piercing and empty as they searched the shadows at the edges of the cathedral. Known as the Butcher of Warsaw, he headed up the dreaded *Einsatzgruppe IV*, a paramilitary death squad whose entire purpose was to kill.

Wherever Meisinger went, peopled died. The rumours that followed him sent a chill down Jan's spine. Mama said she didn't want Jan listening to such rot, but he told her he couldn't help it. People talked and he listened—it was the curse of his open demeanour. When she laughed, he knew he'd won the argument.

Her attempts to keep him a little boy while war waged all around them were futile. They both knew it. He'd grown up the day his father left home and again when the Nazis goose-stepped into Warsaw. Innocence was gone from Warsaw, and in its place languished a black kind of evil that no one could ignore, not even the small boy sniffling beside him against the cathedral wall.

"Quiet or I'll leave you behind," Jan threatened in a whisper as the two Germans raised their voices, arguing loudly.

More shots rang out from the back of the church, the space behind the cathedral where the priests lived and worked. Jan's heart was in his throat as he lowered himself to the floor and crept towards the basilica's tall, arched entrance.

Meisinger slapped the soldier across the face with a shout, the sound reverberating in the basilica. He shoved the paper at the soldier and jogged towards the back of the church, one hand on the holster at his hip. The soldier folded the paper and pushed it into his coat pocket, pressing one hand to his cheek for a moment as he glared at the *Oberführer*'s retreating back, then spun away from the children and headed outside.

This was their chance.

Moving quickly now, Jan crawled closer to the door with the two children not far behind him. He looked at them, gave a nod, then leapt to his feet and sprinted for the door. The children following, he ducked through the doorway even as Meisinger yelled for them to stop. Footsteps thundered as if a hundred elephants were after them, but Jan didn't look back. He leapt down the stairs and ran into the street, nimbly taking cover behind a rickshaw filled to bursting with three men all dressed in black and sporting fashionable fedora hats.

The men barely fit in the tiny vehicle, and the rickshaw driver huffed and puffed along behind them on his bicycle. The man in the centre overflowed onto his fellow passengers, his arms resting down the middle of their chests. Neither seemed bothered by it. All three men ignored Jan and each other.

The two children who'd followed Jan in his escape from the cathedral melted into the passing crowd. Several *Wermacht* soldiers joined Meisinger in searching first one way down the street, then the other. Jan remained behind the rickshaw, keeping up with it at a slow jog, and checking sporadically around the tightly packed men to watch the soldiers in their hunt for him.

Finally, with a nod and a wink at the rickshaw driver, he skipped behind a passing truck and onto the footpath that edged the road. Behind him, guns fired, followed by screams that echoed and caused a panic of people running for cover behind wagons, into shops and around corners. The acrid scent of burning wood drifted in the air, filling his lungs as he sprinted away.

By the time he'd reached the *Hala Mirowski* market, he was puffing hard. He jogged through the marketplace, waving and tipping his hat at the vendors he passed. He couldn't wait to see Mama and tell her what'd happened. The Catholic community in Warsaw had been certain the Germans would leave them alone. They were after the Jews, not the Christians, some had said in hushed voices when concerns were raised about the invaders' intentions for the close-knit community of Old Town, where Jews and Catholics lived side by side in the crowded tenements.

He slowed his pace as he neared Mama's stall. With his chin high and his chest poked out, he walked through the markets as if he owned them. He loved it there, with all the noise and bustle of commerce. Mama had trained under their neighbour, Antoni Wierzbicki, to become a trader. She didn't know how she would provide for her three children after her husband walked out.

In the years since, Jan had come to know the marketplace like it was his own backyard. Every street and alley, each stall and vendor—he recognised them all, and understood how everything worked together to provide food and supplies for the people of Old Town.

Mama's stall was a humble one near the back of the market. To get there, he passed a line of tents where the smallest vendors had set up their fruit and vegetable stands to sell items they'd grown in their kitchen gardens, or shawls they'd knitted at home before the fire.

But the grandeur of the market couldn't be fully appreciated until he stepped inside the looming, two-story building with its curved ceiling and long, narrow aisles. It was a massive marketplace where everything imaginable was bought and sold, haggled and bargained over. Mama was a trader. She shared her tiny pocket of space with Antoni, where they kept the things they intended to trade or the items they'd already traded. They found supplies that buyers needed, they haggled with vendors, and they traded for a profit.

The market was busy with people looking for a bargain. Shoppers stooped over tables, inspecting hand-sewn leather satchels or long coats made from the finest wool. Bags of rice, flour and barley were stacked along the aisles and tucked in corners, while housewives quibbled over the food their families would eat and farmers watched the fruits of their labour walk away slung over stooping shoulders, hidden in cloth bags, or tucked into wagons and trolleys.

Mama was in the middle of a heated discussion with a man. Beside him rested a wooden hand wagon piled high with large bags of flour. Antoni was nearby at a fruit stall, counting coins into the vendor's hand while the man bobbed his head, smiling around a pair of missing front teeth.

Antoni was no longer able to own a stall or trade since the Germans had banned Jews from conducting business, but he still came to Mama's stall each day and helped her, for which she paid him under the table. If the Germans ever came to inspect the market, he would scurry through the door behind their stall into the labyrinth of hallways and storage rooms hidden beyond the wall.

Jan waited impatiently for Mama to finish her trade. He hopped from one foot to the other, the cold afternoon air slicing through his woollen pants and setting loose a trail of goose pimples across his knobby knees. Sweat cooled down the middle of his back, and he shivered.

Mama faced him with a quirked eyebrow. "Janek, you're late."

"I know, Mama. But there's something I must tell you."

She tucked coins into a money pouch and hid it in a secret pocket of her skirt with a deft flick of the wrist that no one else but him could see. "Help me with this flour. It's a good haul. We'll be able to move it before sundown, if I'm right. And for a nice tidy profit."

Jan heaved a bag onto his shoulder and carried it through the stall and out the door to their cramped storage space filled with spices, fruits and vegetables, canned goods and clothing that Mama had traded for that day.

He talked as he worked, Mama overseeing where he put the flour and half listening. It felt to Jan as though she only ever listened to him with one ear. Her brow would furrow in concentration as he spoke, but when he asked a question, she rarely answered him the first time—only after he repeated himself with frustration lacing his voice did she respond to his requests.

"They shot the priests, Mama," he whispered in a furious voice.

He had her full attention. Her eyebrows drew low, and she leaned in close. "What? What are you saying, Jan?"

"The *Einsatzgruppe* was there…with that devil, Meisinger. I lit a candle for Tata."

Frustration flitted across her pretty face.

Jan grit his teeth, but continued with his story. She didn't understand why he held on to the past, and usually his prayers for his father would result in an argument between the two of them that could carry on into the evening hours. But not today. There were more important concerns.

"They came into the cathedral while I was there and shot the priests in the head. Didn't give them a warning. They weren't provoked. They killed some of the old women praying as well."

Mama's eyes widened, and she gasped. Then she crossed herself and said a silent prayer, her lips moving mechanically. "Why? This is wrong. They did nothing to deserve that."

He nodded, feeling a growing tightness in his throat for the first time since it'd happened. "I got out of there."

She squeezed his arm, then kissed his forehead. "It's not safe on the streets tonight. Go home to your sisters and take care of them for me, *mój syn*."

He didn't want to leave her there alone. "But what about you, Mama?"

"I'll be fine. Antoni is here with me. I've got to finish trading." She raised an arm and waved it about at the stock of goods surrounding them. "But as soon as I'm done, I will return home."

Jan hesitated a moment, then with a brief nod of his head, he ran out of the stall and headed for home.

֍ 3 ֍

The mould-covered concrete walls of the apartment building at 9 Mirowski Square hid a happy household inside. The Kostanski home was on the ground floor and opened out onto a courtyard behind and onto a square in front that looked out over the market. The four of them had lived there together since German bombing had forced them out of their home in a housing estate on Krochmalna Street.

Jan raced along the footpath in front of the building, then banged on the door for one of his sisters to let him in. Jadzia, his nine-year-old sister, opened the door with a frown.

"Why all the noise? Use your key for heaven's sakes, Jan." She liked to act as though she was his mother, which irritated and amused him depending on his mood.

"I left it at home," he replied, barging through the door and past her into the dark, cramped space.

The scent of freshly baked bread filled the kitchen, and his stomach growled. He headed for the source of the smell and reached out a hand to take a bread roll cooling on the bench. Jadzia slapped it away.

"Hey," he exclaimed. "I'm hungry."

"It's still hot," she said with a tutting noise. "You'll burn your tongue."

"I don't care," he pouted. "My stomach is caving in. And it smells so good."

She smiled then and her face lit up. Her neatly curled brown hair fell to her shoulders and her blue eyes were large and piercing, just like his own, though his hair was blonder than hers and she often moaned that it wasn't fair because he didn't care either way and she'd always wanted straight, blonde hair just like his.

"Fine. Burn yourself for all I care," she said.

With a grin, he grabbed the bread and shoved it into his mouth. He took a gigantic bite before searching the ice box for some butter to slather over the dark, grainy roll.

"Why are you home early?" asked Danuta, his youngest sister, coming in the back door with a basket full of neatly folded clothing tucked beneath one arm. At seven years old, she had a slight build with dark hair and eyes. Her pale skin made her eyes seem black in her narrow face.

Jan chewed with loud smacking sounds designed to irritate his sisters. "Mama sent me home. The German soldiers shot the priests." He intended his words to shock, but the look of horror on his sisters' faces sobered him momentarily.

"The priests?" Jadzia gaped.

Danuta's eyes filled with tears. She sniffled. "I wish Mama would come home."

"She's fine. She's at the market with Antoni. She told me she'd come home soon. Why don't we go across the courtyard to the Wierzbickas' until then? They won't mind, and I'll bet they have something we can eat."

"All you think about is food," spat Jadzia, wiping her nose with the back of her hand.

Danuta set the clothes basket on the floor and raised her chin. "I want to see Babcia and Papa."

"They're not our grandparents," replied Jadzia, bending over to meet Danuta's gaze and tugging her cardigan more tightly around her thin shoulders.

"Yes, they are," she objected with a sniffle. "Aren't they, Jan?"

He shrugged. "The only ones we've got now. Come on, wrap up and we'll go. It's getting cold in here."

The girls wrapped themselves in woollen shawls and tugged boots over their thick socks. Jan pulled on his overcoat and the three of them shut the back door behind them, then trudged through the small courtyard that joined two rows of apartments.

The shrubbery in the courtyard was dry and bedraggled. Weeds slouched along the base of the building's walls. A bicycle rested on the wall next to the front door opposite the Kostanskis' house. The sky was grey and overcast. It would be hard to tell when the sun set, since the gloaming cast such a dull light over the neighbourhood.

The two families had chosen apartments connected by a courtyard so they could spend time together. If they couldn't live together, they wanted to be as close to one another as they could. Antoni Wierzbicka was a widower. His wife had died years earlier and left him with two children to raise. He lived with his children, Nathan and Nacha, his elderly parents, his brother Berek, along with Berek's wife, Berkowa, and their two children, Fela and Jakob.

Waltrina Kostanska, Jan's mother, was a divorcee. She'd met Antoni years earlier when she was coming to terms with her newly single life and they became close, their families knit together more tightly through the adversity of German assault on their city, and subsequent occupation.

Jan and his sisters burst through the back door of the

Wierzbicka house and into the living room. Nacha and Nathan sat cross-legged on the floor with a small box between them housing a stack of cards piled up like a multi-story building.

Nathan threw up an arm as if to protect the structure. "Watch it!"

Laughing, Jan thundered past them into the kitchen, where he found Babcia standing over a pile of steaming hot *cebularz*, a wheat bun topped with onion. He stopped at the bench, eyes wide, staring at the treats.

Babcia chuckled. "Go on, take one. You need fattening up." She smiled, the creases around her eyes deepening. She wore a dark wraparound dress with a fur trim. Her dark hair was laced with grey, but her brown eyes sparkled with mischief.

He grabbed a *cebularz* and took a bite, relishing the sweet flavour of the onion mixed with the salty bread.

"How was it for Antoni and Waltrina at the market today?" asked Papa. He was the grandfather Jan always wished he'd had. His own on his mother's side had died. His father's parents lived in a remote part of Poland, and he hadn't seen them since the war broke out.

Papa wore a buttoned shirt with a cardigan pulled loosely over the top. His brown hair was carefully groomed to one side, and his cheekbones were accentuated by two red circles that grew more vibrant in the cold weather.

"Good, I think," replied Jan around a mouthful of *cebularz*. Babcia handed him a plate of steaming *pierogi* stuffed with chopped liver and spices and topped with braised sauerkraut. His stomach grumbled in anticipation. He sat at the kitchen table with Papa, who shone his shoes with black polish and a well-used rag. An old towel was carefully laid out beneath his shoes and a pot of black polish.

He dipped a small brush into the polish and rubbed it

across the leather. "Good, good. There are many mouths to feed. It is good the business continues thriving even when the Nazis come. They can't stop enterprise, it seems."

Barek jogged down the stairs, his shirt sleeves rolled up and red suspenders showing. "Oh, hello, Jan."

Jan nodded, his mouth too full to speak. He swallowed the *pierogi*. "Where's Jakob?"

"He's working," replied Berek. "Fela, too. I'm sure you'll see them later. Itching for a game of football, are you?"

Jan's smile gave him away. "If the weather holds."

"Going to be the next Ernest Wilimowski, I'll bet," added Papa as he set aside one gleaming shoe and reached for the other.

"Get those shoes off my table," complained Babcia, playfully flicking a dish towel at her husband.

He clucked his tongue. "Leave me be, woman. I'm not bothering anyone."

She rolled her eyes, but didn't say anything else. Berek winked at Jan, who smiled around a *pierogi*. He loved their playful banter. It was so much better to be here, in the warm apartment filled with love, than at home with his sisters when Mama wasn't there. The three of them agreed on that, at least.

Jadzia had joined Nathan in a game of cards, and Danuta had convinced Nacha to bring out one of her old dolls. They were dressing it and undressing it, arguing over names and setting out chipped cups and cracked plates on the timber floor for a pretend meal of coffee and bagels.

Papa finished polishing his shoes and set them by the front door. Then he quickly cleaned up his mess on the kitchen table. He raised his arms and waved them around, eyebrows arched, as if to say, "See?"

Babcia rolled her eyes again and huffed, but the corners of her mouth twisted upwards.

Papa reached for his violin case where it sat in the corner of the room. He opened it and began tuning the instrument.

"What do you say, children? Shall we have some music?"

Berek filled a plate with *pierogi*, kissed Babcia on the cheek, and sat at the table beside Jan. He hunched over his plate, eating ravenously.

"Yes, please!" shouted Jan, along with a chorus of assent from the other children who'd leapt to their feet and rushed to the kitchen table.

Papa laughed and drew his bow over the strings. "Let's see. What shall I play?"

"*Nigun Cracow!*" called Danuta, clapping her hands together joyfully.

Jan sniffed. "You always ask for the same song."

"I like it," she said, her nose wrinkling as she poked out her tongue at him.

"No fighting," called Babcia from the kitchen.

Papa launched right into the song. He stood to his feet, the bow dancing across the violin strings, and moved into the living room. Each step he took was in steady rhythm with the notes he played. He stood in one corner and, as he continued to play, his foot tapped on the floor in time to the music.

Nacha grabbed Jadzia by the hand and spun her around. She giggled as she slammed into Berek. He picked her up and tossed her into the air until she squealed, then set her down as Danuta begged to have a turn.

Jan finished his meal, his stomach satisfyingly full, and joined them in the small, square room, doing his best impression of a jig around the space without tripping over anyone else or the sparse furniture.

Nacha and Jadzia danced together around the couch, round and round until they collapsed in a pile, too dizzy to keep going. Berek threw Danuta into the air over his head until his arms couldn't manage another toss. Jan and Nathan spun in circles until he could no longer see straight to stand. And all the while, Papa played, his song speeding up with each pass.

Babcia came in from the kitchen and watched them all with a smile as she wiped her hands on a white apron pulled taut around her waist. Then she tossed the apron aside, lifted her skirts, and began to dance. Her feet tapped to the left, then the right, then back again. Before long, everyone else had joined in a circle around the couch. Left, right, left, right, then a shuffle forward and a spin to the back.

When Mama and Antoni came through the back door and hung up their coats and scarves on the coatrack, the expression on their faces made everyone stop. Papa's violin fell silent along with all the tapping feet.

"What is it, son?" asked Papa, his face grim.

Antoni exchanged a look with Mama, who squeezed his hand and offered him a wan smile. "The *Judenrat* has issued a declaration signed by Governor Fischer. They've pasted posters all over the Jewish sector and Old Town."

"What do the signs say?" asked Babcia, coming forward to stand before her son.

"A ghetto," replied Antoni.

Jan frowned, confused. What did it mean? He didn't understand. The adults seemed to know what a ghetto meant. At Antoni's words, their faces fell, and Berek called up the stairs for his wife, Berkowa, to come down. She hurried down the stairs, a question written on her face.

"What is it?" asked Jan. "What is a ghetto?"

Mama wrung her hands together, then kissed his forehead and greeted her daughters. She cleared her throat. "It means all of the Jews in the city must live in one place together."

"Don't we do that already?" asked Nacha, her lower lip trembling.

"But no one else. The Aryans already living in the Jewish

Quarter will have to leave," replied her father, taking her hand in his. "Not only will Jews who leave their designated residential area be punished with death, but the same penalty applies to anyone who knowingly provides refuge to Jews. We suspected it was coming—we paid a lot of money to the Germans last year to prevent it. And now, here it is, despite our best efforts."

"This is unacceptable." Berek's cheeks reddened with anger. "We're not animals!"

Babcia slouched onto the sofa, her face pale. Papa's nostrils flared and he stood behind her, clutching her shoulder with one hand and his violin in the other.

"I'm afraid we have no choice," continued Antoni. "And our friends will no longer be able to visit."

The realisation of what they were saying slowly washed over Jan. Berek and Berkowa embraced one another, Berkowa resting her head on her husband's shoulder, her expression full of fear.

Mama sighed and smoothed her hair back from her fore-head with both hands, then pushed a smile onto her face. "But of course it won't keep us apart forever. We will get through this."

"Yes," agreed Antoni with a brief nod, his eyes and Mama's fixed on one another.

"Where will it be located?" asked Berek as he and his wife separated, only their hands now linked.

"There's a map on each poster," replied Antoni. "It shows the boundaries of the ghetto. This apartment falls within its borders...just. Thank God we can stay where we are."

Babcia stood to her feet and walked to Jan. She cupped his face with both hands, tears sliding down her weathered visage. "My darling boy." She kissed his cheeks, one at a time. Then she moved on to Jadzia and Danuta, whispering loving words to each of them.

His sisters began to sniffle, their faces blotched with red as one by one the adults walked up to them, kissing their cheeks and wishing them well. Jan's throat tightened. He couldn't take in what they were saying. Surely this wouldn't happen. How could the two families be kept apart? They lived across the courtyard from one another. It was impossible for them not to cross paths. How could a group of people be fenced in? This was their city. These were their homes.

An image of the priests falling slumped to the floor of the cathedral flashed across his mind, and he squeezed his eyes shut as panic rushed up his spine. If they could do that to the Catholic priests in the middle of the day, they could do anything they liked. And perhaps they'd done it precisely because of what was to come. They wouldn't allow dissent, and what better way to hobble the Catholic majority than by removing their priests?

"When?" asked Babcia when she had finished her goodbyes. Her hand held tight to Mama's, her knuckles white.

Mama inhaled a slow breath and wiped the tears from her cheeks with the back of her one sleeve. "Those who move have four weeks to do it. But we must say our goodbyes, since we don't know when we will see each other again."

Jadzia and Danuta's sniffling ceased then. They lifted their chins and wiped their cheeks dry. They hugged Nacha's neck, and even threw their arms briefly around Nathan's thin frame. Jan stood to one side, watching as everyone he loved said farewell. When Nacha came up to him, he steeled himself. He didn't want to cry. Couldn't show how angry he was. They all needed him to be strong—Mama, Jadzia, Danuta, Nacha, and even Antoni, who seemed so calm about it all. It was too much for any of them to bear, yet they must. They had no choice.

"Goodbye, Janek," said Nacha, her eyes red, but her expression stoic.

He offered her a half smile. "Goodbye, Nacha. I will see you again."

Hope trickled from her eyes. "Maybe," she said. "And I will never forget you."

He swallowed. "I will find you, no matter what."

She smiled and quickly hugged him, her thin arms making their way around his neck briefly. Then she moved on, embracing his sisters and Mama.

Finally, they were done. Their goodbyes complete, each of them emotionally spent, Jan and his sisters dawdled to the back door. He turned to offer one last wave, then stepped out into the now-dark courtyard. Overhead, the clouds hung low, threatening snow. His breath puffed white in front of his mouth and he tugged up the collar on his overcoat, hunkering down inside it and shoving his bare hands deep into his pockets.

Antoni followed them outside and stood whispering to Mama in the shadow of the doorframe. Mama rose to her tiptoes to kiss his lips, winding her arms around his neck. Jan heard her sob before he turned away, his heart aching.

Another whispered conversation, then Mama left Antoni behind her, reached for Jan's hand, and together the four of them walked across the courtyard and in through their own back door to the cold, dark apartment. Mama slumped into a chair at the small, round kitchen table. She sat in silence, staring at her cold, empty hands.

Jan watched her a moment, then raised his voice. "Jadzia, start the fire. Danuta, the lights, please! Mama, what shall we warm for our supper?" He took her hand and pulled her to her feet, gazing into her eyes.

Please, Mama, don't give up now. We need you.

A shadow flitted over her fine features, and she blinked.

"Of course, you must be starving. Let's get supper on the table and you can tell me all about your day."

Jan sighed with relief and hurried to help Jadzia build the fire in the old stone fireplace. Life would change, but they would adapt. They had to. They couldn't let the Nazis win. They would figure out a way forward, and they would survive. And when this war was over, they would all find each other again.

$$\mathfrak{R} \quad 4 \quad \mathfrak{R}$$

15TH NOVEMBER 1940

Nacha Wierzbicka squatted beneath the grimy window frame, then slowly raised herself up to peer through the dirty pane. Her breath fogged the glass and her heart thudded loudly, nerves squirming in the pit of her stomach.

Although she was only thirteen, she wasn't welcome in school any longer, and she was curious about what was going on after the announcement the previous night.

They hadn't banned her from attending at first. When the Nazis came, they'd removed the Polish textbooks and forced the teacher to use German. They hung pictures of Hitler in the classrooms. It wasn't until later that the Jewish students were told they couldn't return. By then, they'd been harassed and attacked in a feverish escalation for months.

Tata wouldn't talk to her about any of it. He exchanged furious whispers with the other men who stopped by their apartment, but with her, he was silent or offered a bleak smile. He told her everything would be all right and not to fret. But she couldn't help worrying and needed more than empty reassurance, especially now that she knew they'd be forced to stay in a ghetto within the next few weeks.

That morning, he'd paced back and forth across the small living room floor, mouth tight, eyes grim. Whenever Papa tried to calm him with a hand on his arm or a soft word, Tata shouted about Germans and ghettos, and how could it have come to this?

Nacha hadn't seen her father so angry before. A knot formed in her gut, and she'd had to get out of the house. So she'd snuck out when Babcia was busy mending her everyday skirt. She hadn't thought much ahead of time about where she should go, but found herself headed for the school.

She'd taken the same walk every school day for years, and the habit was hard to shake. There had always been something comforting about the classrooms, the teachers, the lessons they learned. She was naturally good at academic work and found it satisfying in a way many of the other students seemed not to. She missed the teachers and was certain they'd miss her too, if only she could see them. But Jewish children had been banned from the school grounds.

Her breath caught in her throat while she peeked through the windowpane outside her former classroom. Desks marched in straight rows from the front of the room to the back. At the head of the class, the teacher, Mr Nowak, stood at the blackboard, speaking words she couldn't understand. His voice was muffled.

He held a pointer in one hand, and every now and then, he aimed it at a white screen where a single image was frozen. He finished what he was saying and stood to one side, holding the pointer down at an angle with his eyes fixed on the screen. Near the front door, an SS officer stood against the wall, hands linked behind his back, hat tilted jauntily to one side.

A filmstrip projector sat on a wooden stool near the back of the room, and Jan hovered beside it. After a nod from Mr Nowak, Jan pressed a button, and the images on the projector screen leapt to life. Still frames flew across the screen, images of people just like Nacha. Her heart in her throat, she stifled a gasp and grabbed hold of the windowsill with both hands. Words flashed over the images, accompanied by grotesque cartoons of hook-nosed men with greasy black hair.

The Jews are vermin. They must be sequestered into the ghetto as a form of quarantine. It is for our own protection that we must separate the Jews from society as they carry typhus and lice. It is for the greater good.

The film ended abruptly, and there were murmurs throughout the group of students. She couldn't see Jan's face, but his shoulders were square and his chin high. What was he thinking? What would he say? Did he agree with the film? Surely not. He was like a brother to her, a son to her father. They were family in every way that mattered.

Tears clogged her throat, but she wouldn't let them fall. Why did people hate her and her family? They'd done nothing to deserve it. And how could all those children, her friends, sit and listen to such lies without saying anything in her defence?

She shivered as the teacher cleared his throat and tapped his pointer on the edge of the screen. "As you see, it is for our own good." She heard his voice clearly that time as it sliced the cold air and reverberated through the glass. Another cough, and he glanced at the SS officer. The officer nodded at the teacher, then stepped out of the room, leaving it in silence as children squirmed in their chairs.

"Right then, class—back to mathematics. Where did we leave things yesterday?"

Nacha stared at the blackboard, eyes glazing over, as the teacher wrote problems with white chalk and students quickly marked them down on sheets of lined paper at their desks. How could the students return to their work as though nothing had happened? As though the world hadn't been torn asunder?

How dare they call her and her family vermin? How could these Nazis label them with vile names and suggest they were dirty or diseased? Why didn't anyone object? She scanned the room, wondering if any of her childhood friends would say something to the teacher about what they'd seen. But each head was bowed over its work, each child focused on the task at hand. Only one set of eyes turned her way—a girl she'd played hopscotch with a hundred times. Someone she'd laughed with, practiced handstands with when the weather was fine. A girl she'd thought of as a friend. The girl met her gaze with a steady look, then leapt to her feet, pointing.

"A Jew!" she shouted. "Look! She's watching us."

Jan swung about, his gaze meeting Nacha's where she crouched. He mouthed to her, "Go!"

Nacha took off at a run, careful to stay close to the wall. She sidestepped a shrub and leapt over an icy puddle. As she closed in on the school entrance, she saw the door fly open and the SS Officer step through it. With adrenaline pumping hard through her veins, she backed up against the building and willed herself to disappear into its brickwork.

The officer stopped at the top of a set of stairs that led down to the road and tapped a cigarette from a box. He lit it and inhaled a deep breath. A puff of smoke appeared before his mouth, and he pushed the hand with the box of cigarettes into his pocket and jogged down the stairs to a waiting car. The vehicle idled at the bottom of the steps, black and shiny with two red flags carrying the swastika attached to the bonnet. Its gleam and the bright red of the flags were a stark contrast to its drab surroundings.

Holding her breath, Nacha watched him climb into the vehicle. As it drove away, she exhaled slowly, her breath visible for a moment before it faded into the frigid air. Shouting emitted from inside the school drove her headlong down the staircase. She sprinted for home, her legs numb inside their stockings from squatting so long beneath the window on the cold, hard ground. She was almost home when a truck rumbled by on the road, its exhaust belching smoke.

Beneath a canvas canopy on the back of the truck, she caught a glimpse of gleaming metal. Soldiers sat on bench seats on either side of the truck bed. Her pulse accelerated. The truck was followed by a line of identical trucks, all packed with soldiers holding rifles between their knees. They were heading for the Jewish District. She had to hurry.

✿

IT WASN'T LONG AFTER NACHA RETURNED HOME THAT SHE heard the sounds of laughter in the courtyard and saw through the window that Jadzia and Danuta had returned home from school. She watched them for a few minutes, forgetting all about the truckloads of soldiers.

It didn't take much for her fear to dissipate, since the invaders had lived amongst them now for six months and so far, she and her family had managed to continue their lives. Of course, she heard all about the beatings and shootings that'd happened in the Jewish District, and she'd seen the burned-out buildings sending spirals of smoke into the sky the next day as the charcoal remains cooled. But Tata told her to keep herself hidden from the Nazis, to be careful where she went and who she saw, and so far, it'd kept her safe.

When she was out and about on her own or with Jan and

his sisters, she passed as one of them, an Aryan. It was only when she was with her own family that she noticed the hateful looks, the women who pulled their skirts aside with a scowl or the men who shouted insults at their backs.

The girls next door took turns skipping with the rope their mother had bought them the previous Christmas. She'd traded for it at the markets with a bag of oats and a hand trowel. Nacha remembered because she'd wished she had a mother who thought of such things. But her mother was dead, and Tata didn't worry himself with frivolous purchases —he had too many mouths to feed. She'd heard him say it often enough. But he said it with a kiss to her forehead and a smile that made his eyes twinkle, so she could never stay angry with him.

Still, it was hard for her to watch from a distance while the girls from next door enjoyed their Christmas gift. Especially since her family didn't celebrate the holiday, which seemed more unfair than anything else in that moment. She knew it was wrong, but she wished she was Catholic. Wished she didn't have to worry about Nazis and could jump rope in the courtyard with her Christmas gift.

Shame washed over her as she pushed the thought aside. There was no point in wishing for something impossible. She couldn't change who she was. And according to Babcia, it was wrong to think that way. They should be proud of their Jewish heritage and faith. But it was hard for Nacha not to wonder about a life where her faith wasn't used to call her dirty and diseased. She wanted more than anything to be invisible. If people couldn't see her, they wouldn't be able to shut her away in a ghetto and call her names.

She glanced over her shoulder to see if Babcia was watching. Her grandmother hummed in the kitchen while she worked on the supper that Nacha was supposed to be helping with. A delicious aroma drifted out to greet her, making her stomach clench with hunger. But what did she care of hunger when there was skipping to be had? Babcia would hardly notice she was gone, and it would only be for a few minutes.

So she leapt from the place by the window where she'd knelt to spy on the sisters and hurried outside, making sure to shut the door quietly behind her. She adjusted her overcoat and scarf as she scampered into the courtyard, a grin tugging at her lips.

"Nacha!" the girls called, clearly glad to see her.

Jadzia laughed while Danuta threw her arms around the older girl and buried her face in Nacha's coat.

"It's good to see you," said Danuta, her voice muffled by the woollen fabric.

Nacha chuckled. "I saw you last night. It hasn't been so long."

"But I thought I'd never see you again." Danuta beamed up at her, eyes glistening.

Nacha huffed. "We live right next door."

"What if the Nazis find out?" whispered Jadzia, looking around as though they might leap out from behind a nearby beech tree and catch the three girls talking to one another.

Nacha shrugged as though she didn't care, but a pang of nerves tightened in her gut. "Let's skip. I don't have long. Babcia will be looking for me to help in the kitchen soon."

"I like your hair curled that way," said Jadzia as she grabbed hold of one end of the rope. "How did you manage it?"

"I tied it in rags last night," replied Nacha. "It was easy enough, although I'm not sure I could be bothered to do it very often." The truth was, she loved the look of the curls that hung against her shoulders. She'd pulled them back from her face, and it made her feel mature and beautiful. But now that she couldn't go to school, or the markets, or even syna-gogue, she couldn't help feeling there was no purpose to any of it—dressing nicely, curling her hair, polishing her shoes. It all seemed inconsequential and pointless. Still, Babcia insisted she keep up her appearance.

Your habits make you the person you are. These little disciplines will keep us going through all of this absurdalność.

So she'd tied her hair in rags each night and she would continue to do it, to keep Babcia happy.

"I'm going to try it too," said Jadzia as Danuta took the other end of the rope.

They began spinning the rope over and over and Nacha watched carefully, judging when she could jump in. She counted in her head, then sprang in to skip over the rope as it spun over her head, then under her feet and back again.

Jadzia and Danuta began to chant in time with the beat of the skipping rope.

> "Snail, snail, show us your horns;
> I'll give you some cheese for pierogi.
> If not cheese, then cabbage;
> From cabbage you will be fat!"

A truck engine gunned up the street. It stopped outside the apartment complex, followed by the shuffling of booted feet. Nacha stopped still, listening. The skipping rope whacked into her ankle.

Danuta whined. "Nacha, what are you doing? You ruined it. We were going for fifty in a row."

"Shhh," begged Nacha.

"What is it?" asked Jadzia, eyes widening.

The side gate on the courtyard banged open, and several German soldiers marched through. Their boots clacked on the hard ground. Their baggy pants stuck out around their legs. With hard hats half obscuring their faces, all Nacha could see was a series of twitching moustaches.

"Move!" shouted one of the men in German. "Back to your homes."

Nacha stumbled away from the girls, her heart in her throat. She didn't dare say a thing. Jadzia grabbed Danuta by the back of her skirt and tugged her towards the door of their apartment.

A trio of men in work clothes ambled into the courtyard. One pushed a wheelbarrow filled with concrete dust. A shovel poked out of the top of the pile of dust. The other two pushed a large timber spool wound about with barbed wire in long, thin strands. They all wore belts about their hips that carried hammers, nails and other tools.

Nacha eased through the door, shut and locked it behind her. She hung her coat, hands trembling on the coatrack, and then ran to the window to peep through the curtains. The men didn't waste any time. They set about digging holes in the middle of the courtyard.

"Babcia!" called Nacha, her voice hoarse with fear.

Babcia came halfway from the kitchen, wiping her hands on her apron, a frown on her face. "Where have you been? You're supposed to be helping. What do you think—I should do it on my own? Maybe you can sit at the table and I can serve you as well."

"Babcia, look!" she insisted.

Babcia shook her head as she shuffled to the window. "Girls these days. You don't know what life was like for us... What is this?" Babcia's face fell. "What are they up to?"

The front door slammed shut and Tata came into the room, puffing hard. "It's a wall." He slumped into a chair at the kitchen table, resting his head in his hands. It seemed as if he would never catch his breath. Nathan stepped inside after him. He, too, was breathing hard.

"They're building a wall around the ghetto," said Nathan.

Babcia's hand flew to cover her mouth. "Through our backyard?"

Tata nodded, letting his hands drop to rest on the table.

A lump formed in Nacha's throat as she turned away from the pained look on her father's face to stare again at the workmen in the courtyard. She'd been so happy only a few minutes earlier. And now, everything had changed. She hadn't really believed it could happen. Surely the Germans couldn't keep her and her family inside a ghetto, away from the world. But now she saw it could be done. If they were willing to build a wall around a city full of people, she supposed they could do anything at all.

"They're sealing us off today," continued Tata, confirming her worst fears. "Over three hundred thousand people."

"How will we all fit?" asked Babcia. "What will we eat?"

Papa stepped slowly down the stairs, his reading glasses hung on a string around his neck.

"Did you see?" asked Babcia.

He sighed. "I did."

"What will happen now?" asked Nacha to no one in particular.

"I don't know," replied Tata, coming to her and taking her hand in his to squeeze it. She leaned against his chest, and his arms encircled her. "But we must do as we're told. We don't want to anger them. Who knows what they might do? And surely this can't last forever. They want us to stay here—we'll do it. We'll keep out of sight. We won't cause any trouble. We will stay home and keep to ourselves. Where is Berek?"

"They went to see the Cykiert family. Jan and Waltrina wanted to say their goodbyes." Tata's lips pulled into a tight line. "I hope they got out in time."

Gunshots filled the quiet, followed by screaming in the distance. Nacha ran to the front door and opened it a crack. She peered outside, her heart beating out a staccato rhythm.

A woman ran by along the street, pulling a small child by the hand after her. A group of five men sprinted past the woman. There were more gunshots. At the end of the street, flames licked at the second story of an apartment building. Black smoke billowed into the sky overhead. The scent of scorched earth and gunpowder filled the air.

When a neighbour shuffled by, blood streaming from a wound on the side of her head, Nacha pulled the door shut with a bang. She clapped a hand over her mouth and ran past Babcia and Tata, through the kitchen. Ignoring their shouted questions, she ran up the staircase. She threw herself down on her bed, pushed her head under the pillow, and bit down on her fist to quiet the groaning sobs that bubbled up her throat.

❧ 5 ❧

There was nothing to do at home. Jan wasn't accustomed to being cooped up inside their small apartment all day long. He longed to be outside. To be doing something. Anything other than staring at the workmen outside building the brick wall directly through the middle of their courtyard and listening to his sisters bicker about inconsequential things.

"You can't wear the blue. It needs mending," said Jadzia to Danuta. They held a blue woollen skirt between them.

Danuta tugged at it, her mouth grim. "I don't care. I want to wear it."

"You're going to worsen the tear."

"No, you are."

"Give it back to me," hissed Jadzia between clenched teeth.

"It's my only warm skirt. Do you want me to freeze to death?"

"It's a tempting idea," replied Jadzia with a grin.

Danuta squealed. She'd done it since she was small. It was her only weapon against an older sister who was bigger and stronger than her. Her squeal pierced the eardrums of anyone within shouting distance, and she used it freely to get her way.

Jan huffed in disgust as he covered his ears. "Stop it. You both sound like babies. There are more important things to worry about than which skirt you wear. Get your coats. We're going out."

Jadzia released the skirt and looked at him with a frown. "Out? We're not supposed to go out."

"Mama said to stay here," agreed Danuta.

He jumped to his feet and headed for the coatrack by the door. "I'm going for a walk. You can either stay here and keep fighting, or you can come with me. I want to see what's going on out there."

Jan waited impatiently for his sisters to wrap themselves in shawls and coats before stepping outside. He stamped his feet for a few moments and blew into his hands while he stood there. Finally, they were ready, and he took off at a clipped pace with them straggling after him.

"Slow down," whined Danuta.

Jadzia shushed her and took her younger sister's hand. Jan could tell Jadzia was nervous about venturing out of the apartment, but he was curious, and there was no better way to satiate his curiosity than to see for himself what was happening. Besides, he was certain Mama would need his help at the market. It was too much for her to do alone. He'd always been her support in the past, and he should be there now. It was silly for him to babysit his sisters instead. They were young, but capable of taking care of themselves, and Mama knew that.

The street outside their apartment usually bustled with activity, automobiles, pedestrians and cyclists. Today it was quiet, with only the occasional truck trundling along or man striding down the side of the road, head bent and hat pulled low.

It was when they got to the first intersection that he understood. The entire street to his left was filled with lines of people. They all trudged slowly forward, unable to move far because of the gridlock. German soldiers stood around them, shouting. While he watched, one soldier yelled at an older woman for taking too long, then hit her on the head with the butt of his rifle. She crumpled silently to the ground, and a younger woman rushed forward with a cry. She knelt by the older woman, lifted her head from the ground, and cradled it in her arms as tears streaked down her cheeks.

The soldier watched for a moment, then turned his rifle around and shot the young woman in the head. She fell on top of the older woman, and the crowd rushed away from the women like a wave.

Jan's heart skittered in his chest. He gaped at the sight of soldiers beating men, women and children. Everyone carried suitcases or cloth bags. Some pulled wooden wagons loaded with valuables and food behind them. All oscillated between sad apathy and rending fear, depending on where in the lines they stood. More shots rang out.

Several men and women took off at a run, heading for a nearby alley. They were shot in the back and fell to the ground. Screaming and wailing broke out nearby. One group of soldiers had a row of men and women kneel in front of them, then each shot their victim. One man only tipped to the side, so a solider kicked him to the ground in disgust. All of them were then pulled away by their feet and loaded into waiting lorries.

A sound at his side, like the mewing of a cat, drew Jan back into himself and he looked down at his two sisters, holding tight to one another beside him. Tears welled in Jadzia's eyes. Danuta was already sobbing. He leaned down to meet them at eye level and looked into Jadzia's red-rimmed eyes.

"Go home. Now!" he said.

She hesitated, her gaze flitting over his shoulder to the chaos beyond.

"Jadzia," he whispered. "You have to take Danuta home and stay there. Lock the doors."

"But what about you?" sobbed Danuta.

"I have to find Mama and make sure she's okay."

Jan pressed himself to the wall of the nearest house and watched his sisters run headlong down the street and back to their house. He saw them close the door, then turned his attention to the soldiers. They'd moved further into the ghetto now. He could see the partially built wall. The lines of Jews crushed around the wall and into their new enclosure. Hunched shoulders, long, dark coats and puffs of white breath in the still, cold air.

Each person wore a white armband with a blue Star of David. It'd been an entire year since the invading Nazis had required every Jew over the age of ten to distinguish themselves in that way. Jan had asked Antoni why he did it—why he conformed to their rules. He'd said, in a tremulous voice, that it was a small thing. It'd been done before, and if it meant they would be left alone, it was a sacrifice he was willing to make.

Of course, it meant no such thing. They were exposed to more violence and hatred than ever before. However, he'd noticed some people would doff their hats in the street at those who wore the stars on their arm. A silent rebellion against the occupying forces and an acknowledgement of their humanity.

Herded like cattle, the men sported wool fedoras, the women leaving their heads exposed or covering them with hoods and scarves. Some were dressed in the very best overcoats with the most stylish skirts and silk blouses beneath them. Others wore soiled rags and crept forward on bare feet. Some carried bags and satchels. Others held carefully wrapped babies or nothing at all in their desperately clenched fists. A crush of humanity surging away from the guns and into the ghetto. Each with fear etched on panicked faces.

Jan turned away from the mass of people and jogged towards the market. He had to find Mama. It was the only thought that kept spinning through his mind.

Find Mama. Find Mama.

As he ran, he noticed smoke coming from the windows of a nearby house. A group of soldiers stood around outside it. One held a jerry can. The others talked and laughed together. He jogged on. *Find Mama.* It was all that mattered in that moment. What if they'd found her? What if they knew about the family's connection to the Wierzbicka family?

After the Nazi invasion in 1939, the Jewish people of Warsaw had seen a surprising increase in harassing behaviour and attacks. Jan had been shocked by the sudden animosity shown by people he'd considered friends to their neighbours. Catholics and Jews had always lived side by side in Warsaw. But after the Nazis arrived, there were some in the community who joined them in their hatred of the Jewish residents of Warsaw. Others simply watched on in horror, peeping through curtained windows, unable to process what was happening and with no idea what to do.

Terror over what he'd seen stole Jan's breath, and he found himself gasping for air. He slowed to a walk and bent at the waist, resting his hands on his knees as his head spun. He couldn't deal with it now—he had to find his mother. Using the back entrance, he snuck into the market and wound his way through the almost-empty building to Mama's stall. She was there, packing dry goods away in the large wooden hand wagon she took everywhere.

"Mama," he whispered, coming up alongside her.

She gasped, pressed a hand to her heart. "Janek, my boy, you startled me. What are you doing here? I told you to stay at home." Her brown eyes were bloodshot, and her eyebrows drew into a single peak above them.

"Mama," he said again, trying to find his breath. "They're burning buildings. They're shooting..."

She shushed him, tugged him into her arms, and pressed his head to her shoulder as she cupped his cheek. "I know. Hush now. We can't talk about it here. The walls have ears. Let's go home. I'm finished for the day, and there's no one about anyway to buy from me."

They took back roads home. Several times they had to hide from the Wermacht in alleys or behind shrubbery. They were jostled by people running for their lives. One man knocked Mama to her knees as he barrelled past. He didn't stop. Jan helped her to her feet again, emotions numb. She wiped the blood from her torn stockings and shook her head, but didn't say anything.

The German military burned and killed indiscriminately, but Jan had seen enough of their work already to know that it was more than that. They were an organised enemy. They kept lists of every person, every resource, and every building. They were meticulous in their planning. There was a clear strategy to their madness. Only Jan couldn't understand why Hitler and his army would show such targeted hatred for a people who had done nothing to deserve it.

It took forever for them to make it the short distance back to their apartment. Inside, they shut and locked the door behind them. Jan kicked off his boots, soles thick with mud, and set them neatly by the door in line with his mother and sisters' boots. He padded across the kitchen floor in woollen socks and slumped into a chair at the kitchen table. He rested his head in his hands.

"My girls," said Mama, coming into the kitchen to kiss his sisters' cheeks. Jadzia was kneading bread and Danuta was stirring a pot of stew on the stove. "How good it is to see you."

There was a red spot on each of Jadzia's cheekbones. Otherwise, her face was pale. She chewed on her lower lip after accepting Mama's kiss.

"I didn't think I'd see you again," she whispered.

Mama squeezed her shoulder. "We're fine, my darling girl. I'm glad to see you stayed at home as I instructed...unlike some."

Jadzia and Jan exchanged a look. There was no need to tell Mama he'd convinced his sisters to go out onto the street with him. That they'd witnessed the kind of brutality he'd never imagined possible. They were safe at home now, and Mama had enough to worry about.

Danuta set the spoon down beside the pot. "Dinner is ready."

"Thank you, *kochanie*. We will eat soon. I need a moment."

Mama walked to the living room and stared out a gap between the curtains, one hand resting on the windowsill. She sighed.

Jan went to her and peered around her at the empty courtyard. The workers were gone. Between their apartment and their neighbours' stood the finished brick wall with two strings of barbed wire pulled taut along the top of it.

"So, it's finished," he said.

She nodded. "They're so close, but we can't go to them. I wonder what they're doing."

He rested his head on her shoulder. "We'll see them again, Mama."

She inhaled a quick breath. "I worry...will they have enough to eat? Antoni can no longer trade at the market. How will they survive?"

Jadzia and Danuta came up behind them. Jadzia shuffled into place in front of Mama to sit with both hands pressed to the window. Danuta slipped in beside her and lay against Jadzia, who immediately began to stroke her sister's hair back from her face.

"It's horrible, Mama," said Danuta, wrinkling her nose. "I want to see Nacha."

"Me too," agreed Jadzia. "What will happen now?"

Mama wrapped an arm around Jan and rested a hand on Jadzia's shoulder. "I don't know, my children. But whatever happens, we must stay together. And we must do what we can to help. We cannot give in to this evil."

❧ 6 ❧

15TH DECEMBER 1940

The smell of smoke still hung acrid in the air over Mirowski Square. Jan traversed around an enormous crater in the centre of the street where German bombers had left their mark during the siege of Warsaw. A woman's body lay on the footpath, her apron over her face, her legs skewed at an angle. He crossed himself and leapt over her legs, taking off at a run.

With a loaf of bread tucked beneath his jacket, he was headed for home after visiting the market where Mama worked. She'd insisted on continuing to spend some time each day there as she believed it would be their means of survival, and she didn't want to lose her standing or her stall to another trader. She'd given him the bread to take home to his sisters, although they still had some flour left in the bottom of the barrel. They'd take what they could get, she said. And today what they got was bread.

Between the siege, the occupation, and now the Nazis'

crackdown on the Jewish population of Warsaw, the city had suffered from food shortages for over a year. The bread lines often stretched around corners and up long streets before they ended. Most people he encountered were thin, many gaunt with skin stretched tight across protruding cheekbones.

Up ahead, a group of soldiers shoved some harried women and children into the back of a waiting truck, smoke chugging from its tailpipe. Jan slowed his pace, then with a frown ducked into an alley and peered around the edge of the building to watch. A horse and cart trotted by, the driver turning onto a side street when he saw the chaos ahead of him. But most pedestrians continued on their way, walking or riding past the crying women and children without a glance in their direction.

Jan wanted to do something to help. Anger burned in his gut, but he stayed where he was. There wasn't anything he could do. If he moved closer to the group, he'd feel compelled to reach out to one of the women, and that wouldn't do him or them any good. He'd be shot, and likely they would be too.

He chewed the end of a fingernail, waiting for the truck to move on. Finally, the tailgate clunked into place and the truck meandered away down the street. The crowd filled the space where it'd been moments earlier, as if the people it carried had never been there at all.

"Janek!" whispered a frantic voice.

Jan turned his head to look into the darkened alley and saw nothing but piles of rubbish and a stray cat licking at something on the cobblestones.

"Huh?" he said.

"Janek," the voice said again. A boy a little taller than he was emerged from behind a bin. "It's me, Walter."

Jan ran to meet him and shook his hand. He noted that

Walter wasn't wearing the armband he usually sported. His red hair was pushed back from his freckled face as though he'd combed his fingers through it over and over again. His bare knees poking out from his shorts were covered in scrapes and bruises. His clothes were dirty and his fingernails bitten to the quick.

"What are you doing here?" asked Jan. "How did you get away?"

"I removed the armband and hid in the crowd," he said. "They took my family—I watched them. But then I realised someone might recognise me and turn me in, so I've been hiding ever since."

"Come with me," said Jan. "You can stay with us. We have plenty of room."

"No." Walter backed away. "I can't risk someone seeing me. If they turn me in, your whole family will be in danger."

"But what will you do?"

"I'm going to sneak into the ghetto tonight. Over the wall. I want to see my mama and tata. I hate it here."

Jan had considered traversing the ghetto's boundaries himself. He'd thought of little else since the wall was constructed. Questions ran through his mind over and over. What were the Wierzbickas doing? How were they faring? Had they been hurt? As much as he loved to tease his sisters that Antoni wasn't their father, he'd filled that role in their family for years.

Jan didn't want to give up on the idea that his own father might someday come looking for them, that he might care how they were surviving the Nazi occupation. But so far there'd been no sign of him, no letter or telegram. Antoni was the man Jan went to when he had a question he didn't wish to bother Mama with, like how to get a bass to take the bait in rainy weather, or the best way to sharpen the pocketknife he got for his twelfth birthday. He even called Antoni's parents Papa and Babcia.

Despite this itching desire to test out the impenetrability of the wall, he hadn't taken the time to examine it closely yet. Soldiers patrolled the wall day and night. If he stayed too long looking it over, he was worried one of them might question him about it. Not to mention what they'd do if he was caught halfway between the Aryan and Jewish sides. But if Walter was willing to try it, the idea was too tempting for him to pass up.

"Let's go back to the square and look at the wall there. When I was with Mama, I noticed it wasn't patrolled as heavily because of all the activity in the market."

Walter smiled for the first time, his colour returning. "We can uncover its weaknesses."

"I'm sure we'll be able to get you across in the dark. I'll come with you," Jan added with a grin. "It'll be fun."

❦

THE NIGHT WAS DARK, WITH SKIDDING CLOUDS COVERING the half moon and bathing the city in deep, ominous shadows. Jan hid in the alley, crouched low behind a rubbish bin, a wool hat pulled down over his ears. The scent of rotting food drifted on the breeze, and his nose wrinkled in response.

He hoped Walter would come soon. His nerves were on edge as he waited in the cold gloom. Mama hadn't stopped him from coming out like he'd thought she would. He didn't want to keep anything from her, so he had told her the moment she got home from the market what he and Walter intended to do. She'd simply pulled him into her arms and hugged him tight, kissing the top of his head and whispering a simple prayer to Saint Christopher for protection.

He blew on his hands and rubbed them together. It wasn't cold enough for gloves, so he hadn't bothered with them. He needed to be able to feel things for what they were. He couldn't risk getting snagged on the barbed wire that topped the ghetto wall.

An image of Antoni, Nacha, Nathan and the rest of the family flashed across his mind's eye. All of them laughing and dancing as Antoni played the violin. Babscia wore an apron around her trim waist. Her eyes sparkled as her black shoes clacked against the hard floor, and she swung a dish cloth to the right, then to the left. Papa sat in his favourite chair, tapping a heel in time to the music.

He smiled to himself and blew on his hands again, listening for the sound of boots marching in unison or the telltale rumble of a line of truck engines. He'd learned how to spot trouble before it arrived during the long months of the occupation.

Suddenly Walter was there, his breath fogging the air and his smile wide. "You came."

Jan nodded, grinning. "Of course I did. You ready?"

Walter's nose was red, his freckled cheeks pale in the dull light. "As I'll ever be."

"Let's go."

They agreed on a system of communication that wouldn't give them away as they tiptoed between buildings and ran along alleyways back to the square. There was still some activity around the market as traders packed their things away from the day's work and furtive late-night shoppers searched the remaining stalls for wares that had already been picked over by a day filled with hungry customers.

Jan and Walter slowed their headlong pace as they drew close to the wall. Jan scanned the area, looking for the glow of a cigarette butt or the glint of light on a rifle from a streetlamp. There didn't appear to be guards in the square, but he knew it would only be a matter of time until the patrol returned. He'd already scoped out the wall and found a location where the workers had used only barbed wire, no brick, for the wall on Krochmalna Street.

He scurried to the fence and ducked low. Walter followed him and used both hands to pull the wire apart. Jan climbed through, careful not to stick himself on the jagged barbs. Then he held the wire open for Walter. As soon as they were through, the boys launched themselves into the space between two apartment buildings. They pressed against the cold brick walls, puffing hard from nervous excitement.

Jan couldn't believe it. They were through, and no one had seen them. It was exhilarating. He flashed a smile at Walter, who offered a mock salute. Then Walter was gone. They'd already agreed—he would go to see his family, then return to the fence in one hour. Jan would do the same, only he would visit the Wierzbickas. He couldn't wait to see the looks on their faces when they opened the door to find him standing on their doorstep. He jogged away into the gloom of the eerily quiet ghetto.

AT FIRST ANTONI STOOD GAPING AT JAN, EYES WIDE. THEN he pulled the boy into an embrace. Their first. Antoni wasn't one for physical displays of affection, but there were tears in his eyes when he tugged Jan into the apartment, scanned the street worriedly and shut the door behind them.

"Look who's here!" he called quietly into the living room.

The entire family ran to greet him, exclaiming in hushed voices over the sight of him, how well he looked, how long it'd been since they'd last seen him. It had only been four weeks, but he agreed that it seemed like a lifetime. Their world had changed so much in the time since they'd all gathered together that last time.

Finally, they let Jan sit in Papa's armchair and crowded around him.

"How did you get through?" asked Berek, Antoni's brother, his brown eyes wide with anxiety.

"Walter Cykiert was stuck living on the Aryan side of the wall. He wanted to see his family, so I agreed to come with him. And here I am." Jan laughed. "It was easier than I thought it'd be."

"No one saw you?" Antoni glanced up at the front door, as if expecting *Wehrmacht* soldiers to burst through at any moment.

"No one saw me. We went through the barbed wire in the square where people were milling about. It's even busier during the daytime hours. I bet we could manage it then as well."

Antoni paced to the other side of the living room, rubbing his stubbled chin. "Do you think you could bring some supplies with you next time?"

Jan frowned. "Are you running low?"

"Everyone is," burst out Fela, Berek's daughter. "We get one meal per day."

"And a small one at that," agreed Nathan, patting his slender stomach.

"There is no medicine, either," added Babcia with a mournful expression. "But I don't want you to risk your life. They are serious about the punishment. They will shoot you. I've seen..." Her voice tapered off.

"I don't mind," replied Jan. "It was fun and easy too."

"You'll need this," said Antoni, removing his armband and securing it around Jan's arm. "Don't move about the ghetto without it. They'll think you're one of us."

Jan patted the band, adjusting it so that the blue star

showed clearly. "Thanks. I'd better go home or Mama will worry, but I'll be back as soon as I can make it. And I'll bring something with me. I'm sure Mama will be able to find what you need if you give me a list."

❧ 7 ❧

The open air on the wide street was eerie after hiding for days in the apartment without so much as looking out a window. Women with scarves pulled over the tops of their heads shuffled by, empty cloth bags hanging from their arms. Men hurried, running a few steps, then slowing their pace to glance around with furtive eyes, then hurrying again. Children hid in the shadows or clung to doorsteps, deciding between playing outside or taking refuge within.

Tata had told them to stay away from the windows and they'd kept the draperies drawn, only letting in slivers of light. They weren't sure what might happen if they were seen. There were so many questions, so much still unknown.

Nacha inhaled a slow breath, willing her heart rate to slow to a normal pace. Adrenaline spiked, making her head light. She'd volunteered to leave the house in search of coal to burn in the fireplace. It was getting colder every day, and they'd need it for the winter ahead. But no one was sure where to look. Tata had been out every day searching for food. He was tired, his face drawn, and he worried about everything—she could see it in his eyes, though he rarely said anything about his fears.

She paced along the street, clutching a heavy saucepan to her chest, looking up each alley she came to. She tugged the blue scarf lower on her head. The cold wind pinched at her nose. Her stockinged legs ached with the pace she kept. But she couldn't slow. The fear of what might happen if the soldiers appeared on the street kept her moving forward.

Some of the Jewish traders had continued to trade in the ghetto portion of the market after the ghetto was sealed ten days earlier. She'd try there first. If they didn't have coal, she wasn't sure where she should go next. But she'd deal with that problem when she came to it. As Tata always said, there was no need to worry about tomorrow when today had enough problems of its own.

Bodies lay strewn in the streets. She hadn't seen them before now. Staying hidden in the apartment had given her a kind of separation from the events going on outside their door, but she couldn't avoid them any longer. Why was no one in the family talking about it?

She strode past a woman lying on her side. Her clothes were old and worn, her hands blistered from hard work. The scarf on her head hid her face from Nacha's gaze. She held her breath as she passed, her heart in her throat. Then she faced forward and hurried on.

It wasn't long before her mind had returned to the task at hand. She had ration cards pushed deep into one of her pockets. There was also money sewn into the hem of her skirts. Babcia had hidden two- and five-zloty coins in the hems of all of their clothing after the decree came through that froze the family bank accounts. But even with the ration cards and money, there was no guarantee she'd find the food or coal they needed. The ration cards only provided for one meagre meal per day for each person. It wasn't enough for any of them to survive on long term. Even after only a few days, Nacha's hunger was almost all she could think about.

The Law and Order Service, a disorderly and cruel group of Jewish men who'd been appointed by the Germans to police the ghetto, conducted regular raids on the ghetto residents, confiscating valuables and food when they found it. Babcia had devised some ingenious ways to hide what little they had left so they wouldn't starve, although Nacha could tell Tata and her grandparents were anxious about how they would manage to feed such a large family despite their few hidden supplies.

A soup kitchen had opened on the ghetto side of the markets, across from the building where Tata had traded not so long ago. It seemed like an eternity since they'd had the opulence of such freedom—to be able to go where they wanted, to trade in the marketplace like a human being. But they weren't considered human any longer, not by the German occupiers. Or by many of their neighbours, who would gladly turn them in to the Nazis if given the chance for no reason other than hatred or fear.

Nacha couldn't understand how people she'd known her whole life could turn on her and her family so suddenly and without provocation. How could they look her in the eye and think her inhuman? She pushed down a welling grief that threatened to climb up her throat. The line for the soup kitchen was long — It meandered along the edge of the street, around the corner and disappeared from view. Perhaps she should stand in line for soup before she went searching for coal. Her stomach clenched, and the faint scent of stewing vegetables wafted on the frigid wind to tickle her nostrils.

Soup first, she decided. She hefted the saucepan higher against her chest, her fingers now almost numb with the effort of carrying it through the cold. She stepped to the back of the queue. It was mostly women and children who formed the crooked line. The women wore shawls and scarves, and the children's heads were covered with knit caps. Each person held a container of some kind, whether a cup or a pot, in their hands.

A girl who seemed a few years older than Nacha was ahead of her in the line. She glanced back and shot Nacha a smile. "Hi."

Nacha smiled shyly. "Good morning."

"This line..." The girl waved a hand in the direction of the crowd of people ahead of her. "It's longer than yesterday. There was no soup left when it was my turn."

"I hope the pot isn't empty today," Nacha said.

"I'll have to get here earlier tomorrow."

"I'm Nacha Wierzbicka."

The girl pushed out a pale hand. "Leah Silverstein. Pleased to meet you." Her brown eyes sparkled and her soft brown hair was combed back from her face and into a high peak, then secured in place with hidden hair pins. It curled around her shoulders in perfectly formed waves.

"You too."

Her hand was cold, but her smile was warm, and Nacha couldn't help returning it.

"Do you like to read?" Leah asked suddenly.

The line shuffled forward, and the two girls moved with it. Leah fell into step beside Nacha.

"Um...yes." It was an odd question, given their situation. But Nacha had always loved reading and learning.

Leah's voice dropped to a whisper and her gaze slid quickly from Nacha's face to the building across the street, down to the first of the market stalls in the distance, and back again. "Because there's a school, you know."

"What?" Nacha's brow furrowed. "A school? But that's not allowed."

"Shhh..." Leah waved to shush her. "Yes, a school. But there's no need to make a loud announcement. It's behind the soup kitchen. If you go through the side door, down the hall, and into the basement, you'll find a teacher and some pupils studying the great poets of old." She chuckled. "Or something like that. I would join them, but I'm hungry. And when I'm hungry, I can't concentrate."

"Do you think I could...?" Nacha gazed longingly in the direction of the soup kitchen doorway.

"I don't see why not. They're setting up schools all over the place. We can't have too many kids in one spot—that's the main issue. They've got small groups tucked away here and there. But you can't say anything or those nasty police will hear about it, and that will be the end of it—and of us, most likely."

Nacha couldn't wait to talk to Tata about it. A school. It was more than she could've hoped for. Perhaps she could go there each day rather than mooning about the apartment waiting for Babcia to give her a chore, like polishing the floorboards again even though she'd only just done them.

"I won't say anything," she agreed.

She shifted the pot to one hip and fingered the ration cards in her pocket to make sure they were still there. She'd worried all the way from the apartment that she'd lose them. Then what would Babcia say?

Shouting broke out at the head of the line. Nacha stood on tiptoe to see what was happening. A truck careened around the corner, and several plainclothes police officers jumped out. Their armbands and hats signified they were part of the Jewish Police, the Law and Order Service, and Nacha's heart leapt into her throat.

"Brutes," whispered Leah beneath her breath. "I'm going. Maybe I'll see you at the school." She ducked her head and scurried away down the street in the opposite direction.

Nacha hated to give up her spot in the line. There were already a dozen people waiting behind her.

The police rushed at a man in the line and pulled him towards the truck. The man stumbled and fell. One of the police tugged a baton from his belt and began to beat the man over the head with it. A woman screamed and leapt at the officer, slapping at him with both hands. Another officer felled her with his baton. All the while, they were shouting abuse and calling the couple thieves. The line broke up, and people scattered as more police officers arrived and set about beating anyone within arm's reach.

Nacha hugged the saucepan close, and with one last wistful glance in the direction of the wonderful smell of soup, she turned to run. She tucked herself close to the building's wall, with the ghetto wall on the other side, and jogged down the street, only occasionally glancing back over her shoulder to make sure she wasn't being followed. She turned down an alley and slowed her pace, puffing lightly.

A terrific thump behind her almost made her scream, but she clamped a hand to her mouth and spun to face the noise.

Jan stood there, feet apart, knees bent and a gigantic grin splitting his face in two. "Scared you!"

He'd jumped down from the top of the ghetto wall in a place where no one else was in sight. On the other side of the wall, she heard the busy sounds of a marketplace on a normal, frigid Tuesday morning in November.

She laughed and ran to embrace him. With the saucepan awkwardly held between them, she threw her arms around his neck and kissed his cheek. The strength of her feelings surprised her. Jan had been a part of her life for almost as long as she could remember. He was like a brother to her, and she'd never considered they might be separated. Her relief at seeing him made her hold him tight a few moments longer than she might have. Before the ghetto, she probably would've been angry with him for frightening her that way. But now she felt nothing but joy.

When she stepped away from him, his eyes sparked. "Glad you didn't scream, though. That might've caused me a bit of trouble."

She slapped his shoulder. "Then don't sneak up on me."

He pulled a piece of white cloth from his back pocket. As he tied the band around his arm, she noticed his heavy backpack.

"What's that?" she asked.

He laughed. "You'll see. Come on, let's go home."

※

ON THE WAY BACK TO THE APARTMENT, JAN TOLD HER about life on the Aryan side of the ghetto wall. She couldn't help feeling some level of gratitude that they were in the ghetto rather than outside it. The Germans would leave them alone now, Papa assured her. They were relatively safe in the ghetto if they did what they were told and stayed mostly out of sight. It was the best place for them. The people who'd been killed since the ghetto was formed, were trouble makers, they'd brought the Nazi's ill will down on themselves by not keeping quiet and doing what they were told.

They'd keep their heads down, stay out of the way of the police and they'd make it through the war. Peace would come and they'd be set free.

She wasn't sure if Papa was right, but it felt true. She felt safer now, tucked away with the rest of Warsaw's Jewish population. As Babcia always said, out of sight, out of mind. And perhaps they would stay out of the Nazis' minds now that they were hidden behind the ghetto's walls. At least they didn't have to face being chased through the streets or shot as long as they didn't steal anything like the couple in the soup line had done.

The police in the ghetto didn't carry guns. So far, she and her family had managed to stay out of trouble, and Tata was determined they'd continue to do just that. He said they would be model citizens, and they'd survive to the end of the war.

"Walter came back with me to the Aryan side," said Jan as he hurried along beside her, his Star of David armband starkly white against his dark brown coat sleeve. "He doesn't want to stay in the ghetto all the time. But he said he'll come with me to visit his family sometimes."

"Will you do it often, then?"

"As often as I can."

They reached the apartment, and Nacha opened the door to walk in ahead of Jan. "Jan's here."

Everyone was happy to see him. He set his backpack on the kitchen table, and Tata shook his hand. Papa and Babcia each kissed his cheeks. Berek slapped him on the shoulder and grinned.

"I brought you some things," Jan said, opening the backpack. "Mama traded for them in the market."

There was much celebration then. He'd brought meat and rice, potatoes and beans, candles and bandages, as well as some vials of morphine and antibiotics.

"This is fantastic," said Tata, holding up the morphine. "You have no idea how much this is needed."

Jan shrugged. "She said she can get more."

"We have money," replied Tata. "I spoke to a few of the others, and they gave me enough for more supplies. There is so much need in the ghetto."

"I'll bring whatever I can." He gathered up what Tata gave him and shoved it into his pockets.

"You will be careful?" asked Babcia, approaching him with a mug of hot tea.

Jan took the tea and sipped it. "I'm careful. They're not fast enough to catch me."

Tata shook his head, laughing. "Ah, the confidence of youth."

Babcia took the food supplies and carried them away to store them out of sight. Nacha shrugged off her coat and hung it on the coatrack by the door. Then she unwound her scarf from her head and let it fall to her shoulders.

"And how is your mother?" asked Tata as he packed the medical supplies into a small box. He didn't look up from his task, but Nacha noted the tension in his shoulders.

"She's fine. Busy trying to find out how long they intend to keep you here and how to get more supplies over the wall."

Tata inhaled a sharp breath. "She does too much."

"She wants to," replied Jan with a smile.

"Take care of her, won't you?" Tata glanced up at Jan for a moment, then returned to his task.

"I will."

8

20TH DECEMBER 1940

Jan pushed the wooden wheelbarrow down the cobblestone street. The front wheel bumped along, jolting his hands. Mama stopped at a stall and haggled with the vendor. He waited impatiently, peering up at the sun as it disappeared behind a cloud. There was no way he'd have time to get to the soccer match being held in the bombed-out ruins of an apartment building a block from their home. It'd be over by the time he made it. He fidgeted with the wheelbarrow's handles, scratching absentmindedly at the timber.

Mama pushed a clutch of potatoes into the wagon. "You're elsewhere today."

"No, Mama," he replied dutifully.

"What are you thinking of?"

"There's a soccer match," he began. But he stopped short when he saw the look on her face. "It's nothing."

"Soccer...but we have to get these things to Antoni. He's meeting us at the wall in less than ten minutes."

"I know, Mama." He knew it was more important to feed their neighbours, but he couldn't help wanting to do something normal. To play a game. To spend time with friends. To do anything that let them forget for a few moments that there was a war being waged all around them.

Mama pinched his cheeks gently between her fingers. "You're a good boy."

He blushed, pulling away from her. "Mama," he complained. There were people all around them, milling through the rows of fruit and vegetable vendors who congregated in rows outside the market building. He'd was fifteen and didn't need his mother to treat him like a baby in front of the world.

She studied his face a moment before moving on. He followed her, the barrow clanking over a rut in the road.

"You should go back to school," she said.

He blanched. "What?"

"School," she repeated.

"But I don't want to go to school. There are far too many things going on, more important things, than sitting in a classroom and learning algebra."

She laughed. "There are few things in life I consider important, and school is one of them. In the last letter you brought me, Antoni says they are finding a new normal way of life in the ghetto with schooling and soup kitchens. They've even set up their own hospitals and campaigned for people to donate sheets and pillows for the patients. They are finding their way, and we must too. You will return to school on Monday. You won't attend for much longer—you're almost a man—but it's important that you learn what you can while there's a chance for it. Your sisters will attend as well."

"Do you think they're safe now?" he asked. "Babcia and Papa were saying it's better, with the walls around the ghetto. Perhaps they'll be secure away from the Nazis' prying eyes."

Mama bit down on her lower lip, her cheeks pale. "I don't know, *mój skarbie*."

They finished their trading, and Jan filled the same backpack again with supplies. He lifted the backpack to his shoulder, and they walked towards the wall that surrounded the ghetto. Where it travelled through the market, it was tall and built of red bricks with a curl of barbed wire along the top. Walter was there waiting in the shadows. He gave Jan a nod then picked up a ladder and carried it casually to the wall.

Jan scanned the market for any sign of a Nazi guard, but saw none. Walter opened the ladder and set it up, then continued walking on his way. Jan stepped quickly up the ladder. On the other side, a group of youths milled about. Several waved at Jan, but none made a sound.

He looked directly down and saw Antoni standing against the wall. He lowered the bag into Antoni's outstretched hands.

"Thank you," whispered Antoni. "We need antibiotics—there's a typhus outbreak. Can you get more?"

Jan offered a nod and quickly descended the ladder. He glanced around the market and saw several men and women staring at him. One of the men doffed his hat. All of the curious onlookers returned to their work. Just then, the man who'd touched his hat whistled.

Jan tucked the ladder beneath his arm and ran along the wall while Mama walked in the other direction, pushing the now-empty wheelbarrow ahead of her. A woman opened a door and Jan skidded through, depositing the ladder against the wall. He glanced out the doorway and saw Nazi soldiers beating one of the men with batons and chasing another through the square.

He pulled the door shut behind him and slid down the wall to sit on his haunches in the dull light, puffing. Adrenaline coursed through his veins, and he tugged the knit cap further down on his head. It'd been a close call. He leapt to his feet and set off at a jog through the rabbit warren of storage rooms and hallways, then emerged into the market building beside Mama's stall. She was there, waiting for him with a smile on her face.

"We must somehow be more careful next time."

He grinned. "You worry too much."

❧ 9 ☙

14TH JULY 1941

There was no school today, and Nacha was bored. She'd attended the school hidden behind the soup kitchen most days, but sometimes it was called off, especially if there'd been a raid on one of the other groups that met around that section of the ghetto.

Besides that, their teacher had been carried away in the back of one of the rumbling trucks with the canvas flaps, according to a whispered message from his son, who'd immediately fled back to his home in one of the old apartment buildings by the hospital. It seemed like almost everyone they knew had typhus, so Tata didn't like Nacha or Nathan going far or mixing with too many people.

And so they did what they could to pass the time. Tata preferred that Nacha stayed home. Babcia had plenty of work for her to do—they were currently embroiled in a project to mend every single missing button, tear or hole worn in every item of clothing in the house. Babcia was determined they not look like homeless people or as if they'd stumbled out of a poorhouse, although the more time passed, the more bony, bedraggled and grimy everyone in the ghetto became.

They'd grown accustomed to stepping around or over bodies lying strewn in the streets. The faces of bloated babies and toddlers sometimes haunted Nacha's dreams, but she rarely thought about them in her waking hours. Her attention was taken up by other things, like how to get hold of some meat and how she might cook it if she did. In the meantime, she occasionally ran into Leah, and they passed the time together.

Today she'd shown up outside Nacha's apartment, waiting in the shadows across the street until Nathan had shouted for Nacha to go and see what she wanted. They'd used a stone to draw lines for hopscotch on the uneven ground. Now they were taking turns at the game, and chanting rhymes as they did it.

Nacha hopped while Leah watched, her chin resting in her upturned hands as she lay on her stomach in the grass.

Leah sighed. "I wish we could get out of this place."

Nacha tossed a small stone, then poked her tongue out the side of her mouth as she hopped on one foot, avoiding the square where the stone had landed. "Me too, but wishing doesn't make it so."

"It's not fair. Our best years, and we're stuck in here. No dances, no boys, not even a nice slice of cake every now and then. What I wouldn't give for a bar of chocolate." She licked her lips.

"I want to go somewhere I can walk around, out in the open, without worrying who might see me."

"Well, I'm going to do it. I'm getting out of this place."

Nacha slumped down beside her friend in the grass. "Will you really?"

"Yep, my parents have already decided. But you can't tell anyone."

"I won't tell, but I'll miss you."

"I'll miss you too."

There wasn't anything else to say. They were both too old to pretend they might see one another again. No one believed that lie any longer. Those who left the ghetto were either caught and killed on the spot, or found their way to a new life and were never heard of again.

Whatever their fate, the residents of the ghetto wouldn't know. It was as if they'd vanished into the ether. Other than through the couriers and smugglers, like Jan, who made their way into and out of the ghetto, risking their lives daily to help the people imprisoned behind its walls, there was no way for anyone living in the ghetto to communicate with the outside world.

Nacha resisted the urge to encourage her friend to be careful, to stay safe. There was no safe place for Jews in Poland any longer. To pretend otherwise would be a hollow and empty platitude and nothing more.

"Goodbye, then," said Leah suddenly. She hugged Nacha, then scurried along the alley and turned onto the main road, staying close to the buildings and out of the street.

Nacha sighed loudly, picked herself up from the cold, hard ground and wandered home. When she got there, Tata was entertaining a visitor in the living room.

Adam Czerniaków was a former senator and head of the *Judenrat*, the Jewish Council. He and Tata were friends and often spoke in hushed voices about the state of affairs they found themselves in and what could be done to improve the lives of the Jews in the ghetto.

Mr Czerniaków was an optimist who believed the Jewish people could survive the war with dignity if only they could organise themselves to maintain a decent level of civilised life and not turn on each other. Tata listened to him politely, but

Nacha could tell he wasn't sure about Mr Czerniaków's hopeful view of their small world.

Tata told her often that they could make it through the war if they did what they were told, but she wasn't certain he believed his own words anymore. Their time behind the ghetto's walls had broken his spirit in some ways and hardened him in others.

She stood as close as she dared to listen in on their conversation. There was something about the cost of goods being three times their value. Then a story about a man found with a homemade radio who was shot in the street by the *Einsatzgruppe* who'd been tipped off by a disgruntled uncle. Tata had shaken his head at that. A tale of family turning on one another was hard for him to comprehend.

Then they spoke briefly of the Polish government in exile, and Mr Czerniaków was certain that there was no hope for them in that regard. Tata's shoulders slumped. He leaned back in his chair.

"The council is meeting in a few minutes. I would urge you to join us," said Mr Czerniaków, standing to his feet and securing a woollen scarf firmly around his neck.

Tata stood as well and nodded. "I will come because you ask it."

They moved in Nacha's direction, so she backed into the kitchen and tugged an apron from a nail on the wall to tie around her waist. Tata and Mr Czerniaków stopped at the coatrack and shrugged into long coats.

"There you are, Nacha. I went looking for you earlier. I'll be out for a few minutes. Babcia and Papa are with Berek and Berkowa at the market fetching our rations."

"Okay, Tata."

She watched them leave, then pulled the apron free and wandered into the living room to throw herself onto the couch in the most impolite way possible. She had few freedoms these days and rarely had the apartment to herself or any privacy at all.

She listened for a few moments, but there was no sound to suggest anyone else was home. They were all out, and she was there alone. What should she do? There was no food to eat, as much as her stomach demanded satisfaction. Otherwise, she might've raided the pantry or the cool box. She could find one of Tata's fiction books and read it. He didn't let her touch his paperbacks usually—tales of war and crime. He didn't touch them either these days.

"No one needs to read about the very things happening to them," he'd said when she'd asked him why he no longer sought solace in fiction.

The idea didn't appeal much to her either, so she pushed it aside. Surely there was something she could do to enjoy the moment. Something that she wouldn't normally get the chance to do.

She vaguely recalled Babcia storing the cooking wine under a loose floorboard in the pantry. She'd tasted it before and hadn't liked the flavour. But now she was older—perhaps she would. She jumped to her feet and tiptoed through the apartment and into the kitchen.

Just as she poked her head into the pantry, there was a loud knock on the front door. The sound startled her, and she almost leapt into the air. She pressed a hand to her pounding heart and hurried to answer it.

"What on earth?" she grumbled beneath her breath.

She flung the front door open and found Jan standing there, a bag in his hands. "Hi."

"Hi."

He pushed past her into the apartment. "This is heavy." He dropped the bag on the kitchen table with a huff. "Phew."

"Thanks," she said.

"Is your father home?"

"No one is," she said.

He cocked his head to one side. "Really? You're here alone?"

She crossed her arms over her chest. "Yes. So?"

His mischievous grin excited and worried her.

"Do you want to do something?" His blue eyes twinkled.

Her eyes narrowed. "That depends." She had no idea what he intended, but his words sparked a tingle in the pit of her stomach.

"Mama traded at the market for two movie tickets. You wanna go with me?"

Nacha laughed. "I can't go to the movies with you. Have you lost your mind?"

He reached for her hand and tugged her towards the door. "Come on. It'll be fun."

She pulled her hand free of his grasp. "Janek Kostanstki, I'm stuck in this ghetto whether you like it or not. If I'm found outside its walls, I'll be shot."

He smiled at her. "Not if you're with me, you won't."

SHE COULDN'T BELIEVE SHE'D LET JAN TALK HER INTO leaving the ghetto. Tata would be furious if he found out what they were doing. Adrenaline coursed in her veins as they hurried through the ghetto in the direction of the barbed wire section of the wall at Krochmalna Street. Nacha had seen dozens of children moving freely back and forth through the wall, carrying goods from the outside or escaping in search of freedom. But she'd never considered taking the chance herself. Tata wouldn't allow it.

"I don't know if we should do this," she murmured. "If we're caught, you'll be killed as well."

Jan huffed. "They won't catch us. Besides, you pass for Aryan. No one will ever guess."

They stopped behind an apartment building and Jan scanned up and down the wall, looking for signs of anyone who might report them to a guard. There was no one around, so he tugged the white armband from his arm and shoved it into his coat pocket.

"You'll have to remove yours as well," he said, waiting.

Nacha glanced down at the white band, her heart pounding. If she removed it, there was no turning back. She pulled it down carefully and folded it into her skirt pocket. Then her eyes met Jan's laughing blue ones, and she smiled.

"I guess we're doing this."

He held the barbed wire up for her and pushed the lower strand down with his foot. She tucked her skirts up around her legs and stepped through, her scarf grazing the top wire. When she was through, she held the wires apart for Jan. Then, they moved quickly, slinking into the shadows of the nearest building.

Gasping from nerves, she stood against the wall, hands pressed to its brickwork, her chest heaving and eyes wide.

Jan laughed at her. "Come on. There's a showing of *Penny Serenade* in fifteen minutes. We can make it if we hurry."

"Cary Grant?" she asked, almost giddy with excitement. She never would've thought she'd get this chance. Every day in the ghetto could be her last—they all felt it. It weighed them down like mud. They couldn't escape it. Death was everywhere. It breathed down her neck and coiled around her heart and squeezed until she had no breath left in her body. But for now, she was free, even if only for a little while. Free to watch a movie starring Cary Grant. She could swoon.

Jan reached for her hand and pulled her after him. They ran together down the street, ducked along an alley and then turned into a main thoroughfare. There were people everywhere—riding bicycles, driving automobiles and walking up and down the street. Nacha's breath caught in her throat as she pulled back on Jan's hand. He turned to face her and urged her forward.

"No one is looking at you. Don't worry so much."

She glanced around and saw it was true. The crowd was busy going about their day—no one paid her any mind. She raised her chin and drew a deep breath. Why should she hide? Jan was right—no one would know she'd escaped from the ghetto unless she was stopped for her papers.

They ran on, weaving through the crowd with Jan in front, hands joined, as he led her to the cinema. Excitement welled inside her as her nerves faded. She was out of the ghetto—she was free. She wanted to shout and dance and cry, but she couldn't draw attention to herself, so instead she pushed her feelings down and followed Jan to the ticket booth outside the cinema.

He showed their tickets, and they marched into the cinema. The entrance was decorated in magenta and gold, with gold trim everywhere. There was a hole that'd been blasted in the ceiling over one of the theatre doors, but it didn't spoil the atmosphere. Nacha couldn't have been more excited about their adventure.

They found seats near the front of the theatre, even though Nacha wanted to hide in the back. But Jan had bought popcorn and insisted they sit up front so they could immerse themselves in the experience.

They sat side by side in the darkness as the last of the commercials drifted across the screen. Nacha reached for a handful of popcorn. The flavour burst across her tastebuds, and her stomach growled in anticipation of the treat. She ate quickly and took another handful. Nothing had ever tasted so good. The opening credits began to roll, and Nacha grinned to herself. It was as if she'd stepped into parallel universe. She couldn't believe her luck.

ॐ

BY THE TIME THE MOVIE WAS FINISHED, NACHA HAD ALL but forgotten about her life, the ghetto and the fear she'd felt on their way to the cinema. It was evening when they emerged from the building. Long shadows darkened the street, and most of the pedestrians had returned home for the day.

Nerves buzzed in Nacha's gut. They couldn't hide now if the Nazis came. They stood out, two teens walking along the footpath. This time she didn't take Jan's hand. She shoved both fists deep into her coat pockets and ducked her head, hunching her shoulders.

Her biggest fear was that they'd be stopped crossing the barbed wire fence that marked the edge of the ghetto, but they weren't. They climbed through without incident and donned their armbands in the gathering darkness. Relief filled her like a deep breath.

"You can go, if you like," said Nacha, her nose cold.

Jan shifted from one foot to the other. "I'll walk you home."

"Okay."

They ambled more slowly now, side by side, their shoulders bumping occasionally. Now that she was back in the ghetto, the excitement of their outing faded, and she was sad it was over.

"Thanks for taking me," she said.

He shrugged. "I thought you might like it."

"I loved it."

"Cary Grant's one of the best," he agreed.

"It wasn't that," she said, but didn't know how to articulate what she meant. It was him, the excitement, the adventure, feeling human for a couple of hours. It was everything.

He seemed to understand.

"Not sure we'll get to do it again any time soon," he said.

"I know."

"But one day..."

"That would be nice." She studied his profile in the gloom. His hands hung loose at his sides. His gaze pushed through the darkness straight ahead. With his shoulders back, he looked so confident, marching along the street beside her. As though nothing could hurt him. She almost believed it. He seemed to glide through life unscathed, laughing at the danger that so many others fell victim to. He'd brought her family supplies every week since they'd been sealed into the ghetto. And he'd smuggled goods to many other Jewish families as well.

No random searches or raids, no roundups or executions bothered him or slowed his pace. She'd never realised how strong or brave he was before the war. The conflict had brought out the worst in so many of the people she knew, but it'd brought out the best in some as well—Jan and his family included. She knew how much his mother risked by helping source the supplies and sending her son over the wall. She also knew he'd never do it without his mother's approval. Everything he did put his mother and sisters in danger, as much as himself.

They stopped at her front door and faced one another for a few quiet moments.

"I suppose I should go inside."

"It's getting chilly," he agreed.

He reached for her hand and held it. His was warm, and his touch sent a thrill up her spine. "Thank you for saying yes."

She laughed. "I'm glad I did. I'll remember this day for the rest of my life."

"Me too," he said with a grin.

The front door flew open, and light spilled out into the night.

"Nacha Wierzbicka, get inside this apartment right now." Tata's voice was low, and his eyes flashed with anger.

Nacha dropped Jan's hand and hurried inside with one last glance over her shoulder. She met Jan's gaze, and the intensity in his eyes made her throat catch. She didn't wait to hear what Tata would say. She knew how angry he would be. He was worried about her. She didn't leave a note or tell anyone where she'd gone. She'd been foolish to do it. But still, she couldn't feel sorry.

She heard his voice, quiet and yet angry. Even in his fear, he wouldn't draw attention.

She threw herself down on her bed and hugged the old, worn pillow her mother had made her years earlier. She'd embroidered a pattern of a flower on the cover, and Nacha always slept with the embroidery facing down and one hand beneath the pillow so she could feel the roughness of it with her fingertips.

Before long, her father's footsteps thudded on the staircase. Then there was a knock at the door to the room she shared with her family. Tata always knocked if the door was shut, even though he slept against the wall opposite her.

"Yes, come in."

He walked in and sat on his own bed. "Nacha, I hope you know how worried you made me."

"I'm sorry, Tata."

"You didn't tell me where you were. Now Jan says you went to the Aryan side to watch a movie. I don't know what to think about it all. How could you do it, after everything we've talked about?"

She sat up and smoothed her skirt. "I know it was wrong and thoughtless of me. But I can't help it—I don't care. I might die tomorrow, Tata. And you know that. But today I got to live." A smile flooded across her features as the memories of what she and Jan had done filled her thoughts.

He sighed. "You're right, my sweet girl. Today you lived."

🪰 10 🪰

10TH OCTOBER 1941

The soccer ball *thunked* against the brick wall of the ghetto. Jan ran to get it and kicked it to Walter, who caught it against the inside of his foot with a grin.

"Two to nothing," he said.

Jan squinted into the sunlight. "No way. That wasn't a goal."

"Yes, it was."

"You were wide," complained Jan.

Walter laughed. "Not a chance. Go again?"

Jan stood close to the wall. He glanced at it, listening to the ruckus taking place on the other side. For days, the Jewish police and Nazis had shepherded Jews away from the wall. Many of the apartment complexes that pushed up close to the brickwork and had made smuggling easier for Jan and the other children had been evacuated.

The Nazis had figured out what they were doing and had moved the residents away from the wall. No one was allowed near it on the ghetto side. Jan hadn't been through for three days and was beginning to think he might not get the chance anytime soon.

He ran over to where Walter was juggling the ball between his feet. He didn't let it hit the ground, kicking it with a toe, then the side of one foot, over his head to the other heel and back again.

"What do you think?" asked Jan, dipping his head in the direction of the wall.

"I guess we'll either have to give it a try or go home."

"I'm not going home," replied Jan.

"Then let's do it," agreed Walter. "What's the worst that can happen?"

"Firing squad," offered Jan.

"Meh," replied Walter. "Piece of cake, as the Americans say."

He'd never let Walter know about the restless nervousness that turned over and over in his gut. But even though he was worried, it wasn't something that would stop him. The thrill of adventure, the call of the challenge—those were things he couldn't pass up. Over the months, he'd learned how to dodge the Nazis, to fool the Jewish Police, to talk his way out of tricky situations. It gave him a thrill every time he escaped death. And besides, what would the Wierzbicka family do without his help? They'd run out of supplies in a few days and starve to death like the thousands of others who collapsed in the ghetto every single day. He'd jumped over or dodged around bodies countless times during his smuggling expeditions. Lately, they were getting so thick on the ground, he'd had to take a different route to get through to Nacha and her family.

That was how he'd begun to think of the Wierzbickas. He tried not to, but couldn't help it. He didn't want to feel the way he did. It only complicated things. But he longed to see

Nacha again. He wished he could spend every day with her. Since their outing to the cinema, she was all he could think about. She was pure and sweet and perfect in every way. She was the antidote to the hatred, darkness and evil surrounding him. The war had sucked all the colour out of his life, but she'd brought it back again.

"Kick the ball over," suggested Walter. "We'll climb the wall to get it back."

"We can each take some of the medical supplies in our backpacks. That way, if one of us is caught, the other will still be able to take them to the hospital."

"Good idea," agreed Walter, his red hair bobbing over his forehead as he nodded. They separated the supplies between their backpacks and slipped them over their shoulders.

Jan took the soccer ball and passed it back and forth between his feet for a few moments, scanning the wall and listening for any activity beyond. He drew back one foot and kicked the ball with his toe, sending it flying over the bricks and barbed wire. It hit the apartment opposite and bounced back into the wall and down to the ground.

With a glance at Walter, Jan ran after it. There was no one around on this side of the wall other than a few vendors packing up their stalls after a long day trading at the markets. They paid no attention to the boys.

Everyone who worked at the markets knew Jan well and understood the role he played in the smuggling network that'd sprung up around the markets and the ghetto. Jan relied on the people around him to keep his secret—and so far, they'd all protected his life with their silence, although he knew he couldn't rely on them continuing to do so if they were caught and interrogated by the Gestapo or the *Einsatz-gruppen*.

Walter held the barbed wire apart for Jan to push through. Jan did the same for his friend. When Jan and Walter straightened on the other side of the wall, his ball was nowhere to be seen. He peered along the wall one way, then the other. There was no one around. The narrow alley that backed onto the ghetto wall was abandoned. Usually it was filled with people, but it'd been emptied by an angry group of Wermacht soldiers and a loyal Jewish Police unit.

"Where is it?" asked Walter, scratching his head.

The sound of a ball being kicked back and forth, followed by laughter and shouts of glee, met Jan's ears. He frowned and followed the noise along a darkened lane. His heart thudded against his rib cage, and each footstep was slow and stealthy.

When he reached the end of the lane, he saw a group of fifty boys. A few had divided into teams and were scrimmaging with Jan's ball. One boy kicked it high over the heads of the other boys, who ran after it with glee, calling "Mine!" or "Got it!" or "Pass!"

All the boys sported a white band around one arm. Some wore woollen caps or fedoras. They shouted and laughed, faces red as they ran after the ball. Quickly Jan and Walter tied their own armbands into place and strode out to greet the boys.

"*Witaj!*" called several of the boys when they spotted Jan and Walter. Others said a quiet "*Shalom.*"

"I've seen you around," said one boy as he sidled up to Jan. His brown eyes were wide and solemn. "My name's Peter."

"I'm Jan, and this is Walter. Yes, I've seen you around as well." Jan waved to several of the boys as they ran past. They grinned but kept moving, intent on stealing back the ball.

"*Shalom*," said Walter.

"Why are so many boys together here?" asked Jan.

"We're waiting for someone." He dipped his head in the direction of the wall. "Your ball, I presume?"

Jan smiled. "Yes, that's right."

"Do you mind if we play? We haven't had a game in ages."

"We don't mind. We've got things to do. But we'll be back in a little while." Jan scanned the street. Something was wrong. It was too quiet. A window slammed shut a few houses down.

Peter smiled. "Want to join us?"

"I don't know," replied Jan, looking around. "Why is it so quiet?"

Peter followed his gaze, his face growing pale. "You're right. It's too quiet." He pressed his fingers to his mouth and let out a whistle.

The game stopped suddenly, and the boys' heads all whipped in Peter's direction.

A deep voice yelled, "Halt or we'll shoot!"

Jan's heart dropped as the group was quickly surrounded by Gestapo, guns raised. Jewish Police were dotted amongst them, thin and peaked-looking. Boys of every age scattered. One moment Walter stood beside Jan, and the next he was gone. Jan ran north along the street, but was halted by a knock to the head that sent him sprawling onto the tarmac.

Pain bit into his lip where it grazed the ground, and his head throbbed. The taste of blood filled his mouth. He pushed himself slowly to his feet and glanced around. The Gestapo had captured most of the group. They stood huddled together surrounded by angry black-clad officers. The soldier who'd knocked him down pushed him back to the rest of the group with a violent shove and an angry shout.

"*Oberführer* Meisinger, we lost three of the little rats. Do you want us to look for them?" one police officer asked, clicking his heels together in front of the man in charge. He looked ridiculous in his thrown-together uniform, the waist cinched by a rope where it was too bulky for his emaciated frame. Jan wanted to scowl at his fawning—didn't he know the *Oberführer* would never recognise him as an equal no matter what he did?

"*Nein.*"

Jan recognised Meisinger from the cathedral as the head of the *Einsatzgruppe* who'd callously shot the priests and other worshipers. His cruelty was renowned throughout Warsaw and all of Poland. Poles trembled when they furtively whispered his name while telling tales of mass graves and burning barns filled with Polish families.

A ball of fear knotted in Jan's belly, and he swallowed hard. Meisinger's cold eyes surveyed the group. His hair was brushed smoothly back in place and secured with gel like a brown skullcap against his head. He paced with hands linked behind his back to study the children as though they were objects to dispose of.

The boys stood in silence, some with heads bowed, others staring sullenly at their captors. Jan looked for a means of escape, but saw none. They were completely surrounded. He took a step backward, and the tip of a rifle pushed against one shoulder blade.

A truck pulled up with a screech of brakes. It had a wire cage on the bed, with a door in the back. A Gestapo officer opened the door and waved a hand at it.

"Get inside," he said.

The rest of the soldiers pushed the boys forward and into the truck. Jan stumbled up the small steps that led into the truck bed. He was jostled back and forth until finally he reached the right-hand side near the front and found a seat. There were two long benches running down the length of the vehicle on either side of the cage. He sat on one and lifted his legs to hug his knees to his chest. The air was cold and the seat beneath him colder still. It sent a chill through his thin frame.

Another truck pulled up beside the first and still more boys were piled into it until all of the boys were crowded together in one of the two vehicles. Peter sat beside Jan, pressed up against him. There were boys all around him. Only about a dozen got to sit, backs pressed against the wire frame of the cage that held them captive. The rest were jammed into any space in which they could stand.

When the truck jerked forward and rumbled down the road, Peter leaned closer to Jan. "You should tell them."

"Tell them what?"

"That you're Catholic. They'll let you go."

Jan rested his chin on his knees. The rattling of the truck made his teeth chatter. "But they won't let *you* go. And besides, they'll ask me what I was doing in the ghetto wearing a Star of David armband. They'll try to get me to talk, to betray my family. I won't do it."

Peter sighed. "You're right."

Jan felt an affinity with the group of boys. Some of the younger ones sniffled into their sleeves. The older boys sat or stood with pale faces, not speaking, only staring into the distance. He couldn't leave them. Even if the Gestapo cared whether he was Catholic or Jewish, he had no intention of telling them. It wasn't likely they'd let him go. But if they did, he'd be leaving the other boys behind or betraying his family.

He'd heard the rumours about what happened to the Jews rounded up in the ghetto and taken away in trucks. No one knew for sure what happened to them, but there were whispers. The only thing they were certain of was that none ever returned.

Nacha chewed the end of her fingernail nervously. She scanned the alley one way then the other, looking for any sign of police or Gestapo. But no one was around. Many families in the area had heard about the raid earlier that day.

They'd rounded up around fifty boys from the neighbourhood and taken them away in trucks. Everyone else was holed up in their apartments, grieving the loss. Nacha didn't know what to think. They had to talk to Waltrina, Jan's mother, about what had happened, and she wasn't looking forward to their conversation.

They'd communicated early on with Waltrina through Jan that if something should happen to him to meet by the wall in the marketplace. So, Nacha and her cousin Jakob had paced the area for an hour in the cold and dark as soon as the sun went down, waiting for her to show up.

Finally, they heard movement against the wall. A scrape and a squeak, and Waltrina's pale face showed above the barbed wire.

"Nacha," whispered Waltrina.

"I'm here."

"Is Jan with you?"

Nacha swallowed. "No, the Gestapo took him."

Waltrina gasped and covered her mouth with one hand, the other steadying the wobbling ladder. "No."

"Walter was with him. They took dozens of boys at once, but Walter managed to escape, and he told us what happened. He's in hiding with his family for now."

Waltrina raised her chin. "Do you know where they took him?"

"No, but it was Meisinger. Walter saw him."

"The *Einsatzgruppen*," murmured Waltrina. "Thank you, Nacha. Go home now and stay safe."

"What will you do? We have to do something." Nacha couldn't bear to be locked inside the ghetto. She wanted to run after Jan, to chase down the truck that drove him away from them. What if he was gone forever? She hadn't said goodbye. It wasn't possible that she'd never see him again.

Waltrina scanned the marketplace on either side of the fence, then leaned closer. "I'll bribe a guard. They like diamonds and jewels. I'm a trader. I can find whatever I need easily enough."

"Will it work?"

Waltrina sighed. "I don't know, but I have to try. Meisinger is a cold-hearted killer, but perhaps one of his underlings will be open to a gift. I'll get in touch when I can. But if you don't hear from me, know that I'm doing everything I can. You should go home to your father. He'll be worried."

Nacha waved goodbye to Waltrina and met Jakob's gaze. He blew on his bare hands in the darkness, his breath a fog of steam in the cold air.

"What do you think?" he asked.

She grimaced. "I don't think. I hope."

✻ 12 ✻

They were taken to the Gestapo headquarters. There was no sign, but Jan recognised it. The lines of flag-bearing staff cars parked outside and in the courtyard gave the place away, along with the constant stream of black uniforms. Clouds gathered in the sky, obscuring the sunlight and giving their surroundings the look of twilight even though it was only afternoon.

The building itself was intimidating, with towering columns around the driveway. A pale cream colour, it rose above the trucks as they drove into the courtyard, like a sentinel on watch over prey that would find no escape. Jan shuddered as the shadow of the columns fell over him, then was gone again as quickly.

The trucks parked in front of a massive doorway, and the engines fell silent. The boys whispered amongst themselves, shuffling to pull back from the gate. None wanted to be the first to step out of the vehicle. So, Jan pushed himself forward through the crowd to wait for the gate to be opened.

Peter followed him, his breath warm on the back of Jan's neck. He looked over his shoulder to give Peter a nod. The boy's brown eyes were wide, but his jaw was set and head high beneath a jaunty grey fedora.

Overhead, the first raindrop fell. It landed on Jan's nose, and he dashed it away with the back of his hand. His heart hammered against his rib cage, and his rapid breathing made his head feel light. He didn't allow thoughts about what was to come to cloud his mind. Unlike the sky above him, he wanted a clear head. No matter what happened, he'd never betray his family. It was the only thought that occupied his consciousness in that moment.

Tell the Gestapo nothing. Tell them nothing.

A guard lumbered to the back of the vehicle and unlatched the door. It swung open, and he indicated for Jan to climb down. Jan took the steps carefully, his eyes on the ground. If he staggered or stumbled, he knew the guard would take it out on him. He'd seen the way they treated the Jews in the ghetto, and the guard saw him as Jewish. The guard wouldn't hesitate to assault Jan. His best approach would be not to draw attention to himself.

The moment his foot hit the pavement, he felt the first strike to his head. The guard's baton came down again, this time smiting one shoulder. He pitched forward and covered his head with both hands as he fell. The baton came down again and again, this time on his forearm, the next on his back. He grunted with the pain of it and scrambled away from the guard, out of reach. The man turned his attention to Peter, and after him the next boy. Each of the boys received blows as they scuttled from the truck bed and into the court-yard. But none so bad as Jan. It was the generally recognised curse of going first.

Jan nursed his bruised arm, holding it against his side as they were shuttled through the courtyard and into a darkened doorway. The boys jogged along in pairs, the guards rushing after them shouting in German, punishing them with blows and kicks.

Finally, they were pushed into a series of cells side by side along a hallway. Jan sank gratefully to the ground, his back leaning against a frigid stone wall. Peter landed beside him. The heavy door swung shut. Boys crowded towards the back of the cell, shivering. A few sobbed, but most were silent.

It was soon after that the first boy was taken. The door creaked open with a suddenness that surprised the group. Guards grabbed the nearest boy, a tall lad with gangly legs and a pointed nose. They pushed him roughly from the cell and let the door clang shut behind them.

A chink of daylight gleamed dully on the floor through a small barred window in the wall behind Jan. He studied the window. He stood on tiptoe to test out the strength of the bars, but could barely reach them. Peter lifted him up and he shook them with all his strength, grimacing at the pain in his arm, but it was no use. The bars were too strong and the gaps between them too small. Even the slimmest boy in the group wouldn't be able to squirm through.

He slid to the floor with a grunt of disappointment.

"I'm going to look around," he whispered.

"I don't think you'll find anything useful," Peter said.

Jan knew the Nazis had every possibility covered. They were meticulous, systematic and thorough in everything they did. But he couldn't sit still and let himself think. His thoughts would go to his mother and sisters, to Nacha and her family, and he'd lose his resolve. He had to stay busy and keep the images of the people he loved from his mind.

He walked around the small room, fingers to the wall. He felt something rough and looked closer to see messages scrawled into the paintwork. Written in Polish and Russian, Romani and Yiddish, they were everywhere. It was difficult to read them in the dim light, but he could make out some of the Polish words.

Peter joined him, running his hands over the scratched surface. "'*I love you, Mama and Papa,*' this one says."

Jan swallowed back a ball of emotion that climbed up his throat.

"Don't give up on me."

"I wish I'd left when I had the chance."

"I am here because of you, Alek."

"Never surrender to them! Those maggots dressed in black with their long, snivelling faces."

"If only you'd let me go."

"Mother, your daughter is here and I don't have long. Farewell."

The boys whispered the etchings, carved with the end of a nail or screw, back and forth to each other. Soon, other boys crowded around them, joining in reading or listening to the words. Some began looking for implements and carved their own messages into the walls.

THEY SPENT THEIR TIME SHUFFLING BACK AND FORTH around the cell that first day and night. There was little room to move and none to lie down. They dozed where they stood or sat, leaning on the walls or each other for support.

Thirst clenched at Jan's throat, suffocating him with its longing. He swallowed repeatedly, seeking relief, but found none. Several of the boys cried for their mothers throughout that first night. But by the second day, they were all silent, and the shuffling had given way to lethargy and hopelessness.

"I'm so hungry," said Peter, his back pressed against Jan's.

They'd slept that way for a few hours, but with other boys standing or sitting up against them, they couldn't find a more comfortable position. So their sleep was interrupted constantly by shoves and knocks, or by their own head dropping from where it'd rested on their knees.

"I'd love a cup of water," replied Jan.

"Do you think they'll bring us something?" Peter asked.

"I don't know. But I'm not sure how long we can go on like this."

It was cold in the cell, exacerbated by the stonework and the open window. Their collective body heat helped, but unable to move much and without food or water, Jan found that his joints had stiffened.

That evening, when the sunlight peeking through the window into the cell dimmed, the door opened and a pot of soup was shoved inside, along with a pile of bowls and spoons. They boys rushed hungrily for the pot, but Jan stepped forward, hands raised.

"There's no rush, no rush," he said in a soothing voice. "Let's take our time so we don't spill a drop."

The boys listened to his words and waited as he and Peter dipped the watery potato soup into bowls and handed it around. They ate hungrily, though by the time Jan finished his bowl, his stomach had begun to grumble for more. It didn't satisfy, but it was better than nothing, and the broth had quenched the worst of his thirst for now.

During the daylight hours, boys were taken one by one. They were each returned to the cell beaten and bloodied. When Jan questioned them about what'd happened, they didn't want to talk about it. A few said they hadn't told the

Gestapo a thing. They were adamant about that. None wanted to condemn their families. Some didn't say a word to him, but cried in the corner until they fell asleep.

On the fifth day, Jan was reading the carvings on the walls again. He'd barely slept in days. His hunger had abated on the fourth day, although his thirst had only grown until it fairly ravaged his waking hours. He could think of little besides finding water. Reading the messages scrawled by other desperate inmates in the Gestapo's prison was the only thing that distracted him from the cloying thirst.

Jan found himself by the cell door still reading, with boys crowded all around him so that he felt as though he'd never had a moment in his life without someone touching him, when the door was flung open. He staggered away from it into the crowd of prisoners, but the guard caught him by the collar and threw him into the hall like a piece of luggage.

"Come on. Your turn," he snarled.

The boy they'd taken earlier that morning stood in the hallway. His face was swollen and distorted. Jan barely recognised him but for the floppy brown hair that fell over his forehead. His eyes were swollen almost shut. He was missing teeth. Blood dripped from his chin and stained his torn shirt.

The boy staggered past Jan and fell onto the dirt in the cell. He lay there unmoving. The door closed, and Jan was pushed forward.

"Let's go."

There were two guards. One led the way, the other pushing him forcefully from behind. They took him down several corridors to a large room with a table on one side and a chair in the middle. He was told to sit in the chair and then he waited.

They didn't make him wait long. They tied him upside down to the chair and took turns beating him. One had a thick wooden club. The other carried a horse whip around with him, whacking it against his own thigh gently as he paced back and forth. When it came his turn to beat Jan, he did so with a smile.

Jan watched it all upside down, sweat dripping into his eyes along with the blood.

"Tell us who smuggles food into the ghetto." They asked their questions over and over.

"Who is the leader of your group?"

"What are you plotting?"

"Why do you conspire against the Reich and your esteemed *Führer*?"

"Give us a name!"

Jan said nothing in response. His silence only further enraged his torturers. They were puffing hard before too long, but it didn't slow the frenzy of their assault.

One kick, landed by the guard with the horse crop, knocked Jan's front teeth out. He lost consciousness then, and didn't know how long he remained that way. He woke up hours later in the cell again, with Peter watching over him, a worried expression on his pale face in the dull moonlight that sifted through the window above them.

"You're awake," Peter said with a sigh.

Jan couldn't speak. Pain rushed into every part of his body at once. His mouth throbbed, his head ached, his limbs were bruised. He clenched his hands and wriggled his toes. At least he wasn't paralysed. For that he was grateful.

Peter nursed him back to health, spooning the insipid soup into his bloodied mouth. He wiped Jan's face clean with his own shirt as best as he could.

"You've got to tell them," he whispered so the others couldn't hear. "Tell them you're Catholic."

There were tears in the corners of his eyes, but they didn't fall.

Jan shook his head. It would make no difference. He had a

death sentence, no matter what his religious beliefs or background. The etchings on the walls of the cell confirmed that. Gypsies, Christians, Muslims, atheists, agnostics and Jews had all gone before him. All had died at the hands of the demons in black who'd taken it upon themselves to rid the world of all that was good.

When they took Peter early the next morning, Jan was finally sitting up and had even spent a few minutes standing during the night. His heart fell as he saw his friend marched away and the heavy wooden door fall back into place, obscuring everything from his view. The morning sun hadn't yet risen, and so the cell lay in pure darkness. There was no light from the moon, nothing to break up the blackness that swallowed them whole the moment the cell door shut.

None of the boys whimpered or cried any longer. Six days in the dank cell with only a bucket in the corner in which to relieve themselves, and one bowl of watered-down potato soup in the evenings, had rendered all of them weak and thinner than they'd already been. Several of the boys hadn't returned from their interrogations and Jan feared the worst, although he couldn't bring himself to worry about them or about anything other than the pain that he knew was coming the next time he left that room.

It was all-consuming. The torture was worse than he'd been prepared to suffer through. He'd known it was coming, but he couldn't have imagined how much his body would hurt and how intensely he wanted to tell them everything he knew so the pain would stop. But he hadn't said a word. He'd kept his family safe and his secrets remained hidden in his heart. He only hoped his body would give out and die before it got so bad that he cracked.

"Where's Peter?" asked one of the smaller boys, his voice grating on Jan's nerves.

"I don't know," he replied shortly.

He didn't want to take it out on them, but he couldn't think about Peter. It was too much. Too hard.

The door swung open again and Peter stumbled into the room a short time later. They hadn't spent as much time questioning him as they had some of the others. The guard surveilled the room in the faint morning light, disgust turning down the corners of his mouth beneath a short black moustache.

"Get up, all of you. Come with me."

The boys staggered out of the dank cell and into the corridor. They jogged or shuffled in line, two by two, along the hallway and found themselves once again in the courtyard outside. Jan recalled their arrival in that same location six days earlier. It seemed like another lifetime. He was a different boy than the one who'd driven through the archway in the back of a truck, full of trepidation but excited to prove he was strong enough to withstand his fate. Whatever it may be.

Now he knew—his fate was death at the hands of the Gestapo's *Einsatzgruppe*. The cruelty of the men whose purpose was the torture and murder of anyone they deemed a threat went beyond anything he'd seen or believed possible before they snatched him off the ghetto's streets.

The boys whispered amongst themselves.

"Where are they taking us?"

"What will happen now?"

"Are we going home?"

"Will they kill us?"

So many questions. None with any answers. Jan didn't believe they'd take the boys home, not after all they'd been through. But he wouldn't say it. Wouldn't steal hope in their final moments. He steeled himself, his jaw tightening as he fought back the tears. If only he'd had a chance to say goodbye to Mama and to Nacha. They didn't know where he was, wouldn't know what'd become of him. The thought brought a lump to his throat.

"He's Catholic," Peter said. His voice was too soft, raspy. It was lost in the noise.

Jan frowned. What was he doing?

"Catholic!" shouted Peter, gaining strength as he spoke. "Jan Kostanski is Catholic."

A guard wandered closer, his brow furrowed. "Which one of you is Jan Kostanski?"

Jan raised a shaking hand. His shoulder ached from the effort.

"Come with me. I've been looking for you." The guard spun on his heel and marched from the courtyard out to the street. The sun glanced above the buildings on the other side of the road, temporarily blinding Jan as he followed the man.

He stepped through the archway, tenting a hand over his eyes to shield them from the glare.

"Don't be shy, boy. What were you doing in the ghetto? Never mind, you're free to go. Your mother waits for you over there." The guard pointed across the road to where a vehicle lay idling. An old black BMW Dixie sat with one door open. Mama stood beside the door, her hands pressed to her mouth.

When Jan saw her, he began to run. His legs didn't work the way they should, but he ambled and hurried the best he could across the empty street. He reached her and collapsed into her arms.

"Mama," he groaned.

She cupped his cheeks between her hands and kissed him all over his face. "My darling boy. What have they done to you?"

He gasped at the pain of her touch. She released him, tears streaking down her cheeks in rivulets.

Just then, a series of shots rang out behind him. There

were screams of terror and pain, then more shots fired. Five, ten, twenty, then on and on. He lost count of how many there were. It fell silent for a few moments, then more shooting followed. He covered his ears with both hands, his tears turning to rivers.

Mama pushed him quickly into the passenger seat and shut the door behind him. She climbed in the driver's side and pushed the car into gear, accelerating away from the curb.

They didn't speak. Instead, each of them sat in silence, crying, Jan with his hands still covering his ears. He rocked back and forth in his seat, willing himself not to think about what had happened, what he'd escaped from with moments to spare. And all because the words of a friend had given him freedom. A friend he'd never see again.

Mama glanced at him as she wiped the tears from her eyes with the back of one gloved hand. "I bribed them days ago, but they said they couldn't locate you."

"I was there all the time," he said.

13

30TH MARCH 1942

At seventeen years of age, Jan had smuggled regular supplies into the Jewish ghetto in Warsaw for two long years. He'd learned every place to scale the wall or push his way through. Every weakness in the structures of the ghetto, every tunnel built by resistors and every member of the Jewish Police who could be trusted, bought, or was dangerous to his cause.

Nathan held the barbed wire apart for him and he stepped through, then paused to look at the camera. Edek held the Rolleiflex camera steady atop a tripod. He peered down through the second lens and held up his free hand.

When his hand dropped, Jan sighed with relief and finished climbing through the wire. "Have you got enough photographs?"

Edek packed the camera away into a satchel slung over his shoulder. "That's enough for now. Thanks for posing. I'll add these to my collection."

"What will you do with all these photos?" asked Nathan.

Edek had followed Jan several times over the years, keen to document the smuggling operation that kept the Jews in the ghetto from starving to death on the meagre rations provided by the Germans. He'd photographed Jan riding in a rickshaw with Jakob, standing at the dividing wall with Antoni, one arm around Nacha in an awkward embrace that still made the heat rise to Jan's cheeks when he recalled the moment, and a profile shot of him and Walter when they were considering the best way to get back to the Aryan side of the fence one day during a particularly nasty bout of raids.

In the end, they'd simply marched through the open gate with a work crew and ducked into a nearby alley before running home. Thankfully, the guard on duty at the gate knew them well, had a predilection for fine chocolate that Jan was able to satisfy on a regular basis, and looked away at just the right moment.

"I have them hidden beneath the floor of my apartment. I hope to smuggle them out to send to the Allies, or perhaps they will be revealed when the war is over and I am gone." He offered them a wan smile.

Jan didn't like it when his friends spoke that way. "Don't say that—you'll still be around then. The Gestapo likes you. They've given you a job, after all."

Edek's face clouded over. "It isn't a kindness. You can trust me on that."

"What is it you do?" asked Walter.

Edek studied his expression. "You wish to know?"

"I do too," replied Jan.

Everyone in the ghetto knew of the favouritism Edek received. That he put his camera bag over his shoulder and set off in the gleaming black staff cars with various Gestapo officers. Once he even went on an outing with Meisinger. But he never told them what he did on those expeditions outside the ghetto walls, only that the Nazis paid him to take photographs for the sake of their records and for posterity.

"You may come with me now, then. I have a small job to do, and if you keep out of sight, I don't see how it will hurt. You should know, I think. You should see for yourself what I see. Too many still believe they can survive this war if they keep their heads low. Never mind all that—we won't speak of it now. You can witness for yourself and make up your own mind about the fate of my people."

Edek's black moustache twitched as he spoke, and there was a deep sadness behind his almost-black eyes. His fedora was pulled low and tipped to one side. Dark brown hair curled out from beneath it.

He adjusted the satchel on his shoulder and beckoned them to follow him. Jan and Walter exchanged a curious glance. With a shrug, Jan trotted after the photographer. Walter waited a moment, chewing his lower lip, then followed them.

"Wait for me," Walter called.

Jan slowed his pace and the two of them walked together, side by side, several paces behind Edek. The photographer paid them no attention. He walked with slumped shoulders and a swinging gate. He hummed beneath his breath all the while, waving occasionally to people they passed in the street.

Everyone seemed to know Edek, although he was a quiet, studious type who generally kept to himself. He was well-liked in the community, as well as something of a curiosity. People weren't sure whether or not to trust him, although in Jan's experience, he was a man of deep integrity and compassion. Still, anyone favoured by the Gestapo was immediately under suspicion in the ghetto.

They walked a long time until they'd passed through the entire ghetto and out the other side. The boys caught up to

Edek to make it through the ghetto gates, where he simply doffed his hat to the guards and they waved him through.

Jan shoved his hands deep into his pockets and chewed on the stem of a long piece of grass to pass the time. He was missing his front teeth, but had learned to manage with the rest of the teeth he'd retained after surviving the Gestapo's beating the previous October.

"I have a favour to ask you," Edek said.

"What is it?" Jan asked.

"The photographs in my collection—will you take them? Will you get them to the Allies? Will you get them into the hands of the right people so the world will see what is happening here in Warsaw to my people?"

"Of course I will."

"Can I give them to you soon? I don't know how much longer they will tolerate me."

Jan nodded. "Tomorrow? I'll return then, if you like."

"Yes, tomorrow."

They came across a field between two bombed-out buildings and Edek stopped them at the outskirts. On the other side of the field were two trucks and a black staff car. They were parked on the grass.

The sun had set behind them and black shadows hung over them and lengthened across the field, giving the entire scene a sinister look with the remnants of a building in sharp relief behind them.

Edek beckoned Jan and Walter deeper into the ruins of the first building and pushed a finger to his lips.

"Circle around the outside of the field and you can watch from the building yonder. Do you see it?" He pointed to the outline of the partially collapsed building behind the Gestapo soldiers, who milled about in the field smoking cigarettes that glowed red in the failing light.

Jan nodded.

Walter scratched his nose. "What are they doing?"

"You'll see." Edek's eyes darkened. "When I'm finished, I'll return and meet you here. Make sure no one sees you."

Jan was beginning to think they shouldn't have come. Why had Edek encouraged them if they weren't supposed to be here? The last thing he wanted was another close encounter with members of the Gestapo. The memory of his visit to their headquarters still haunted his dreams at night, leaving him in a cold sweat with tears on his cheeks.

They watched as Edek lumbered across the field, shoulders rounded and hands hanging loosely by his sides.

"What do you think?" asked Walter.

Jan spat the grass stem from his mouth. "Let's go. We can keep out of sight if we stay in the shadows of the trees and buildings. They've got their vehicle headlights illuminating the field, so they won't be able to see anything beyond. If we're quiet, they'll never know we're there."

The two boys jogged through the bombed-out building, navigating around the crater at its centre and leaping over piles of bricks. They skirted around the field, making sure to stay in the shadows.

Walter tripped on a pile of bricks and almost sprawled into the dirt, but Jan caught him by the arm and steadied him. They waited in silence a few moments, breaths held in their lungs, to see if they'd been heard. But the Gestapo were talking and laughing loudly amongst themselves and didn't seem to notice the clatter of bricks that skidded across the broken timber floor.

Jan and Walter exchanged a silent look, then continued on their way. They stopped close to the soldiers and crouched down behind a half-destroyed wall. The building they were in looked as though it'd been a store of some kind, but there was no roof, and everything had been looted from the shelves. The front entrance was nothing but a crater in the ground.

It was difficult for Jan to remember a time when his home hadn't been under siege or occupation—it felt as though it'd always been that way. He didn't give himself the luxury of sifting through memories or dreaming of the future. He inhabited each moment with the will only to live and to ensure his loved ones survived. Nothing else mattered.

When the ghetto was built, he'd been intrigued by the adventure of smuggling goods to his Jewish family. But ever since his arrest, he hadn't been able to shake a growing sense of doom that hung over him daily and invaded his sleep.

"What are they doing?" asked Walter, shuffling forward on his haunches to get a better look.

Jan didn't respond. He had a clear view of the field. The staff cars were parked so that the beams of light from their headlamps illuminated a patch of dirt in front of them. The Gestapo officers were gathered in a semi-circle around the lit-up space, puffs of smoke issuing from their mouths in bursts.

In the middle of the lighted ground was an enormous pit. Dirt was piled up around it, and on those piles of dirt knelt dozens of people. A group of emaciated men stood back from the rest. They were dressed in striped rags. Some of those kneeling sobbed, and others were silent. Several women held children close with desperate arms.

All waited while the men guarding them smoked cigarettes and made jokes behind them. Several of the men were speaking about a night out at a *wirtshaus,* or tavern, on the outskirts of town. Jan had picked up enough vocabulary over the years to understand the gist of their conversation. They'd met some girls and were discussing which of the girls was the prettiest. One of the men thought it was the blonde girl, but the others chose the brunette.

Walter's face fell as he took in the scene.

"We should go," said Jan. A sense of foreboding pushed

him to move, to go anywhere else other than there. Why had Edek brought them? What was his purpose?

"No," Walter said. His voice was quiet but firm.

They saw Edek talking with one of the soldiers. He stood off to one side. Then the soldiers raised their machine guns and began to fire. Jan couldn't watch. He bowed his head, squeezing his eyes shut tight as the row of men, women and children who knelt along the edge of the pit were shot in the back.

When the shooting stopped, he looked first at Walter. His friend hadn't turned away. He surveyed the carnage before them, face pale and eyes devoid of emotion.

Jan's heart thundered against his rib cage. He couldn't bring himself to look up. To take in what he knew he'd see. Finally, he raised his eyes and looked. Several officers were walking down the line, turning their victims over so they lay face up.

Any who had fallen forward were rolled over by hand or a swift kick. The Gestapo continued their conversation about the previous evening, discussing whether or not they should return to the same *wirtshaus* that evening.

Bile rose up Jan's throat.

Walter still hadn't moved.

"Where's Edek?" asked Jan.

Walter stared at him, eyes blank. His lips opened, but he didn't say anything.

Then Jan saw him. Edek was on the edge of the glow from the vehicles' headlights. He held up his camera and snapped a shot of one of the victims. Then he moved onto the next. He was documenting the dead. Jan's throat tightened.

"There he is," he whispered.

Walter's gaze followed Jan's pointed finger.

They waited in the dark as the cold seeped into Jan's joints. Edek moved down the line, taking photos, one by one.

He took his time. And as he drew closer, Jan could see his face was expressionless. The Gestapo ignored him.

Once Edek had taken a victim's photograph, the men in rags moved forward and took turns pushing the victims into the pit until they were puffing from the effort. Edek went through several rolls of film before he was finished. Then he ambled back across the darkened field as the group of thin men finished their work at the pit while the Gestapo watched on in amusement.

Jan and Walter hurried quietly back to their meeting place and caught up with Edek. The trio didn't say a word, but trudged silently to the ghetto and through its gates.

Finally, Jan spoke up. "Why did you do that?" He wanted to scream, to cry, to hit Edek for what he'd done. A stone of emotion sat heavy in the base of his throat that he couldn't swallow no matter how he tried.

Edek sighed. "I do this often. I don't wish to do it, but I believe it is important to capture the faces of these people, my people. They make me document their victims so they can keep their meticulous records. But I do it so that one day the world will know what they have done, and who they are. And so we can all remember the lives they've snuffed out. Who will remember them if not us?" His voice trembled with emotion.

He stepped up to Jan and grabbed him by the shoulders. His gaze found Jan's, and the intensity behind Edek's eyes scared Jan into silence. "Who will remember them if not you?"

❦

THE NEXT MORNING, JAN ROSE EARLY AND STRODE through a foggy dawn to the ghetto wall. He traversed it quickly and pulled on his armband as he ran along the empty streets. When he reached the corner where he and Edek had arranged to meet the previous evening, he found it deserted.

He shifted back and forth from his right foot to his left, blowing hard on his hands to warm them while he waited. The silent empty streets were eerie and he scanned them constantly, his ears pricked and nerves taut.

Footsteps hurried up the street behind him and he spun around to see Nathan striding towards him through the fog.

"Nathan, what are you doing here?" he asked.

Nathan hushed him with a hand to his mouth. "Our voices will carry this morning."

Jan fell into step beside him as he continued walking.

"I came to tell you something," said Nathan, his voice low.

His brown eyes found Jan's and he stopped suddenly with a sigh. "Edek is gone."

"What?"

"They took him this morning. There was a transport to Treblinka, and he was rounded up along with many others. I'm sorry."

Jan shook his head. "We were supposed to meet."

"I know. He told me."

"Did he give you anything for me?"

"No, I'm sorry."

They said their goodbyes, and Jan watched as Nathan jogged back in the direction of his family's apartment. Anger surged up his spine and he blinked back hot tears.

Then he shoved his hands deep into his pockets, hunched his shoulders against the cold and walked home through the gloom as the city wakened around him.

❧ 14 ❧

Tata left with Adam Czerniaków early in the morning. Nacha watched them leave from her bedroom window. She pressed her nose to the glass and followed them with her gaze until they were out of sight. Adam gesticulated wildly with his hands as he spoke, the sound of his voice echoing down the street even though she couldn't make out the words.

Something was happening. Her father had looked unusually worried, his normally stoic expression replaced by a palpable fear as he strode mechanically beside his long-time friend. The *Judenrat* was meeting urgently to discuss something of importance—that much she'd gathered from their frantic discussion at the front door. But what could it be?

Life in the ghetto had found its own rhythm. There was school to attend, although it was sporadic and poorly resourced. The latest outbreak of typhus had claimed many lives, but her family had managed to escape its reach yet again. Jan brought them regular supplies and so they were able to live, however humbly, on more food than most had.

The Council, run by Adam Czerniaków, had established a semblance of a functioning community. Even with the amount of death surrounding them, the ghetto had swelled in size over the years, and according to Tata's estimation, it held around 460,000 Jews. Nacha's family's apartment was already crowded to capacity, but every other apartment or home in the small ghetto district housed almost ten people per room.

The ghetto was cramped, but it was also an escape from the worst of the violence. The Jews within its walls were sick and starving, but they had each other and even though they no longer spoke of it, Nacha knew they carried the hope of liberation in their hearts.

Nacha had grown accustomed to the constant police presence and the unmarked dead bodies carried by families to lie in the street so they could continue to collect their loved ones' meagre rations for as long as possible after they died. She understood the rhythm of the ghetto and how to survive in the midst of it.

But something had changed, and she knew Tata wouldn't talk about it with her. He rarely told her anything he thought might worry her. He still seemed to think it possible to guard her innocence, although why he believed that, she couldn't say. Her innocence had died the day the Nazis occupied Warsaw and torched the synagogues with the rabbis still inside.

Nacha wanted to see for herself what it was that drew her father from the warmth of his bed so early in the morning. She dressed quickly and quietly and hurried downstairs without disturbing Babcia, who was in the middle of her *shacharit,* morning prayers.

Nacha knew she should also be saying *shacharit,* but God

would forgive her this one omission, since she couldn't let her father and Mr Czerniaków get too far ahead or she'd never catch them. She could guess where they were headed, of course. To the room above the barber shop where the council always met. But she didn't want to risk the possibility of them going elsewhere.

So she skipped out the door, pulling it softly shut behind her, and then ran down the street after her father and his friend, tying her scarf in place as she went.

The sun rose slowly over the buildings to the east, warming the ghetto as it went. The scent of decay and rotting corpses rose with it and she steeled her empty stomach against it, slowing her pace to clench her nostrils shut with her fingertips.

Soon she passed the smell and was able to run again. And before long she saw her father and Mr Czerniaków up ahead. She resumed a fast walking pace, keeping her eyes glued to the men as they wove through the foot traffic that had begun filtering into the street for the morning rush to soup kitchens and the market after prayers.

She followed the two men to the brick wall surrounding the ghetto and separating it from the *Umschlagplatz* at the train station. The *Umschlagplatz* was the area adjacent to the train station where Jews were assembled for transportation to Treblinka.

Nacha didn't know exactly what Treblinka was, or what happened to people when they arrived there, but she'd heard the whispers. It was some kind of camp, and according to women in the line at the soup kitchen she'd overheard months earlier, no one ever returned to the ghetto if they were sent there.

Nacha had stayed away from the *Umschlagplatz* since then. But now she was close to it, and a glimpse through its open gate sent a shiver up her spine. She continued walking until she could look through the gates directly, and what she saw turned her stomach.

Hundreds of Jews from the ghetto were seated on the ground. They wore layers of clothing in the heat of the summer morning. Beside them or in clenched hands were suitcases and satchels. Children squatted by their parents or lay quietly in their laps.

The murmur of voices carried to her on the breeze. Her father and Mr Czerniaków marched up to the gates, and her breath caught in her throat. What was Tata doing? They might arrest him and send him away as well if he wasn't careful.

Mr Czerniaków spoke to one of the guards, and the man spun on his heel and walked away. He soon returned with a Gestapo officer dressed in black with riding pants tucked into long, black boots and carrying a walking stick that he held tucked against his side. His black cap was pulled low over his eyes, and his stomach protruded over his pants.

She tiptoed closer and pressed herself to the wall, willing the guards not to see her. Then she peeked around the edge of the opening where the wide gate led to the train yards.

"We ask that you cease this transportation. Our people wish to stay in the ghetto," Mr Czerniaków said.

The Gestapo officer addressed him politely. "Of course. I understand, Herr Czerniaków. But unfortunately, the orders come from above. You understand. Everyone must do their part. There is a war on, after all."

"But we can manage here. We're not causing any trouble."

"The resettlement to the east of the entire ghetto's occupants will continue as planned. You have nothing to fear, Herr Czerniaków. I assure you we will take every precaution necessary to transport your people to their new home. The ghetto has become overcrowded. We're doing what we must to make certain of your safety."

Mr Czerniaków hesitated, his voice trembling when he spoke again. "And what is their destination, Herr Müller?"

"I can't say, I'm sorry to tell you. But I do know they're going east. Now, if you'll excuse me, I must get moving. I have a lot to do if I'm going to manage the task set before me." The man offered a half-hearted *heil Hitler* and was turning to go when Mr Czerniaków addressed him again.

"I apologise for the intrusion, Herr Müller, but one last request." His voice wavered. "The children. May they remain behind?"

"The children? Surely not. Who will care for them without their parents?" Herr Müller barked.

"What about the children in the orphanages? Will you let them remain behind? They can care for themselves, or their carers could stay with them."

Herr Müller's brow furrowed. "It's not possible, Herr Czerniaków. I have my orders. You will follow the directions of my men. I give you my word, that is the best way for everyone."

The officer marched away, deep in conversation with one of his subordinates. Nacha watched as Mr Czerniaków and her father exchanged words in voices too low for her to hear. Tata's face was pale. He had aged badly over the past two years and had lost a lot of weight. His pants hung low around his hips, and his shirt billowed around thin arms.

They returned to the ghetto and Nacha watched them, her stomach churning. They would all have to leave. If the rumours were true and the train took them to Treblinka, they would never return.

She scanned the ghetto, taking in the familiar faces on the busy street. The rickshaws riding by the shops selling their wares, the soup kitchens and the schools, the hospitals and doctors, the musicians who held the occasional secret revue —all would be gone. The ghetto would be a ghost town.

❧ 15 ❧

23RD JULY 1942

Jan watched his mother pacing up and down the length of the living room in their cozy apartment. She wrung her hands together and her nostrils flared. Then she paced again.

"Did you hear the news?"

"What news?"

"Himmler has come to Warsaw."

The sound of the man's name sent a tremor through Jan's body. He didn't know much about Himmler other than that he was *Reichsführer* of the *Schutzstaffel*, the dreaded SS. Jan had seen enough of the SS to know that their leader was an evil and dangerous man.

"What is he doing here?"

"They say he's overseeing the operation of Treblinka. The camp where they're sending the people on the transports from the *Umschlagplatz*. Poles, Jews, Gypsies...they're all being sent away to a camp we know little about. I've heard rumours that there is something worse still, another secret camp beyond Treblinka. Even the guards aren't allowed to enter. But that's where they send the Jews. It's where Antoni and his family will go if they get on that train."

Jan's heart thudded. Would the Nazis stop at nothing? What did they have against the Jews in the ghetto? They'd done what they'd been asked to do. They'd kept the peace and had been compliant. Why was this happening?

"We have to get them out. It's the only way." She stopped to look at him. "Is it possible?"

"Maybe. But where would they go?"

"I don't know." Mama strode across the room again. "We will find a place for them. But there is a glaring issue."

"What's that?" Jan could think of a dozen glaring issues, starting with the fact that they had no actual plan. He could smuggle the family out of the ghetto—he was fairly certain of that, although the Nazis had stepped up their activity as they undertook what the Jews were calling *The Great Deportation*.

This made movements into and out of the ghetto more problematic than they usually were. They knew the ghetto residents would try to escape and had round-the-clock surveillance sites set up along the wall. Still, Jan wasn't worried about getting them out so much as he was about what to do with them once they *were* out.

"There are so many of them," Mama replied. "We might be able to squeeze three or four into our apartment without anyone noticing, but there are ten adults to hide. Besides that, Fela is eight months pregnant. I'm not sure she could manage climbing over the wall, let alone whatever else she'll have to do to get to a hiding place. Plus, Jakob will not pass as a Gentile." Mama chewed on a fingernail. "If our neighbours see him...or any of them..."

"They'll report him," Jan added. "We can't trust them not to."

"No, we can't trust anyone."

"So, what should we do?" Jan would do whatever Mama decided. The risks were clear; there was no way to escape what the Nazis had planned. He knew his future was dire no matter what.

He'd already risked his life every single day of the occupation. He was more hesitant to do so since his arrest, but he also didn't want to risk Nacha's life, or the lives of her family, by doing something stupid or thoughtless.

"If we're going to get them out, we have to plan it first."

Mama agreed. "You should talk to Antoni. See what he thinks."

Antoni could help decide the issue of how many they should attempt to smuggle out of the ghetto, or if they even wanted to try it. They may not want to take the risk.

Perhaps he should tell Antoni about that last night with Edek, or what'd happened in the Gestapo headquarters. So far, he'd managed to keep those things to himself. Mama had pried a little, but when he hadn't wanted to talk about it, she'd left him alone. It was time to share what he knew. It might help Antoni make a better choice.

Jan slipped through the wall and into the ghetto. He was almost discovered by a Gestapo officer who caught him donning his armband and chased him into a group of Jews headed for the train station. He melted into the group and pulled his cap down over his eyes. The Gestapo officer looked for him, but couldn't pick him out from the crowd.

It was bedlam in the ghetto. Bodies lined the streets. Jewish Police rounded people up in small groups and shepherded them in the direction of the train station. Gestapo officers watched on, occasionally pulling out their pistols to shoot any who were too slow or failed to comply. Families huddled together, each member carrying a small suitcase and wearing layers of clothing despite the heat.

The crowd carried him with them, finally ending up at the

Umschlagplatz. Jan ducked out of the crowd and found a space behind a pile of garbage to hide as he watched through the fence. Families huddled on the platform, joining the thousands who were already there. Guards chased them onto open cattle cars, beating the recalcitrant or elderly with batons and shouting obscenities at them.

His stomach roiled at the sight of children shoved into the open carriages until they were fairly bursting at the seams. Each car had bars over the windows and hands protruded, grasping for air. He could only imagine how stifling it must be in those metal carriages as they boiled beneath the summer sun, packed to the brim with humanity.

The train finally full, the doors were pulled shut and the train chugged away from the station. There were guards seated on the roof of the train, armed with shotguns.

As the train left the station, a man slipped from one of the barred windows to the ground below and sprinted away from the train. One of the guards seated on the roof of the train raised his gun and shot the man in the back. He fell to the ground.

All Jan could hear as the train pulled away from the station were the cries of the people and the firing of the guards' shotguns as they felled escapees. He turned to one side and heaved his breakfast onto the ground beside the stinking pile of garbage. Then he wiped his mouth and ran in the direction of the Wierzbicka apartment. He could watch no more.

Jan did his best to stay out of sight, shrinking into the shadows and dashing between buildings. When he knocked on their door, it took a moment before it was answered. Nathan pulled him inside, his face pale.

"What are you doing?" asked Antoni as he hurried to greet Jan. "It's too dangerous for you to be here." He shook Jan's hand and held it.

Jan offered a shaky smile. "I came to get you."

"What do you mean?" asked Nacha, who stood in the kitchen holding a bowl, an apron around her waist.

"Mama says we should try to get you to safety outside the ghetto. It's dangerous for you to remain here. They'll put you on a transport, and that will be the end of you."

Antoni pressed both hands to his head. "Is it even possible? The Gestapo is everywhere."

"I can get you out, but we'll have to move quickly. I went to the *Umschlagplatz,* where they were loading up Jews by the thousands, bound for Treblinka. Only I'm not sure I can manage the entire family at once."

Antoni scanned the room, exchanging looks with each adult member of his extended family. His expression was pained. "We could be walking directly into a trap."

"That's true," Jan said. "It isn't safe, but neither is staying."

Babcia and Papa smiled at one another. Papa's gravelly voice broke through the strained silence. "We will stay. We are too old to run anyway."

"You should go," Berek said to Antoni. "If we go, we'll only make things worse for you. And besides, we haven't received our orders yet. Perhaps they will allow some of us to remain behind. Surely they can't mean for everyone to leave."

Antoni shoved his hands deep into his pockets. "I didn't want to say anything. But you should all know—Adam Czerniaków took his own life last night."

A collective gasp circulated around the room.

"No," whispered Babcia, covering her mouth with one gnarled hand.

"He wrote a note to his wife that said, *'They demand that I kill the children of my people with my own hands. There is nothing left for me to do but die.'*"

The room fell silent. Jan's stomach clenched and bile rose in his throat. Adam was a good man. He'd done his best to lead the ghetto community after their imprisonment. Jan couldn't imagine the ghetto surviving without him. It was time he shared what he knew with the family.

"I've seen what the Gestapo and SS do to the Jews they take out of the ghetto," Jan said. "Walter and I followed Edek one night. We saw a large group, families of all ages, shot in the back and dumped in a mass grave."

"So the rumours are true, then," Nathan said, his eyes wide. "It's not just scaremongering."

"They say there's a secret camp beyond Treblinka. That's where they're sending the Jews. Even the guards have never seen it." Jakob's voice was low, his dark eyes focused on Jan's face.

Jan nodded. "I have heard that too. I will smuggle out as many of you as I can. Walter has offered to help. He wishes to rescue his family as well. But on the other side of the wall, there are dangers too. Our neighbours could report you, and us along with you. The SS are waging a war on the entire city. Even Himmler has come to Warsaw. Perhaps I could take you in smaller groups. It would be less risky."

Nacha's eyes glistened in the dull light. She bit down on her lower lip. Jan wanted to tell her everything would be okay, but it would be a lie. He'd do his best, but he couldn't guarantee her safety. He was just a boy, rebelling against an entire army on his own.

Fela stroked her pregnant belly thoughtfully, her brow furrowed. "You should take Antoni, Nacha and Nathan first and get them situated. Then come back for the rest of us when you can."

Berek took his wife's hand and squeezed it. She smiled up at him.

It would be a big operation to smuggle the entire family out of the ghetto. But Jan couldn't stomach the idea of leaving anyone behind, not after all he'd witnessed.

First, he would have to find a way out of the ghetto. With the current state of affairs, it seemed virtually impossible even for him on his own, let alone with a family of Jews in tow.

ॐ

EVERY DAY, JAN, WALTER AND THE WIERZBICKA FAMILY haunted the ghetto wall, each with a small bag and Antoni carrying his precious violin. Antoni, Nacha and Nathan waited in the shadows, out of sight, while Jan and Walter paced the brick and barbed wire structure, looking for a way out.

Jan had never seen the ghetto so well guarded. Walter's eyes were dull as the two of them worked. He'd arrived in his family's apartment to find they'd already left. They'd been ordered onto a transport the previous day, according to one of their neighbours, and would be in Treblinka. He was too late.

Jan's heart ached for Walter, but he had to focus on the task at hand. If he made a misstep, they would all die. The responsibility weighed heavy on his shoulders, and he found himself with a burgeoning headache that worsened as the day went on.

It seemed as though they'd never find a way through. But on the third day, he stumbled across one of the guards he'd managed to bribe previously when smuggling goods into the ghetto. He approached the guard without making eye contact, then offered him a can of salmon. The guard looked at the salmon, raised it in a kind of salute, then shoved it into his back pocket.

"I need to get over the wall," he said.

The guard sucked on a mouthful of tobacco, then spit a stream of juice at the dirt. "You and everyone else."

"What do you need?"

"Jewels, diamonds, anything of value," replied the guard.

Jan had come prepared. He tugged a single-carat diamond ring from his pocket and handed it discreetly to the guard, who took it with wide eyes. "Where'd you get that?"

"A family friend," he replied. It was Babcia's. She'd offered it to Jan before he left the apartment on the first day.

"You might need this," she'd said. "It's not likely it will do me any good." She'd kissed his cheeks then and headed outside to bring in the dry clothes hanging in the courtyard.

The guard nodded. "You'd better hurry before my shift ends."

Jan beckoned to Walter, who brought the family to the wall. Jan climbed the fence, then helped Nacha, Nathan, Antoni and Walter climb over behind him while the guard studiously ignored them.

"Hurry," Jan whispered as he ducked into the back of an open stall in the Hala Mirowska Market.

Just as they hid behind a stand of curtain fabric and tore off their armbands, a guard marched past, a gun slung over his shoulder, his black boots thudding in a steady rhythm on the tarmac. He turned back suddenly, then stopped at the stall and fingered a piece of fabric, calling to the owner. The man came running, his balding head gleaming beneath the hot sun.

"Yes, sir, how can I help you?"

"Has anyone crossed the wall here?"

The man ran his fingers over his long, black moustache as he considered the guard's question. "No, sir, I witnessed no one. But I've been very busy serving customers, as you can see." He gestured in the direction of a line of three customers waiting in front of his stall.

The guard grunted. "Well, make sure to report any Jew you see breaking the law. You know the punishment for assisting a Jew?"

"Of course, sir. I will do what you ask."

The guard moved on, with one last suspicious glance in the direction of the line of customers. The customers included Jan, Walter and the stall owner's wife. Jan thought his heart might burst from his chest, it pounded so hard against his rib cage. Adrenaline spiked through his veins. He had no time to waste.

"Thank you for your kindness," Jan said to the man and his wife.

They waved away his thanks. "It's a travesty what those pigs are doing to our land and our countryfolk," the man said.

Jan led the way back to the apartment, although his travelling companions knew it just as well as he did. But they held back in case he had reason for them to halt their journey and could raise a hand in warning. They made it home by sticking to alleyways and small roads and taking refuge in the shadows. By the time they arrived, they were all puffing hard and had streaks of sweat running down the sides of their faces.

Mama threw the door open silently and ushered them all inside. Then she embraced Nacha and Nathan, welcoming them quietly into the Kostanski home. Finally, she cupped Antoni's cheeks between her hands, tears flowing from her eyes.

"It has been too long," he said.

She could only nod. As Jan led the others into the kitchen, she stepped into Antoni's arms.

16

The day was bright and sunny. Nacha leaned her back against the wall as she stared out the window at the world below. They were seven stories up, but it felt like a thousand. It might as well have been, for all the good it did her.

She could see a green park from her window. It was unkempt, with long, weedy grass and rusted play equipment, but it was a park and there were children playing in a dirty sandpit. Their laughter was too far away to be heard, but she could imagine it. And she longed to be out there, enjoying a sunny day in the park, even if she was too old to play.

With a sigh, she leaned her head back and let her eyes drift shut as she hugged the embroidered pillow her mother made to her stomach.

"What are you mooning about?" Nathan asked, taking a seat beside her. He sat half on her feet, and she quickly pulled them out of his way.

"Don't be annoying." She frowned. "What are you eating?"

"Bread," he replied around a bite.

"Ugh. Don't talk with your mouth full." She rolled her eyes. "I'm bored, that's all."

"Me too," he said.

She offered him a smile. "Cards?"

He grinned. "Okay."

She'd brought a pack with her out of the ghetto to Waltrina's apartment, and from there to Irka's. Waltrina's brother had been imprisoned by the Nazis for supposed crimes against the Reich, but his wife remained behind in their apartment and had room enough for the Wierzbicka family to stay.

"Only for a few weeks, though," she'd said when they first arrived as she wrung her hands together. "My neighbours are nosy, and I'm afraid it won't take long for them to work it all out."

They'd agreed to four weeks, and their time in the apartment was almost at an end. As bored as Nacha had been for the past few weeks, she couldn't help fearing what was to come. So far, Tata hadn't told her the plan. She was fairly certain he didn't have one. And Jan was no better. The two of them hadn't been alone since their trip to the movie theatre, so she couldn't weasel any more information out of him.

All she knew for certain was that he'd continued working at the market with his mother and Walter every day in hopes that he'd find a way back into the ghetto. But so far neither he nor Walter had managed it. There were guards everywhere, he'd said. It was hopeless.

He didn't tell them more than that, and she wondered if it was because he wished to shield her. She wanted to know everything—what was happening, what was it like, who remained in the ghetto after all this time? But he was reluctant to talk about it and she didn't have the chance to pry any deeper, since Tata was always there, hovering nearby, shooting her disapproving looks.

Waltrina rarely came to the apartment other than to bring them supplies. She was worked off her feet at the market and doing what she could to help those Jews who managed to escape the ghetto.

She'd taken it upon herself to give as much food and as many medical supplies as she could manage to whoever needed it. They had money to pay, and she had connections at the market. So far, it'd worked well for all of them—no matter what else was going on, Nacha's family had never gone hungry, thanks to Waltrina and Jan.

Waltrina's sister-in-law, Irka, was also frequently gone. She worked as a seamstress at a local fabric shop, which paid a pittance. But it kept her occupied and gave her enough money to buy food. Waltrina had made sure Irka was taken care of ever since her husband went to prison, and Irka showed her gratitude by allowing the Wierzbicka family to stay.

Nacha and Nathan played a game of Hearts for the next hour, only stopping to fetch a glass of water from the small kitchen. Nathan cheated, or at least Nacha accused him of cheating, after which he put her in a headlock and she beat him with her palms against his back until he let her go, laughing.

It wasn't fair that he was so much bigger and stronger than she was. He treated her like a baby most of the time, and she longed to trip him over or put him in a headlock sometime just to show him how it felt. But for the most part, they got along.

Only now they were stuck inside a small single bedroom apartment together with nowhere to go and nothing to do besides the few chores that it took to keep the place tidy and prepare food for the group.

When Jan knocked on the door and Irka let him in, kissing him on each cheek, Nacha wanted to shout for joy.

Not only because she was glad to see Jan, but because she was grateful to have contact with anyone from outside of her immediate family.

She missed her grandparents desperately and there was a constant irritation burning in her gut over where they were and what they might be doing, since she hated not knowing. But now Jan was there. Surely he'd have some good news for them.

"Jan," she said, rushing to see him.

She embraced him before remembering herself and that everyone was watching them. She backed away awkwardly, her cheeks blazing. He grinned, his own face red.

"I'm happy to see you," she said.

"I am too," he replied.

Tata shook Jan's hand with a broad smile. "It's good to see you, Jan. How are your mother and sisters?"

"They're well. I brought you some turnips and a sack of potatoes." He lifted a string bag onto the kitchen bench.

Irka unpacked the bag quickly and offered Jan a cup of hot tea. He took it and sat at the kitchen table while the family plied him with questions. Nacha was content to stand nearby, watching him speak and absorbing the news from their side of town.

Jan and his family lived in Old Town, but Irka's apartment was in Praga, almost five kilometres away. And with the state of transportation the way it was, Jan would've walked all the way there unless he was willing to pay for a taxi, but money was tight for them all.

"The transports continue each day," said Jan in answer to a question from Tata about the *Umschlagplatz*. "I've watched from nearby, and it seems to me they take about five or six thousand Jews per day. There are other trains too, taking Poles, Gypsies, Russians and other prisoners down the same track. They're headed for Treblinka."

"The labour camp there must be rapidly filling up. How long can it go on like this?" Tata glanced around the room, his question lingering in the air. But none of them had an answer for him.

Nacha couldn't imagine how large a camp must be to hold so many Jews, not to mention the Poles and others who were also being sent. "It must be very big."

Jan's gaze met her own for a moment and his blue eyes crinkled at the edges. "I'm grateful you're not on the train, but I can't help worrying for Babcia and Papa, along with all of the others."

Tata ran fingers over his smooth, dark hair. He slammed a fist down on the table, startling them all and making Nacha jump. "We've got to find a way to get them out of there."

"I've tried, but I can't find a way into the ghetto. It's too heavily guarded, and even the guards I usually bribe are refusing to help. None of the smugglers are getting through any longer." Jan shook his head. "I'll keep trying, though. In the meantime, we've got to come up with a solution for all of you. The four weeks is almost at an end."

Tata paced across the kitchen and back again. "Where can we go? What are our options?"

"I've been thinking," Jan said. "I could smuggle you into the Otwock ghetto. It's smaller and still peaceful."

"How far away is that?" Nathan asked.

"About twenty-five kilometres. We'd have to hire a taxi, but Mother and I have been saving for it."

Tata rubbed a hand over his stubbled chin. "It's a possibility. We wouldn't stand out. But what are the chances they'll begin to deport Jews from there to Treblinka as well?"

"Probably high," admitted Jan. "But I could smuggle you out again if that happens."

"I'm not sure where else you could go," Irka added. "People are turning in any Jews they see. They're afraid that if they don't, the Gestapo will come for them and their families."

Tata sighed. "It is our best option. We'll do it. Let us know when, Jan. We'll be ready."

❧ 17 ❧

20TH AUGUST 1942

The ghetto in Otwock was a smaller facility than the Warsaw ghetto, and wasn't as heavily guarded. It contained two sections divided in half by the railway tracks that ran from there north to Warsaw and beyond to Treblinka to the northeast.

Jan investigated the ghetto from the outside the day before their journey and found an easy way in beside the sanatorium, an enormous white five-story building that backed onto a thick, green wood. Patients wandered in an outside garden during the warmth of the summer days, and Jan was certain he could get Antoni, Nathan and Nacha into the garden easily enough.

He arrived at his Aunt Irka's apartment early in the morning, when the sun had not yet heated the day. A crow cawed rhythmically nearby, and he shuddered at the sound. He wasn't one for superstition, but he'd never liked the black birds.

The sooner he had the family safely ensconced in the

Otwock ghetto, the sooner he could relax. He'd seen the way the neighbours looked at him each time he visited his aunt's apartment, and he didn't trust them not to become more inquisitive over his motives.

He slipped into the apartment while the family was still eating breakfast. Then they washed the dishes quietly and finished packing their small suitcases. Nacha tied a scarf over her head, and they were ready.

They said their goodbyes to Aunt Irka, who cried over them, kissed them each on the cheeks, and told them she'd be praying for them. Irka was the only one with wet cheeks when finally they left. The others were each too lost in their own thoughts and worries about what lay ahead for tears.

The mood was grim. Jan did his best to calm their fears, but it was no use. They were in danger, and he couldn't predict what would happen to any of them. Even the cab driver could report on them to the Gestapo or they could run into a group of SS soldiers in the street. Anything was possible. And the possibilities were the things that kept Jan on edge.

"Perhaps we should catch a train to Otwock instead of wasting money on a taxi," suggested Nathan as they hurried down the street.

"The same train station where Jews are being herded into cattle cars for Treblinka?" hissed Nacha.

Antoni stopped their headlong pace with a hand on Jan's arm. He faced his children with a look of warmth and compassion on his lined face. "We can't turn on each other now. We're all we have."

Nacha's mouth turned down at the corners. "I'm sorry, Tata. I don't mean to snap."

"We're all anxious," added Nathan, reaching out to squeeze his sister's arm lovingly.

She offered him a half smile. "You drive me crazy, but I love you still."

He laughed. "I'm glad to hear it. I guess you're not so bad either. Although you do have a sharp tongue at times."

"I'll work on it, I promise. Tata is right. All we have is each other," she said, and pressed her lips together.

Jan scanned the street, looking for any sign of trouble. Pedestrians dodged between vehicles and carts as they ran up and down the street.

Nearby, a horse pulling a large wooden cart filled with produce stopped and dropped its head towards the ground as though exhausted. The driver lashed its back with a whip, and it plodded onwards.

A police officer directed traffic at the nearby intersection, his black uniform and black gloves contrasting with the pale sandstone building behind him. A woman pedalled a rickshaw past, ferrying a fashionably dressed woman with her teen daughter in front of her.

As soon as there was an opening, Jan hurried the family across the road, and they merged into the crowd on the other side.

"The train is a good idea. But we don't have the identification we need," whispered Jan as they strode together along the street. "We'll have to pay for a cab, I'm afraid."

"Of course," agreed Antoni. "There's nothing we can do about it now."

As they neared the intersection, Jan noticed the police officer's eyes on them. He studied them intently, even as he changed hand signals to steer traffic in the right direction. His brow furrowed beneath his smart black cap, and he took a step in their direction.

"You there!" he called.

Jan pretended not to see him. All his attention was focused on the passing vehicles as he searched for a taxi to take them away. Nacha stepped down into the street just as a motorcycle whizzed past.

Jan raised an arm to stop her. "Wait!" he cried.

She gasped as his arm impacted against her throat. "Ouch."

"I'm sorry, but that motorcycle almost hit you."

"There's a taxi rank," said Nathan, pointing to a line of people waiting at the curb ahead of them.

"Hey, you!" shouted the officer again, his voice growing louder. "Wait right there. I want to see your papers."

"Hurry," whispered Antoni.

The four of them scurried along the footpath, dodging and ducking between pedestrians. As they drew closer to the taxi rank, the last of the people in line stepped into a shiny black cab. They were at the head of the line.

Jan stood on tiptoe and saw that the policeman had left his position in the intersection and was pursuing them down the street at a clipped pace. He scanned the road for any sign of a taxi. He saw one making its way slowly towards them behind a large truck full of sheep. The truck lurched and swayed as it ground down the gears, then back up again.

"It's as if he's never driven before," spat Antoni in frustration.

The policeman marched closer, almost within speaking distance now, as Jan waited impatiently for the cab to pull up to the curb in front of them. Finally, the truck inched its way past them, and the taxi parked in front of them.

Without waiting for the driver to get out and open the door for them, the four quickly piled into the back seat.

"Otwock, and in a hurry!" shouted Antoni.

The driver's eyebrows rose in surprise, but he complied with a quick shift of pace, pressing his foot to the accelerator and pulling away just as the police officer rushed towards them through the press of the crowd. He reached out a hand to grasp the door handle, but he was too late.

As the car merged into traffic, Jan lay back against the seat with a sigh, his heart thudding so loud, he could feel it.

"Phew! That was close," whispered Nathan.

"Shh," admonished Antoni with a glance at the driver.

"Where in Otwock?" asked the man as he changed gears.

"The sanatorium," replied Antoni.

"That's in the ghetto now. But I can get you close."

⚜

SMUGGLING THE WIERZBICKAS INTO THE OTWOCK GHETTO was easier than Jan had thought it would be. The guards were relaxed and didn't follow protocol when it came to walking the fence line. The locals ignored them completely, and the Jewish Police inside the ghetto were nowhere to be seen.

Once they were in, Jan helped the family locate an abandoned apartment. The houses in the ghetto were like nothing Jan had ever seen before. They passed by wooden *Świdermajer* villas that looked as though they'd fallen from the pages of a fairy tale. The villas were large, with wide wooden verandahs on the bottom and top levels.

"Wow, look at that one," said Nacha, pointing at a particularly impressive blue building with glistening glass windows on three levels and sweeping gardens.

"This is where the wealthy used to come to relax. It's close to the sanatorium, and holiday makers would come here in the summer months to bathe and rest in the sunshine. Of course, all that was before the war and before they turned Otwock into a ghetto."

Before long, they found a small grouping of apartments and one that was empty. They carried their suitcases up the dark stairwell and into the apartment.

Antoni and Nathan explored the adjoining rooms in the small, dank space. Nacha pulled open the curtains to let light in, but the window was stuck. Jan helped her open it and their hands touched for a single moment, sending a spark of electricity along his skin and up his arm.

He blushed and offered her a brief smile.

"I suppose you'll leave now," she said.

Jan thought she sounded disappointed. Likely she was sad to have to move on yet again, and into a ghetto so far from everything she knew. They'd be strangers here, would know no one. He hated to leave them, but he had to get back to Mama and his sisters.

"Mama will be waiting for me."

"I know she's worried."

"Not so very much. She's grown accustomed to it." He laughed. "She says I don't give her a chance to relax between attacks of anxiety and so she's become immune to their effects."

Nacha grinned. "I wonder if that's what's happened to me as well. I can't seem to feel afraid any longer, only despondent."

Jan studied her face—brown eyes so full of light and warmth, long brown hair pulled back into a braid with a blue scarf wrapped neatly over it. Her smile was delightful and her laughter contagious. He'd known her for as long as he could remember, but something was different now.

Antoni returned from the other room with a sneeze. "Well, there is plenty of dust, but it is safe and dry enough. Thank you, Janek."

Jan nodded. "I will return as soon as we find a better place for you to stay."

"Is there anywhere else?" Nathan asked.

"I don't want to get your hopes up, but Mama is looking for an apartment where we might all perhaps live together."

Antoni's eyes lit up. "I told her not to bother with that. It's too risky."

"But she won't let that stop her," replied Jan with a grin. "If she can find a place where no one knows any of us, but also close to the market, she will rent it. Then I will come back to Otwock to get you."

"We won't see you before then?" Nacha's hands twisted together in front of her brown dress.

"You will, no doubt. We all intend to take turns visiting you, bringing supplies and so on, and since we have papers, we can take the train. It will be a much easier and more affordable journey than the one we took today."

"That's good to hear." Antoni cleared his throat. "Tell your mother we are well, and thank you for all you've done and are doing to care for us."

"I will."

Jan left after embracing each of them, a knot lodged in his throat. They would be safe in the ghetto for now. Still, he hated to leave them knowing they would be so far away from home and in the company of strangers and Nazis.

He said a Hail Mary and offered a prayer to Saint Christopher on their behalf as he jogged through the ghetto in the direction of the train station. He found a place to sneak through the fence when no one was looking and removed the white band from his arm, shoving it into his pocket as he walked.

When he reached the entrance to the ghetto, there was a single guard standing beneath a flimsy-looking archway with a sign overhead announcing the ghetto and its purpose.

Jan stopped beside the guard and lit a cigarette. He inhaled a deep breath of smoke and watched the guard from the corner of his eye.

"Do you have another?" asked the guard in German.

Jan flashed a grin. "Of course. Here you go." He tugged a

cigarette from the packet in his shirt pocket and handed it to the guard. Then he lit it with a match, which he extinguished with a flick of the wrist and threw to the ground.

"*Danke*."

"Hey, do you know how long this ghetto is going to be here?"

The guard shrugged as he drew on the cigarette. "They will empty it soon enough."

"You have orders?"

"We have our duty to perform. Although it will be a big job." The guard looked wistfully over his shoulder into the ghetto.

"When?"

"In a few months. That's all I know. They're working on the Warsaw ghetto first."

Jan's heart dropped. Mama had to find an apartment for them all soon or the Wierzbickas wouldn't last long enough to need it. "Where's the train station from here?"

The guard directed him towards the station, and Jan took off at a jog. As he ran, he considered his options. If Mama couldn't find a place for the family to stay and the Wierzbicka family was sent to Treblinka, everything he and his family had done for the past two years would've been for nothing.

❧ II ❧

Bees build around the honeycomb of lungs,
Ants build around white bone...
The roof and the wall collapse in flame and
　　heat seizes the foundations.
Now there is only the earth, sandy, trodden
　　down,
With one leafless tree.

> — "A POOR CHRISTIAN LOOKS AT THE
> GHETTO" BY CZESLAW MILOSZ

18

15TH JANUARY 1983

MELBOURNE, AUSTRALIA

I often wonder whether my husband has a gift for slumber that I missed out on. He sits still where we drank our tea on the porch outside. His eyes are closed, his mouth slightly ajar, and there is a soft snoring sound emanating through the screen door to where I stand at the kitchen sink, washing our cups.

I love that he can fall asleep anywhere. It's probably a skill he learned when we were in hiding, the bombs dropping overhead, as the war neared its end. If you can sleep through a Russian invasion, you can sleep anywhere.

He's nervous about the ceremony. I am too, a little. But I'm more concerned about his mother and how she'll cope with all the attention. She's getting older now and is not always fond of large crowds. Who can blame her, after all she's been through?

All this talk of the past has me remembering things I'd pushed out of my thoughts so long ago. Memories rise to the surface unbidden, catching me by surprise when I'm doing the crossword or playing with my grandchildren.

I think about that apartment where we were prisoners for so long. Prisoners and yet free all at the same time. It's a difficult thing to comprehend, especially for a teenaged girl. And yet it saved us, that apartment. The bird on the windowsill had more freedom than I did. Yet I lived, and that is what matters most in the end.

I walk to my bedroom and pick up the pillow with the embroidered flower on one side. It's old and faded—the white pillow slip is yellow. The embroidery is no longer rough, but smooth to the touch and coming apart in places.

I still sleep with it sometimes, my cheek against the soft cotton slip as I feel the flower beneath my fingertips. It's the only thing I have left from my mother. Everything else is gone. Even my memories of her have faded until I can barely make them out.

Tears wet my cheeks and since I am alone, I let them fall unhindered. The pain and anguish of a teenager still resides deep in my heart. I never really dealt with the trauma. It wasn't something people did at the time. Life had enough problems of its own without borrowing past troubles.

We moved on—it was healing enough. I had so much to do. Migrating to Australia, raising my boys, helping with the businesses. No time for dwelling on the past or dredging up memories to sift through and cry over.

But there is time now, and I suppose it is better to face the past eventually than not at all. And I'm grateful, of course, for a long life filled with so much joy that sometimes it makes my heart feel as though it could burst.

So many we knew didn't live another day, let alone the many decades given to me and my family. The memories bring pain, but also relief. I face them square on as I dry my hands on a tea towel embroidered with a kingfisher and sprigs of wattle.

There's a knock at the front door, and I amble down the hall to answer it with a smile. I know who it will be. The children are here for Babcia to babysit.

It's the thing I enjoy most and of course I'll sneak in some Polish words—I want them to understand their heritage and to learn a little of their own language. But I know it will come with a strong Aussie accent and a disinterest only the young can perfect. It is the way things always are. The way I was as well when Tata tried to instil an understanding of our Jewish heritage throughout my childhood years—in the before time.

I regret so much, especially my indifference. But indifference is the privilege of youth, and so I pay no mind. My grandchildren rush through the door and embrace me before tearing towards the kitchen chattering about *szarlotka* and *pączkis*.

I love to bake, and they know without asking that the pastry tin will be full of treats. As I embrace my son and kiss both his cheeks, gazing into his hazel eyes with love, I picture also their cheeky faces garnished with powdered sugar and their lips gleaming with grease.

"Come in, come in," I say, ushering my son inside, and then embracing his wife, who carries bags of food and homework as if she's a pack mule.

"My goodness, you must share the load," I admonish my son. "Look at your poor wife."

He grins. "Sorry. Let me have one of those."

They follow me into the kitchen, telling me all about their day. My husband is awake on the porch now, with one grandchild in his lap and another standing nearby telling him a story in a loud voice while munching on a fresh *pączki*.

The house is full of love and laughter, and for a moment I

let my eyes drift shut and simply absorb every wisp of it. There's no fear or anxiety, no pain or anguish.

The memories that I'd run through had brought those feelings back like the darkness that comes when storm clouds rush across the sky and cover the sun. But the clouds are pushed back by the sound of my grandchildren laughing at their grandfather's antics. The sky is clear again, and the sun warms my face as I watch life unfold with a smile.

It was in that apartment my life was saved. But it was there I thought it would end. I was sure of it. We wouldn't make it. There was no chance of salvation. But I was wrong.

19

5TH NOVEMBER 1942

The day came when Jan saw a guard he knew standing by the entrance to the Warsaw ghetto. It was the same man who'd been on duty when Jan and Walter had taken the Wierzbicka family out of the ghetto months earlier.

He'd visited the extended family several times since then but wasn't able to smuggle them out since the wall was so well guarded. Lately it'd been difficult for him to get through, and the Nazis had stepped up their efforts to deport as many of the Jews as possible. Still, Jan hadn't been able to convince the family to leave with him. It was too risky, they'd said.

They were certain they would be able to remain behind even with the evidence in front of them that the Germans were deporting the entire ghetto. The resistance in the ghetto had grown, and thousands of Jews had built tunnels and hiding places where they could go when the police came knocking. The Wierzbickas planned on using a tunnel dug by their neighbour.

Jan plied the guard with chocolate in hopes the man would let him back through with any of the family who might accompany him and hurried through the gates, slipping on the armband as he went.

It'd been so long since he'd scurried through the streets that he barely recognised the place. Entire buildings had been burned to the ground. Most of the streets were empty. Black smoke wafted in the air, the acrid scent singeing his nostrils.

He ducked around a pile of rubble and leapt over the edge of a bomb crater in the middle of the street. His heart thudded against his rib cage as his anticipation of being reunited with loved ones slowly transformed into a cloying dread.

The apartment building was still there. He was grateful for that at least. As he drew closer, though, it didn't look as though anyone remained in the apartments. There were several open doors along the first balcony, and no lights on within any of the units. None of the chimneys smoked, and he couldn't hear the sound of voices within. It was as though the complex had become a ghost town.

He slowed his pace and pressed himself up against the outside wall of the apartment, scanning the street for any sign of movement. There was none, other than a crow pecking at something on the street a few metres away.

He glanced inside a broken ground-floor window and saw that the dining room and kitchen remained basically as they had been when he was last there. He opened the door and crept inside. It was darker than usual, with no light in any of the gloomy corners.

There was no fire in the hearth, no scent of bread coming from the oven. No Babcia dancing in the living room, or Antoni playing the violin. Papa wasn't sneaking a *pierogi* from the chipped jar on the kitchen bench and Nacha was nowhere to be seen, playing with her doll or helping in the kitchen, her hands coated in flour and a smile lighting up her pretty face.

He brushed away the loneliness that washed over him and moved into the living room, then up the stairs to the two bedrooms. There was no sign than anyone had been here for some time. And there was a terrible stench that almost made him heave halfway up the staircase.

His eyes watering, he pushed open a bedroom door. Papa and Babcia's bed was where it always had been. The covers were pulled back and only the sheet was in place. There were two figures beneath the sheet. Jan tiptoed closer to get a better look.

It was Papa and Babcia. They were in their pyjamas. Both had been shot in the head. Dark blood splattered the headboard and stained their pillows. Their eyes were shut. Their bodies bloated. The smell was overwhelming.

He ran from the room and threw up in the hall. Pinpricks of light danced before his eyes, and he thought he might faint. A ball of grief welled in his throat, and he threw up again. Then, without a backward glance, he ran down the stairs and through the living room.

He stopped and glanced around for a moment. What should he take? Antoni, Nacha and Nathan might want something from their home to remember it by. But there was nothing he could carry, and all he wanted to do was to get out of there as quickly as possible.

A framed photograph of the family, along with Jan, his mother and sisters, hung on the living room wall. He reached for it and tucked it under his shirt and into his pants. Then he sprinted from the apartment, leaving the door swinging on its hinges.

He didn't stop until he reached the guard, who waved him through with a smile. Then he ran home, his laboured breathing making his throat ache.

He pushed through the door and into the apartment, tripping on the threshold and landing on his knees with a thud against the smooth stone floor.

"What on earth?" Mama asked, hurrying from the kitchen as she wiped her hands on the white apron that covered her blue floral dress.

Jan looked up at her, silent tears falling from his eyes.

"What is it, Janek? What's happened?" Her voice was smooth, warm like honey eaten from a hive on a hot summer's day.

She knelt beside him and held open her arms. He fell into them, sobbing. "They're gone," he said. "They're all gone."

❧ 20 ❧

7TH JANUARY 1943

There were clouds covering the sky like a blanket of grey when twelve-year-old Jadzia Kostanski skipped out of her apartment with a group of friends that shifted like a flock of gulls in the direction of the movie theatre. She was glad to get out of the apartment.

Ever since the Nazi occupation, she'd spent more and more time at home and was sick of the confinement. School was one of her few means of escape, but now that she was older, Mama had said she could go out with friends if she was careful, and the liberation filled her with a euphoric feeling that made her giddy.

"Which movie are we going to see?" Hanna asked, a plump girl with a ruddy complexion who laughed a lot.

"I think it's a Tarzan movie," Jadzia replied. "But I don't honestly care. It could be the three little pigs, for all I'm concerned. I'm so glad to be out of the apartment and having some fun with my friends!" She pushed her arms out and twirled in a circle. The other girls laughed.

"Me too," Julie, another friend with red curls and a freckled nose admitted. "Mama says I have to come straight home after, but I thought we could go for a walk. There's a park near the theatre that has some wonderful trails."

"Good idea," Jadzia agreed. "Mama will kill me if she finds out, though."

Hanna giggled. "So we won't tell her."

The group of five girls couldn't stop giggling the whole way to the movie theatre. They chattered so much that the ticket saleswoman almost lost her cool. Finally, they had their tickets, and Jadzia marvelled at the red velvet upholstery on the couches in the reception area and the gold gilding on everything. It was luxurious and beautiful, and she couldn't believe she was able to be there without so much as a parent in sight.

It was too good to be true.

They each bought a box of popcorn and found seats in the front row. Jadzia stared up at the large screen above her with wide eyes.

"This is so great," whispered Hanna. "I can't believe we're actually here."

"I know. I've been so looking forward to it."

"Do you think your mother would let you come over to my place next weekend? I'm helping Mama mend first thing, but after that, I'm free as a bird. And Julie says she can come."

"I don't know. Mama works at the market, and weekends are her busiest time." The truth was, Jadzia wasn't sure when her family might move, and Mama had warned her not to tell anyone about it. It was hard to keep the secret, especially from her friends who had no idea. But she knew it was a life-and-death matter for Nacha's family, and for hers.

It was important that no one in their lives knew about their plans to help the Jewish family escape the ghetto and live with them in an apartment in another part of the city. But it meant Jadzia wouldn't get a chance to tell her friends goodbye, and that thought caused her smile to fade.

"That's okay—maybe another time. We hardly see each other these days. Especially when school is cancelled or during the break."

"I know, but maybe things will get better when the war is over."

Julie shook her head. "Whenever that is. I know I shouldn't say it or even think it, but part of me believes the war will never end."

"Of course it will," Jadzia said. "It can't go on like this forever. And besides, I heard…"

There was a bang at the back of the theatre. The dancing boxes of popcorn on the screen slowed, then faded to black. and the lights in the large, sloping room flickered to life.

"Raid!"

A woman screamed. A man shouted. Then there were more screams coming from outside the theatre and shots rang out.

Jadzia leapt to her feet and tugged a frozen Hanna after her, spilling their popcorn to the floor. "Let's get out of here."

The other girls ran ahead of them, squealing in fright. Jadzia and Hanna lost sight of them as soon as they melted into the surging crowd. Everyone had bolted from their theatres at once and converged into the velvet and gold reception area. Gestapo guards raced after them, beating those within reach with batons.

"Over here!" Jadzia led the way to one of the exit doors, Hanna and Julie following close behind.

She sprinted for the door, her heart in her throat. She was always so careful, rarely going anywhere without Jan or her mother. And today, she finally had a chance to do something with friends, something for herself, and the Gestapo had chosen to raid the theatre right at that very moment. If she wasn't so panicked, she might've laughed at the absurdity of the situation.

When she reached the doorway, she found it blocked by two Gestapo guards with guns pointed directly at her chest. She halted and raised her hands over her head.

"Aryan," she puffed, her head light. "I'm Aryan." She reached for her papers inside her skirt pocket and held them out.

The guard took the papers, looked at them, then tore them to shreds in front of her. As the pieces of her identification floated to the ground, realisation dawned that she was in deep trouble.

"But I'm Aryan," she said.

The guard laughed. "Do you think I care, little girl?" He shoved her so that she stumbled.

She found herself at the end of a long line of people of all ages. Some whimpered, and others openly cried. Still others shouted.

I'm innocent, I'm Aryan. I've done nothing wrong. I have papers. Please let me go!

It was no use. The Gestapo officer in charge wasn't listening. He wore a jaunty black cap, and his black moustache was perfectly groomed to curve down over the corners of his mouth. Two dark brown eyes glittered beneath the peak of his cap as he studied the crowd, walking slowly along each line as he tapped a riding crop against one tall black boot.

"Well, well, well, what a good group we have here. No, no—there's no need to cry or to shout. Everything will work out. You'll see." He offered Jadzia a smile, but his stare was vacant and sent a shiver down her spine. "I'm *Oberführer* Meisinger, commander of the *Einsatzgruppe* IV.

Do as you are asked. Please don't resist. It will not help your cause."

Jadzia had lost sight of Hanna and Julie. She scanned the crowd for her friends' cheerful countenances, but saw only a sea of frightened faces. The Gestapo pushed them all forward. She struggled to keep up the pace at first, then it slowed as they headed towards the ghetto. Where were they being taken? Into the almost empty ghetto? From what Jan had told her, the Nazis had deported virtually everyone. Only a small group of Jews remained behind.

They were herded to the *Umschlagplatz*. A train waited at the station with cattle cars in a row. The windows were barred by strands of barbed wire. The gaping double doors opened to reveal a black emptiness. The guards ushered the people into the yard and had them sit in lines. Then they began the methodical task of going down the lines and writing every person's details into a large paper ledger.

Jadzia stared longingly at the ghetto and back towards home. If only she'd stayed with Mama, Jan and Danuta today, as she had done every other day. None of this would've happened. And now she would be sent away and her family wouldn't know where.

❦

THE APARTMENT WAS EERILY QUIET WHEN JAN GOT IN FROM working all day at the market. He frowned as he hung up his coat on the nail by the door. In the kitchen, he found Danuta reheating a pan of *pierogi*. She looked up as he came in, then her face fell.

"I thought you were Jadzia."

He grabbed an apple from the fruit bowl and took a bite. The sweet, tart flavour burst across his tongue. He and Mama had managed to trade for a few crates of apples the previous day. They'd proven very popular that morning and had been the first thing they'd sold out of.

"What do you mean? Where is she?"

"She hasn't come back from the movies yet."

Jan's heart thudded. "What? She should've been home hours ago."

"Where's Mama?"

"Right behind me," he said. "She's talking to one of the neighbours."

Just then, the front door opened and Mama stepped inside. "Next time Mrs Nowak stops me to talk, please fake an injury or an emergency, Janek. Anything to get me out of it —she won't stop talking and my feet are killing me." She glanced around the living room. "Why has the fire died? And there are no lights on in here."

Jan strode to meet her. "Jadzia isn't home yet."

Mama's face whitened. "She should be home by now. Jan, will you go and look for her?"

He nodded and hurried to fetch his coat. Outside, the world was dark. It'd happened quickly and early, since winter clouds hung low in the sky. As though the sun had simply given up.

He ran in the direction of the cinema, hoping to come across Jadzia and her friends deep in conversation and unaware of the time. But there was no sign of her. When he reached the shopping district around the theatre, he stopped suddenly at the sound of gunfire and shouting.

He slipped into an alley and peeked around the corner. Gestapo and *Einsatzgruppen* rounded people up and herded them in the direction of the train station. If he went any closer, they'd pick him up as well, and he couldn't risk that.

Just then, a girl stepped out of the shadows beside him. "Jan?"

He startled. "Is that you, Julie?"

She began to cry. "I don't know how to get home. There are soldiers everywhere."

He rested a hand on her arm. "It's okay. I'll go with you. But where is Jadzia?"

She sniffled into her sleeve. "They got her. I don't know where she's gone, but they came to the theatre and rounded everyone up. They took them somewhere. I didn't dare follow."

His heart fell. "But she's not a Jew. Why did they do it?"

"They tore up her papers." Julie sobbed loudly. "They didn't care. I only managed to escape because the guard was distracted by a man falling down."

He didn't know what to say. Julie's tears made him uncomfortable. He shifted from one foot to the other in the darkness, his thoughts on his sister.

"Come on—I'll take you home. I've got to find Jadzia."

He took Julie to her street and watched as she slid through her apartment door and inside. Then he sprinted home to tell Mama what he'd learned.

Mama listened with a stern look on her face. "I have a friend who is dating an SS officer. I will drive over to her place to ask if he will help us get her back. You see if you can discover where they've taken her."

A few minutes later, Mama was in the neighbour's borrowed car. The same one she'd used to pick him up from Gestapo headquarters. She drove off with a wave, leaving Jan with Danuta. He gave her instructions to lock the door and go to bed. Usually his little sister would argue with him and tell him he couldn't give her orders, but this time she gave a solemn nod, her eyes wide.

He added a scarf and gloves to his outfit and tugged his woollen cap down low to stave off the cold. Then, with a quick prayer to Saint Sophia for wisdom, he ran back the way he'd come earlier.

When he reached the place where the Gestapo was dragging people from storefronts and churches and pushing them in groups along the street in the direction of the ghetto, he followed them at a distance, sliding into shadowy doorways and crouching behind piles of rubbish or the remnants of dark, brittle shrubbery that'd somehow survived the violence of war.

They herded the crowds of prisoners to the *Umschlagplatz,* where a train awaited them. Half of the cars were already packed with human cargo. The sounds of their cries and shouts echoed through the still night air. Jan wanted to cover his ears, wanted to be anywhere but there. He hated the sound, hated thinking of his sister shoved into that cramped car between desperate strangers and gasping for air.

He lingered closer to the gate and listened to the guards. They spoke of the ledger and what they'd recorded there— how many men, women and children were already on board. How many more they could fit.

"Some of them are not Jews."

"We have a quota to fill, and we will fill it."

Rage formed a knot in Jan's gut. His sister had been taken to fill a quota. She would die because of the greed and corruption of an evil government. In that moment, he wanted to kill them all. If he could have, he would've pushed them into a pit of lava, or mowed them down with a machine gun.

He'd never been violent, never felt the urge to harm another human being until this very moment. But he'd do it. He'd kill them all if he had the chance, to save Jadzia from the Nazis.

Then came the revelation Jan was waiting for.

"These are going to Majdanek Vernichtungslager."

"Not to Treblinka?"

"Not today. See to it that every person is accounted for. I won't have Meisinger say I'm bad at my job."

Jan hurried away without looking back. He'd heard of Majdanek only recently. It was originally a prisoner of war camp in Lublin, but lately they'd been sending the Jews from the ghetto there rather than to Treblinka. From everything he'd heard about the camp, the SS who ran the place were particularly brutal.

The guard had referred to it as *vernichtungslager*, which in German meant extermination camp. He had to get home to wait for Mama so he could tell her what he'd discovered. If Jadzia was at Majdanek, they could rescue her. He didn't know how, but together they'd find a way. Mama would know what to do.

8TH FEBRUARY 1943

J adzia had been interred at the *vernichtungslager* two
kilometres outside of Lublin for the past four weeks. It
might as well have been four years. It seemed longer
than a lifetime. At first, she'd hoped they would realise
their mistake, that she wasn't a criminal or a prisoner of war
or a Jew, but a normal Polish Catholic girl who shouldn't be
there. She'd done nothing wrong, she told them. Why was she
here? It was a mistake.

Over and over, the response was—*where are your papers?*

When she said a guard had torn them to shreds, they'd
laughed and moved on to the next person, clipboard in hand
ready to take down the prisoner's details. She'd wanted to
scream in frustration. It wasn't fair. They could call her
mother and speak to her—please could someone call her
mother? But her request had resulted in a swift blow to the
side of her head with a baton, and she'd soon learned to keep
silent.

She'd long since given up paying attention to pangs of

hunger or dehydration. Listening to her physical senses would only get her in trouble. Instead, she had to pay attention to what was going on around her in the world outside her own pain, suffering and inner torment. Pay attention and do what she was told or die.

At four a.m., she was already awake. Her body had adjusted to the new schedule within a few days of arriving at Majdanek, and she woke minutes before the guards arrived. As the barracks doors burst open, Jadzia was already climbing to her feet.

Her body screamed a silent objection, pain shot through her legs as her almost-frozen feet hit the cold concrete floor. She ignored the pain with a grimace and was already smoothing her hair back from her face the best she could.

She still had her clothes. They hadn't processed her or Hanna yet. The rest of the prisoners in the camp wore only a thin cotton sheath and shivered about their labour for the duration of the short, cold days spent toiling outdoors.

Any of the women and girls who failed to leap from their beds were beaten with clubs by the female SS guards until they were on their feet. Sometimes the beatings lasted longer, depending on the moods of the women in charge.

"Hanna," whispered Jadzia. "Get up."

Hanna groaned and rolled over. "Just a few more minutes, Mama."

"It's Jadzia, not your mother, and you have to get up or the guards will deal with you."

Hanna's hazel eyes blinked open and she quickly slipped off the short, hard mat that served as a bed on a bunk made of wire and metal pipes.

"Oh, I was having such a nice dream," she complained.

"Hush." Jadzia didn't want to see her friend suffer the wrath of Braunstein, the guard currently tormenting a girl at the other end of the bunkhouse for hiding a piece of bread beneath her pillow, and who was known for her cruelty.

Jadzia reached up to tap the woman asleep on the bunk above her own but found the woman's arm was cold. She was dead. Jadzia shrank back, recoiling in horror.

"What is it?" Hanna whispered, eyes wide.

"I think she's dead."

"We have to carry her out for roll call."

Jadzia knew it was true. She wanted to cry. But if she and Hanna left the woman's body where it was, they'd be the ones blamed and they might be beaten, whipped or worse. She'd seen enough in the past four weeks to know that it was better to carry the cold, dead corpse out to the yard than leave it behind.

She gave a quick nod. They'd have to move fast.

Hanna reached for the woman's feet and Jadzia took her under the arms. Between the two of them, they dragged her from the bed to the ground with a sickening thud. Then they half carried, half pulled her through the rows of bunk beds as they followed the other women and girls outside to the cold, grey yard. Drifts of snow clung to tussocks of grass, the eaves of the buildings and filled the hollows. Puddles sparkled with shards of ice.

The women lined up in front of the guards and shouted a response when their name was called. Jadzia and Hanna set the dead woman on the ground beside them. She was dragged away after her name was called and thrown into the back of a nearby wagon on top of a growing pile of corpses.

The rest were dressed in the striped prison uniforms. Only the middle-aged woman from their barracks wore civilian clothing and had long, brown hair that'd fallen from her bun in wisps.

Braunstein eyed the group as she paced up and down in front of them, her baton dangling from one hand as she went.

Her SS uniform was impeccable, her countenance pleasing. She smiled as she walked, and there was a dimple in one of her plump white cheeks.

If Jadzia saw her in the street out of uniform, she'd assume the woman was kind and sweet. But the truth couldn't be more divorced from the guard's appearance. She looked for opportunities to torture the prisoners and often joined in with other guards to kill them for sport, laughing and joking as death came in the most degrading ways.

A shiver ran down Jadzia's spine as she recalled some of the things she'd witnessed since arriving in the camp. But she couldn't think about it. Remembering would drive her crazy. Instead, she pushed the thoughts out of her mind and focused on the task at hand—to work all day in the damp cold and not draw any attention to herself.

At six a.m., they were all marched from the camp to a field nearby and given shovels. They were told to dig a long trench. Jadzia did what she was told without complaint. If she worked hard and didn't make a fuss, she'd found that the guards left her alone.

The ground was frozen, and her shovel bounced off the soil the first few times she attempted it. But she put her weight behind it and used her foot to push down on the blade, and it entered the ground a few centimetres. The work was backbreaking and slow. How long could the older women in the group manage?

The prisoners in uniform who'd already been processed were marched off into the distance to do some other form of work. She knew her time for that would come just as soon as the SS managed to wade through the enormous amount of administrative work required to keep their meticulous accounts.

She'd heard Braunstein complain to one of the other female guards that the camp was full to bursting and they'd have to give more of the prisoners special treatment soon or they'd have nowhere to put the new arrivals.

From where she worked, Jadzia could see the entire camp. It covered almost three square kilometres of land and was surrounded by two curled rows of electrified barbed wire fence.

There were six fields, each separated from the others by barbed wire, a guard room at the entrance, and twenty-four barracks per field that each accommodated over three hundred prisoners.

Dotted throughout the fields were warehouses, work-shops and three large buildings from which a constant stream of smoke emitted. The smell was sickly, and there was a steady rain of ashes that came down on the prisoners' heads when the wind turned.

All around the camp, tall watchtowers looked out. And in each of the towers was stationed a pair of machine-gun-armed sentries. Throughout the camp was a large contingent of SS troops to guard the prisoners at all times, as well as over two hundred German Shepherd police dogs and a contingent of auxiliary police, the *Kampfpolizei*, who seemed to Jadzia to be mostly comprised of lowlifes and criminals with a fetish for violence.

The dogs were particularly frightening to Jadzia and the other prisoners. She'd already seen them tear apart several prisoners who'd made a run for the camp entrance when it was opened to allow a transport through, or had upset the SS guards in some other way. They were well-trained and vicious.

Around eleven a.m., the guards brought the two hundred and fifty women in Jadzia's bunkhouse back to the camp for dinner. The striped prisoners returned as well from wherever they'd been taken. The ones who'd left in the backs of trucks, however, were nowhere to be seen.

The trucks had returned earlier, their beds empty and

freshly washed, and were parked alongside the entrance to the camp. When Jadzia passed through the open gates, she felt as if she might be sick at the sight of three guards standing beside the empty trucks. They were joking and laughing as they harassed a prisoner with one of their dogs, and the woman, on her hands and knees, cried, streaks of dirt mixing with the tears in rivulets down her cheeks as the dog growled in her face, its teeth bared and saliva dripping from its chin.

They lined up outside their barracks and were treated to a cup of coffee made of roasted turnips, a mug of soup made from grass, and a chunk of bread, adulterated with sawdust. Jadzia and Hanna sat side by side, their backs against the barracks walls.

They ate slowly. The meal was meagre, but it was all they'd get until suppertime and they didn't intend to waste a crumb. Jadzia had already lost weight since their arrival; her clothes were loose on her thin frame. And Hanna's cheek-bones protruded, making her look austere.

"We have to get out of here," said Hanna as she studied the bread in her hand.

"I know, but how? They'll shoot us if we try to escape. And the dogs..."

"Yes, but we can't stay. Why hasn't anyone come for us? Where are our parents?"

"I'm sure they're trying. Mama will do everything she can."

"Do you think so?"

Jadzia nodded. "I know she will. And I'm sure your parents are working to free you as well."

"But they haven't succeeded." Hanna's face fell. "We might die in here."

Jadzia tried not to think about it. She'd held onto the hope that her family would do something to get her out of this hellhole. But she should face facts—it'd been four weeks and she was still there. Hanna was right—it was likely they'd die in the *vernichtungslager*, just like so many of their fellow prisoners did every day.

Just then, the prisoners in striped uniforms lined up. Their guards walked down the lines and tapped several of them on the shoulder. Those prisoners they tapped walked forward. Jadzia's stomach curled into a knot. She hated this time of the day. Any prisoners the guards regarded as slacking in their work were punished before the afternoon shift. It was sickening and horrifying all at the same time. And soon, Jadzia would be processed and would be part of the striped crews.

When they brought out the whips, she turned away, preferring to look up at the sky and make a game of guessing the animal shapes she saw there. She and Hanna could play the game together for the rest of lunchtime and never see the punishment meted out on their fellow prisoners, many of whom had grey hair and were so thin, she thought a gentle breeze might bowl them over if they turned sideways.

But she couldn't block out the sound of the whip as it slapped across bare skin, or the wails of the prisoners as they lay in the dirt, dying.

❦

JAN WAS FRUSTRATED. THEY'D BEEN LOOKING FOR apartments for months now and hadn't found anything suitable. Every place was either too exposed and likely to result in them being reported to the SS, or too expensive, too small or too mouldy.

Mama rubbed both hands over her face, then set her hands on her hips to survey the room. The apartment they were inspecting was old and the walls were full of holes. The unit next door had been bombed in the siege and there was a breeze blowing from somewhere through the living room. Not only that, but the owner wanted a small fortune for the place. It was more than they could afford.

"We're never going to find anything suitable," Mama said, her shoulders slumping.

Jan sighed. "I can't think about it anyway. Not with Jadzia still locked up in Majdanek."

Mama faced him. She had dark rings beneath her eyes and a look of defeat on her face. "I know. I can't either. But we have to—we've got to find somewhere before Otwock is emptied and all its inhabitants are sent to Treblinka."

"I don't know why we're even doing this. We have to rescue Jadzia." Jan slapped the wall in frustration.

Mama began to cry. "I know we do. I'm working as hard as I can to get her released."

"We can't think about anyone else now. She's our priority. I shouldn't have been sneaking into the ghetto—I should've been with her instead. If I was there with her, this wouldn't have happened." Jan's entire body burned with anger.

He wanted to face the men who'd taken his sister and beat them to a pulp. He wanted to run, to shout, to do something, anything other than mindlessly, pointlessly looking at apartments that would never be theirs.

Mama cupped his cheek with one hand. "It isn't your fault, Janek. And if you were with her, you'd have been captured as well."

"I can't do it anymore, Mama." He swallowed around a growing lump in his throat.

"What can't you do?"

"Help them. I'm only a boy. I can't save anyone."

She sighed. "None of us can save anyone. All we can do is try."

"But if it's futile, why go on?" He wanted to know the

answer, longed for someone to tell him that risking his life and his family every single day wasn't for nothing. That it wouldn't end the way so many other stories had, all the lives he'd seen cut short despite their bravery and their innocence.

"We go on because we must. What else can we do?" Mama shrugged. "You're a good boy. I'm proud of you."

"What if I can't keep going, Mama? Will you be proud of me then?"

"Of course, my son. I love you and always will."

He felt better on hearing her words. The weight of expectation had given him sleepless nights and anxious days. He didn't know if he could keep it up, or even if he wanted to.

"This place won't do, so let's try again tomorrow after work." Mama smiled, wiping her cheeks dry with her sleeve.

Jan nodded and followed her out of the apartment, his heart heavy.

They'd been working so hard at the market and spending every spare moment on getting Jadzia released from the concentration camp and looking for an apartment that they'd barely slept in weeks.

"You're right. Let's go home."

Danuta was in the hallway, playing with a handful of rocks and sorting them into their various sizes and shapes. She'd learned to adapt to their new life. Without Jadzia to take care of her, she spent most of her time with either Mama, Jan or one of the neighbours and had grown accustomed to working at the market with them. She was almost as good as Jan at closing a deal.

The three of them wandered home, too tired to think about anything other than bed, although Jan's stomach grumbled as they passed a bakery and the scent of freshly baked bread drifted out to them on the breeze.

He missed Jadzia's bread. She made the best sourdough in the world. And he missed her laughter, her gentle teasing.

Everything about her. He hated to think what she must be going through, and there was nothing he could do about it. The frustration of that ate at him like acid.

When they reached home, the short day was almost over. The sun had never really shone, but had glowed behind a bank of dreary clouds. The land was cold and the air damp. A greyness hung over it all, exacerbated by the bombed-out craters that pockmarked the city and the bullet holes that punctuated walls.

"I'm lazy today," said Danuta, echoing Jan's mood.

"I think we all are. Let's build a nice fire and eat some left-overs around it." Mama rubbed her gloved hands together. Her face looked pale beneath her blue scarf, and Jan thought she had aged in recent weeks.

There was a woman standing outside their front door. Jan didn't recognise her at first. He tensed and held back, but Mama surged forward.

"Magdalena, you are here!" She kissed the woman's cheeks.

"It's good to see you, Waltrina. Even in these circum-stances. I don't get out much anymore, at least not around my own people, as you know."

"Yes, it is dangerous when the enemy decides you are his friend."

"Dangerous on both sides," Magdalena agreed. "There are many who don't understand what I'm doing."

"I'm grateful for you." Mama grasped her friend's hands and squeezed them. "What is your news?"

"Let's go inside," the woman replied, glancing around. "The walls have ears."

"And eyes," Mama agreed. "Come in, come in. Jan will build us a fire and Danuta will make tea. We can talk together and warm up."

• • •

AFTER MAGDALENA LEFT, JAN HURRIED TO HIS MOTHER'S side and plied her with questions. She laughed and cupped his cheek with one hand, then ruffled Danuta's hair with the other, since his sister was just as curious as he was about what the woman had said.

"Give me a moment to breathe and I will tell you everything." Mama leaned back in her chair, her cheeks pink in the glow of the fire from the hearth. "She says her boyfriend, the SS officer, will help us. He wants a diamond ring, a mink coat and two hundred American dollars."

Jan's stomach tightened. How would they get so much? "What did you say?"

"I agreed."

"But?"

"We will do it, Jan, because we have no other choice. Leave it to me, my son. I will go to the market first thing tomorrow and I will get what we need. This is one time where I don't need your help." Her eyes glowed with love as she stroked his cheek. "You're such a good boy. Always doing everything you can to help others. And I will need your help again—there is no doubt of that. But not for this. Do not let your heart be troubled. There is one thing she mentioned, though."

"What is it?" Jan's brow furrowed.

"He told her that if Jadzia has already been processed, he can't help us."

"How will we know if that's happened?"

Mama sighed. "He said she will be wearing a striped tunic. If she's still in her own clothes, he can get her out. If she's not, it's too late and there's nothing he can do."

15TH FEBRUARY 1943

I t took Mama a week to get the things she'd promised Magdalena's boyfriend, but she finally managed it. Every single day, Jan helped her at the market, took care of Danuta and went with her to look at apartments. And every day they got further and further away from a reconciliation with Jadzia. She could be processed at any moment and there was nothing they could do about it.

Finally, Mama had every item they needed and had given it all to the SS officer. She stood outside at the curb with him while Jan and Danuta watched through the window of their apartment.

They couldn't see his face, but his black uniform and cap sent a shiver down Jan's spine. Having an SS officer so close to their home made him nervous. And putting his sister's life in that man's hands was the last thing he wanted to do, but they had no choice.

They had to trust in a *Schutzstaffel* officer, a member of Hitler's elite guard. The most cruel and inhuman group of men on the face of the earth. Otherwise, they might not see Jadzia again in this lifetime. He prayed to all the saints he could think of, one by one, and recited the Hail Mary in his head over and over as he watched the officer drive away in a shiny black staff car with a Nazi flag flying from the tip of the bonnet.

Mama came inside and slipped out of her coat, hanging it carefully on the wall. Then she pressed a hand to her chest.

"Oh, my heart is racing."

Danuta ran to her, throwing her arms around her mother's waist. "Mama, I was so scared."

"Me too, my darling. But he's gone now, and he says he will do what he can. If she hasn't been processed, he promised to bring her back to us. Now it is in God's hands."

"And a Nazi's hands."

Mama swallowed hard. "Yes, and that too. Heaven help us."

Jan stared out the window again, his head light. Nacha was out there, in the Otwock ghetto with her family, abandoned by society and afraid. Now Jadzia was a prisoner in an extermination camp. The world didn't make sense anymore. And maybe it never had.

"This is no good," said Mama in a bright voice. "We can't all stand by the window and wait. Who knows how long it will take? Let's get some supper together and play a game of cards. I bet I can beat you, Danuta."

Danuta grinned. "No, you can't. I win every time."

"Maybe this time is different." Mama winked and hurried away to the kitchen with Danuta close behind.

Jan wandered to the cupboard where the pack of cards was kept beside the few books they owned. Mama and Danuta took the cards, while he flicked through the pages of the books. It was time to build up the fire and bring in firewood from outside. But when he got outside, there wasn't enough cut, so he cut firewood until the stack was high against the side of the apartment. He carried an armful inside and piled it in the hearth, then prodded it with the poker until it burned just right.

By that time, supper was ready, and they all ate at the kitchen table. Mama and Danuta chatted quietly together, but Jan ate in silence. He'd been so hungry lately, it was often difficult to think about anything other than helping his sister, rescuing Nacha's family, and food. Even now, while he was eating, he wanted more, and his thoughts wandered to visions of pastries covered in whipped cream and custard, or mountains of fresh bread dripping with butter and honey.

After supper, they cleaned up and then played a hand of cards. Followed by another and another. Soon, Danuta was yawning, and the hands on the clock passed her bedtime. But Mama didn't say a word about sleep. Jan's eyes blinked shut and he almost drifted off where he sat, but jerked himself awake and slapped his own cheek.

"Getting tired?" Mama asked in a kind voice.

"No, I'm fine."

"Me too," replied Danuta, with another gigantic yawn that threatened to split her face in two. Her golden hair fell in two straight plaits on either side of her face and her blue eyes were hooded.

Just then, a car pulled up outside the apartment and a door slammed. There were footsteps on the path, and a loud knock at the door. Jan leapt to his feet and Mama hurried to answer the door.

She flung the door open and there stood Jadzia. She was dirty and dishevelled. Her clothes were torn and stained. She looked thin, with strands of soiled hair hanging down either side of her gaunt, wind-burned face.

Mama thanked the SS officer, who hung back. He murmured a few words then hurried away. Once he was gone,

Mama pulled Jadzia into a bear hug. Jan and Danuta rushed to join in. Jan shut the door behind the officer and locked it, then threw his arms around Jadzia and Mama. Danuta did the same.

All three of them stood there, embracing Jadzia and crying together while the fire crackled in the hearth. Jadzia didn't cry. She stood in silence, her arms by her sides, her eyes vacant. She didn't look like herself, but she was home. And Jan had never felt so relieved.

🕸 23 🕸

18TH FEBRUARY 1943

The world was a snowy, glistening wonderland. Nacha leaned against the window of their Otwock apartment and studied the landscape below. Snow had fallen all night long and was falling still. It was silent and beautiful, and she couldn't help feeling hopeful that everything was going to work out somehow.

Danuta had ridden the train to the ghetto and was currently ensconced on a chair beside Nacha, telling her all about what had transpired.

Jadzia was home from the extermination camp, something everyone said wasn't possible. Jadzia was like a sister to Nacha and she'd been terrified that she would never see her again. She still hadn't left the apartment since coming home, according to Danuta. She was tired and quiet and had lost a lot of weight. She wouldn't talk much about what'd happened or what she'd seen, but she was safe and she was with Waltrina, and that was what mattered most.

She'd asked about her friend, Hanna. But Mama didn't want to tell Jadzia that she hadn't come home.

"And Jan is working with Mama today at the market. So, I said I would come and tell you all what happened. I caught the train on my own. Mama said I had to come straight here and right back home again without stopping."

"I hope you were careful," Nacha replied.

"Of course. I know my way around now. Besides, if it wasn't for this stupid war, I would've been catching trains on my own long ago. I'm ten years old, after all. Jadzia was doing a lot more than me when she was ten. It's really not fair."

"The war has changed everything," Nacha admitted. "I'm fifteen and I can't catch trains, or go to the movies, or see my friends…"

A stone lodged in Nacha's throat.

Danut's face fell. "I'm sorry, I didn't think."

"It's okay. It's not your fault. The war has affected all of us."

Screaming erupted outside the apartment building, followed by several loud shots. Nacha leapt up from her seat and scanned the neighbourhood. A man lay on the ground, red seeping from a wound in his head into the white snow. Nearby, a family wailed as a pair of guards ushered them away.

"What's going on out there?" Tata asked, coming to the window.

"I don't know."

Danuta whimpered. "I want to go home."

"You should go," Tata said. "I will walk you to the fence."

"Don't leave us, Tata," Nacha begged.

"We'll all go together."

Another group of Jews were herded past the window. Then suddenly the snowscape was filled with the trudging dark bodies of Jews bundled up in coats and scarves with booted feet.

Tata frowned. "On second thought, everyone get in your coats and warm things. Get your suitcases. It looks like we're being deported."

Nathan got up from where he was reading at the kitchen table and hurried into the bedroom. Nacha stood, frozen in place.

"Nacha, come on," Tata said gently.

"But where will we go?"

"We will try to get out with Danuta. We have to take her to the fence. Come, be quick about it."

They got ready quickly. Nacha felt numb. She couldn't understand why this was happening. It was cold. There was snow on the ground. Winter had always been magical to her, but this wasn't magic. This was terror, it was evil, it was a frozen tundra ravaged by the boots of thousands of Jews marching to their deaths and stained in the blood of those who'd fallen behind.

Dressed and with their small items of luggage in hand, the family hurried out of the apartment. Everywhere around them, people were peering out of doors or scurrying down staircases. There were shouts in the distance and the occasional firing of a rifle or a machine gun's rat-a-tat.

They'd come for her family soon. Their only chance was to get ahead of their persecutors and scale the fence with Danuta. But after that, where would they go? They couldn't put Danuta's family at risk by attempting to travel all the way back to her place with her. They wouldn't be allowed on the train without papers. They'd have to walk through the snow for twenty-five kilometres. The realisation made her stomach clench with fear.

"Let's go," Tata said.

The four of them hurried down the stairs and out across the snow in the direction of the sanatorium. It soon loomed over them, rows of windows glowering like so many eyes. The fence was close by and they ran the last few metres. Tata helped Danuta over, but just as he was about to boost Nacha over the fence, a guard rushed at them, gun raised.

"Halt, or I'll shoot!" he cried.

His grey overcoat reached almost to his feet and his grey helmet matched his grey eyes. He sported a small, square black moustache. Nacha's heart fell. It was over. There was no escaping now.

The dejected group marched along with the others from their neighbourhood in the direction of the train station and out through the ghetto gates. Nacha glanced over her shoulder for one last look at the place where they'd lived for months. She had no affection for it, only a fear of leaving.

They gathered with the growing crowd on the platform. It began to snow again, and flakes accumulated on Nacha's eyelashes. She didn't bother to brush them off. What did it matter? She could freeze to death at the station waiting to board the train and it would be a sweet relief compared to what she knew lay ahead for her and her family.

It wasn't for herself that the tears came, but the idea of being separated from her father and brother, and what would almost certainly become of them. The grief of knowing the loss that was ahead overwhelmed her for a few moments and she wept silently but openly in the falling snow.

When the time came, they were herded together onto an empty carriage with large sliding doors on both sides. The far side was locked, but the near side wide open, and the Jews from the ghetto scrambled up into the cavernous space.

"Quick, stay together and get to a window," Tata instructed.

So the three of them hustled to the back left side of the carriage and pressed themselves against the wall beneath a small rectangular window crosshatched with barbed wire. It wasn't long before the carriage was full to overflowing.

The doors slid shut and they found themselves in the dark. The train chugged away from the station and travelled for ten minutes or so. Several children began to cry, their parents doing their best to comfort them in their own fear. Adults cried as well, some shouted for help, and still others banged open palms against the walls.

When the train pulled to a halt, Nacha stood on tiptoe to look out the window.

Behind her, Tata whispered, "Can you see anything?"

"Just another platform. There are more guards, some Gestapo, a small station house."

The train sat idle for a long time. There were shouts outside, but the doors to their car remained shut.

Tata grunted. "I wish I knew where they were taking us. Most probably it will be Treblinka, but it might be Majdanek, where Jadzia went."

Nacha shivered at the thought. The few things Danuta had managed to tell them before the roundup began had chilled her to her core. And now they were being driven to the same fate as Jadzia with no chance of the same salvation.

"Waltrina!" she whispered.

She spied her through the crowd on the platform in the distance. Waltrina, Jadzia and Jan. All three of them were there. They were scanning the crowds of Jews—looking at every face. Looking for them.

They were too far away—they wouldn't hear even if she called to them. They were surrounded by Gestapo. The last thing they needed was for her to give them away by yelling their names across the tracks. Waltrina turned to a guard nearest her and spoke to him. She pointed along the platform, and he nodded.

"Where?" Behind her, Tata leaned forward, desperately looking for them.

"She, Jadzia and Jan are there," Nacha said, pointing. She

reached both hands up through the barbed wire that covered the window to wave, but they weren't looking in her direction. "They're here to find us."

Nathan sighed. "It will do no good. Don't get your hopes up, Nacha. They can't save us now. It's too late."

Tata rested a hand on Nathan's shoulder. "He's right, Nacha. They can do nothing."

Nacha's eyes pricked with tears as she watched Jan veer off from his mother and sister and jog away along another platform, searching for them. Searching for her. She knew it deep in her heart. He was looking for her. She wanted to scream, to cry, to call out his name. But it would only mean death for him if he came to her.

On the platform, guards beat a family of Jews. One guard lifted his gun and shot each of them in the back of the head one by one. People screamed and cried. In the carriage, someone fainted, and those around him trampled on his still form as it lay on the floor of the train. Waltrina and Jadzia made their way towards their carriage. Perhaps they would see her if they looked up soon.

"Mother! Mother! Water, please!" Nacha shouted suddenly.

Jadzia jolted at the sound of her voice and spun about until her eyes met Nacha's through the opening. Nacha's hands waved through the wire, her fingers reaching for her friend. Jadzia's hands clenched at her sides, but otherwise she didn't move, her gaze firmly fixed on Nacha's. She mouthed something, but Nacha couldn't understand what it was.

Waltrina came up beside Jadzia and scanned the carriage, searching the window, but the train began to move and Nacha knew she hadn't seen her. A great sob wracked her body. Tata held on to her as the train jolted, then pulled back, jolted forward again.

"There was nothing they could do for us," he repeated.

"I know," she sobbed. "But I wanted so badly for Waltrina to see me, and Jan..." She couldn't finish the sentence. It hung in the air between them, unspoken.

Nathan looked away, his jaw clenched.

Nacha stood in silence then, her face upturned towards the window, the fresh air from outside drifting in and filling her nostrils with the sweet smell of snow. She tugged off her gloves and shoved them in her pockets.

As the train lurched forward, she reached up a hand and clenched her fingers around the barbed wire. It was cold and hard against her flesh. The fingers of her other hand, she pushed through the opening between strands of wire and felt the air rushing over them as the train gathered speed.

Nathan turned towards her, his eyes full of pain.

"Are you okay?"

She smiled at him through a veil of tears. "I'll miss you."

He nodded, swallowed. "We'll try to stay together."

"You know they won't allow that. But you and Tata should keep close. Maybe you can make it, if you stick together."

Tata grabbed her and pulled her into a hug, burying his face in her hair. "Don't talk like that, *moja córka*. You will make it too, and we'll be together again before you know it."

It wasn't true. She knew that, and he did too, but it was nice to hear him say it all the same.

It took her a few moments to realise that she was holding a strand of barbed wire in one hand. When Tata released her from his embrace, the wire snagged on his coat. She frowned at it.

"Where'd that come from?" Nathan asked.

She looked up at the window and saw a space where the wire had been. "From there."

Both men followed her pointing finger. Tata gasped. "The wire came away."

As the train rattled along the tracks, and with no one else

paying them any attention, the three of them worked and jiggled, pulled and twisted the barbed wire covering the window until every last piece was either laying on the floor of the carriage or bent back away from the opening.

They worked in silence, not willing to speak about their hopes in case they might be dashed away or some fellow passengers heard what they were doing and crushed them in a rush to get to the window. But their eyes gleamed as they smiled at one another.

It was a small chance, but it was something. Nacha had seen the guards seated on top of trains in the past, waiting to shoot anyone who dared to escape. But it was cold and this train had a layer of snow on its roof, which had only grown thicker while they waited at the station.

Perhaps the guards had decided the weather didn't merit a ride on the roof today. She couldn't be certain, but it was worth the risk to make a run for it if they could manage to get out the small window. A shot in the back was preferable to whatever awaited them in Treblinka.

When the train blew its whistle, the sound jolted Nacha. Her nerves were frayed. She stood on her tiptoes, trying to see out the window to get some idea of where they were.

"We're in Warsaw, at the main station," Tata said.

"How do you know?"

"The direction we travelled, plus the distance. It would be the first big station, and the place they'd be most likely to stop to take on more passengers. As soon as we stop, we get out. Nacha first. Me last. Got it?"

They all muttered their agreement and waited in silence as the train slowed to a stop with a screech of brakes. It shuddered a moment, then was still.

Tata boosted Nacha and she pushed her arms through the window first, followed by the rest of her body. It was an easy fit, but she knew Tata would struggle to make it through the opening. He was bigger than she was, his shoulders much wider.

When her legs were partway through, she pushed against the carriage with her hands and fell away from it, tucking into a somersault. The gravel bit hard into her back and she stifled a grunt of pain as she rolled away from the train.

Quickly she leapt to her feet and scurried back to the shelter of the carriage. She helped Nathan down so he didn't have to land on his back the way she had. Then they both reached for Tata. He wriggled and squirmed while they pulled and tugged until finally all three of them were standing beside the carriage.

There was no platform on the other side, only a few trees, bare of leaves, and beyond them a fence and some residential buildings. No one had seen them escape.

Tata gave them a nod and they all ducked low, then ran along the tracks, passing the carriages at the back of the train. It'd grown dark as the train travelled, and the darkness hid them from the guards on the platform as well as their fellow prisoners, who didn't seem to notice they'd escaped, much to Nacha's surprise.

Perhaps they were all so busy looking at the doors, waiting for them to open on the other side, that they didn't see the wriggling forms slipping out through the last window. What-ever it was, when Nacha, Nathan and Tata sprinted away from the platform and slipped through a hole in the wire fence, no one saw them leave and nothing stopped their escape.

They ran through the streets of Warsaw, glancing back the way they'd come every now and then to see if they were followed. Eventually they slowed their pace and tugged the bands from their arms, stowing them in their pockets.

They walked in silence, turning right, then left, then right again. Nacha's pulse slowed the further they got from the train tracks. She still couldn't quite believe they'd done it. How was it possible? The God of her ancestors was watching over them. Or perhaps it'd been Jan, Waltrina and Jadzia's prayers that'd saved them.

Whatever it was, whoever had blinded the eyes of the thousands of people who'd inextricably missed their escape, she was grateful.

They hid in shadows and scurried along streets until finally they climbed the stairs to Aunt Irka's apartment and knocked on the door. When she opened it, she gasped and then ushered them inside with tears in her eyes.

She hugged them one by one and kissed their cheeks, exclaiming that she'd never seen such a thing in all the days of her life. How on earth had they managed such a miracle?

Nathan excitedly told her about their escape as she boiled a pot of tea and reheated some pork stew, which was light on the pork, but was the most delicious meal Nacha had ever eaten in her entire short life.

24

J an was on his way to Aunt Irka's apartment with a box
of groceries and a message from Mama that his aunt
had called and wanted one of them to stop by for some
news. He wondered what it could be. He'd been
despondent ever since the Otwock ghetto was cleared by the
Germans a few days earlier. He, Mama and Jadzia had rushed
over to the train station the moment Danuta got home and
told them what was happening. But they were too late.

Mama intended to bribe the guards and take the family, or
at least as many as she was able, back with them. But by the
time they got to the station, the Wierzbickas were already
loaded into a cattle car. Jadzia swore she locked eyes with
Nacha through a window, but Mama and Jan didn't see any
sign of the family.

All of them had been living under a cloud of grief and pain
ever since. Mama wouldn't come out of her room to go to the
market. Jan felt as though there was a great weight in his

chest. He regretted the things he'd said about helping the family.

They were his kin, no matter if they didn't share blood. He loved them more than he'd been able to put into words, and now they were gone. If he could do anything to bring them back, he would. Meanwhile, his sisters snuck around the apartment quietly, doing what they could to take care of Mama.

Jadzia in particular felt the horror of what lay ahead for the family since she'd only recently returned from an extermination camp herself and knew what they'd face. She seemed overwhelmed by it every now and then and would cover her head with her apron and rock back and forth in silence.

Jan didn't know what to do to help her. He could only continue going to the market, working and visiting the ghetto in the hopes that he might stumble across his friend, Walter, who he hadn't seen for a while.

He'd often asked Walter to live with them over the years, but his friend turned him down, saying he had a place to stay. Jan didn't know where he was now—he'd lost track of him in all the German raids and deportations. But he hoped they'd find each other again.

He trudged across the street with the box of groceries balanced on his head, then up the stairs to Aunt Irka's apartment. He set the box on the ground and knocked on the door. When Irka opened the door, he picked up the groceries.

"I brought you some things."

"Aren't you the sweetest nephew in the world? Thank you, Janek. Bring them into the kitchen for me and set them on the table. I'll put them away while you tell me everything."

She loved to hear about his life and always wanted to chat. But the truth was, Jan didn't have much to say this time. He didn't want to talk about the Otwock ghetto or the Wierzbickas. And there was nothing else on his mind.

"I'm so glad Jadzia made it home," said Irka, leading the way to the kitchen.

He set the box on the table just as someone behind him said. "Hello, Jan."

He spun to face the voice and found himself face-to-face with Nacha, Nathan and Antoni. His face lit up with joy and he rushed forward, then shook hands vigorously with Antoni and Nathan before kissing Nacha's cheeks.

"I can't believe it. How did you manage it? Jadzia was certain she saw you on the train bound for Treblinka."

They all sat around the table and ate a variation of *wuzetka*, made from whatever ingredients Aunt Irka had available and without fresh whipped cream. It was delicious and filled the hole in Jan's stomach that had turned to ravenous hunger the moment he knew the Wierzbickas were safe.

They told him all about their escape, and he updated them on everything that'd happened in their neighbourhood and the ghetto.

He hadn't told them yet about his discovery in their apartment. The moment wasn't right. He hated to be the one to bring it up, and especially when they were all so happy.

"Have you been into the ghetto lately?" Antoni asked.

"Not lately. I've been busy, and besides, they made it difficult for me for a long time. But it's better now."

"Oh?" Nathan took a bite of cake. "What's changed?"

" Himmler himself came to the ghetto last month. Everyone thought the deportations were over and the remaining Jews could stay behind, so they were surprised when he ordered more deportations. Eight thousand, I heard."

"What happened?" Nacha asked, eyes wide.

"They didn't report to the *Umschlagplatz*."

Antoni smiled. "Really?"

"Nope. The resistance has organised since you left. They call themselves the *Żydowska Organizacja Bojowa*—the ŻOB. People hid in holes and tunnels and the ŻOB fought back."

"They fought the Germans?" Nathan asked, his eyes gleaming.

Jan nodded. "And they won."

"What?" Antoni frowned. "What do you mean?"

"I mean the Germans pulled out. They stopped the deportations. There haven't been any more since then. The ŻOB fought on rooftops and in cellars, and the Germans weren't willing to do that. They were afraid of being ambushed."

Antoni clapped his hands together and Nathan grinned. Nacha laughed.

"Well, how about that." Antoni stirred his cup of tea with a silver spoon. "I didn't think I'd live to see it. But I'm glad they're finally fighting back. Someone had to do it."

"The ghetto seems safe now. There aren't any more deportations. Very few Jews are still living there compared to before. So, I was thinking—maybe I should smuggle you back in. You could go to your apartment and live there."

Nacha's eyes widened. "Oh, please, Tata. I want to see Babcia and Papa again. Could we please go home?"

"It's too dangerous," Antoni replied.

"It's up to you, but you can't stay here long term and Mama hasn't found an apartment for us yet. There are so few available, and even when we find something suitable, it's snatched up by someone else before we get it leased. If you go back to the ghetto, I will help you get out again just as soon as we locate a place to live."

Antoni scratched his stubbled chin. "And the deportations have stopped?"

"They haven't removed anyone in over a month."

"I suppose we could try it. It would be nice to see family again after all this time."

Jan swallowed and studied the table. He couldn't let them continue living in hope. He had to tell them the truth. He'd wanted to let them enjoy happiness for a while, but if they returned with him tonight to the ghetto, they'd learn about what'd happened soon enough.

Nacha jumped up from the table and embraced her father with a squeal of excitement.

Nathan reached for another slice of cake, grinning from ear to ear. "It will be good to go home again. I didn't much like Otwock."

"Me neither," Nacha agreed with a wrinkled nose. "It never felt like home to me."

"There's something I have to tell you before we go." Jan wanted to walk out the door and leave them at Aunt Irka's, happy, laughing and eating cake.

"What is it?" Antoni asked.

"It's about your family." Jan inhaled a deep breath. "They're gone."

"What?" Antoni's brow furrowed.

"I'm guessing they were deported to Treblinka. But I can't know for certain. I visited them three months ago and discovered the apartment was empty. They'd been there before that—I saw them several times."

Nacha began to cry. She covered her face with both hands and sobbed quietly. Nathan's face clouded over, and Antoni slammed a hand down on the table.

"We knew it was likely," Jan continued. "And one more thing. I found Babcia and Papa there. They were in bed."

Antoni met his gaze. "Dead?"

Jan nodded.

Nacha wailed and hid her face against Nathan's shoulder.

Nathan's nostrils flared, but he didn't speak. Antoni's eyes glistened with tears. Irka patted her cheeks dry with the bottom corner of her apron and shuffled into the kitchen to boil the kettle for more tea.

25

4TH MARCH 1943

Time ticked by so slowly. Nacha sat on her bed and stared out the window at the street below. Her street. Her home. The place where she'd spent years of her life. It wasn't the same anymore now that the rest of the family was gone. When they'd returned to the apart-ment, Babcia and Papa's bodies were missing. Someone had collected them. But their bloodstains were on the pillows, and the stench still filled the closed apartment.

Since then, they'd cleaned the place from top to bottom. It gave Nacha and Nathan something to do. Tata spent each day meeting with the ŻOB leaders and shouting about revolu-tion and fighting back against the Nazis. He came home tired, his hair dishevelled and his tie askew. But he rarely spoke to either of them about what he'd done or what'd been discussed.

With a sigh of boredom, Nacha skipped down the stairs to the kitchen. She might as well get started on making *golabki*, the little cabbage rolls Nathan loved so much, for supper. There was nothing else to do. No one around to spend time with, even if Tata would let her out of the apartment.

She was entirely alone, especially when Nathan accompanied Tata to the ŻOB meetings. She'd asked if she could go, but Tata still saw her as a little girl and didn't want to place her in danger. She wanted to point out that she was a prisoner in a Nazi ghetto with the constant threat of deportation to an extermination camp hanging over her head, danger was her everyday reality. But she held back the retort, knowing it wouldn't help him feel any better. He had enough stress to deal with, let alone an argumentative daughter.

Besides, she didn't really want to be part of the ŻOB meetings. She'd only asked to go, to give herself something to do and so she might have someone to talk to other than her brother and father. She looked forward to each of Jan's visits more than ever before. He came almost every day to bring supplies, check in on them and update them on Waltrina's search for a suitable apartment.

When he showed up at the front door an hour later, she was up to her elbows in mashed potato dough.

She called out, "Come in. The door isn't locked."

He pushed through the door and shut it behind him with a frown. "Why isn't the door locked?"

"I was hoping you'd come, and I've got my hands deep in this pastry." She grinned and blew a lock of hair out of her face with a puff of air.

He laughed. "You have potato smeared all over your cheek."

She tried to brush it away with the back of her hand, but it adhered to her hand as well.

He stepped closer with a chuckle. "No, you made it worse." He reached up a hand and brushed her cheek gently. He was so close, she could feel the warmth of his breath on her face. His eyes were blue and sparkled as they met her gaze.

She blushed. "Thank you."

He took a step back. "I came to give you the good news."

"What's that?" she asked as she kneaded the dough with both hands.

"We found an apartment. It's time for you all to come home."

THE CELEBRATION AT THE NEW APARTMENT THAT NIGHT was enthusiastic, but quiet. They chatted and laughed, drank and ate. There were the *golabki* that Nacha had made and packaged up to carry with them to the Aryan side once Tata and Nathan came home from the ŻOB meeting. Waltrina had made piles of *pierogi*, steaming hot along with mounds of vegetables fresh from the market.

They sat around in their new kitchen, at the Kostanskis' table, and ate until they could eat no more. Nacha couldn't remember being so happy in all her life. The Kostanskis were there, they were together again. The only dampener on her joy was the fact that Babcia, Papa, and her aunts, uncles and cousins couldn't be there.

She prayed any that had survived so far were safe and that she might see them again when all this was over. It was a pipe dream, she knew, but so far they'd managed to survive against the odds when it seemed impossible.

"I'd like to propose a toast," Tata said, raising his glass of black-market wine in the air.

Everyone stopped talking and eating to raise their glasses high as well. Nacha couldn't stop smiling.

"To Waltrina, Jan, Jadzia and Danuta—we are so very grateful for you. We wouldn't be here without you."

"To the Kostanskis," echoed Nathan and Nacha.

They all drank at once. Waltrina gazed lovingly at Tata, and they all pretended not to notice that the two of them held hands beneath the table.

"I miss Babcia," Nacha said, her heart aching. "But I'm glad I have all of you."

Everyone fell silent and the mood shifted.

Waltrina jumped to her feet with a forced smile. "I have a surprise." She bustled into the bedroom and returned with Tata's violin, still in its case. "You left this at Irka's the first time, since you didn't want to take it to the ghetto with you. She gave it to me months ago, and I haven't had an opportunity to return it."

Waltrina handed the violin case to Tata, who opened it and lovingly brushed his fingers over the strings.

His eyes glistened. "Thank you."

"Play something, please, Tata," Nacha said.

He took the violin and tuned it for a few moments, then sat it beneath his chin and began to play. The notes that emitted from the instrument were slow, long and mournful. The music filled the small space, bringing tears to every eye. Then Tata changed pace, shifting into a fast-paced song that had every foot tapping in no time.

Jan reached for Nacha's hand and spun her away from him, then back again. They danced together, in time to the music, until they were both out of breath. Nathan danced with Jadzia, and Danuta made up her own dance, spinning around the room until she fell over on the couch laughing. Then Waltrina joined her and they danced together, with Danuta stepping on Waltrina's feet so much, she declared she'd need to ice them in the snow outside after they were done.

After they'd finished celebrating, Jan led them all to the small room he and his family had built for them in the centre of the house. It was hidden behind walls that made it look as though it was part of the bedroom next door, with no visible doorway. Anyone who walked into the apartment wouldn't notice it—at least, that was their hope.

Nacha surveyed the room with trepidation—this small, dark space would be their home. For how long? It was safe, dry and warm. There were mats on the floor for sleeping. She shouldn't complain—she knew that. She glanced at the nearby window.

It was dark outside, and snow fell silently beyond the glass pane. Out there were people, and birds, animals and trees. In spring, there would be flowers. Would she get to see them? Or would she still be hidden in this dark, cramped space waiting for the world to end?

❧ 26 ❧

2ND APRIL 1943

The entire family fell into something of a routine before long. They lived freely in the apartment, but the Wierzbickas slept on the mats in the hidden room in case anyone surprised them all at night. They also used the room if a neighbour came to visit or a friend showed up unexpectedly for tea. However, Waltrina, Jan, Jadzia and Danuta gradually stopped seeing their friends. They didn't want to risk exposing the Wierzbickas, and besides that, they genuinely preferred to spend time only with each other now that they were all back together.

It was a happy time. Nacha took on the task of cooking the meals the family would eat. Jadzia kept house, while Danuta ran little errands and did what she could to help. Jan and Waltrina continued working each day, trading at the market for the things they'd need. But they'd also formed something of an alliance with the ŻOB through Antoni's contacts and had begun supplying them to keep the resistance going.

Jan knew it was a great relief to his mother to have the Wierzbicka family under the same roof. And yet the danger was still there. It lurked on every corner, as the Germans stepped up their campaign to harass and debase the Polish people and wipe out the Jews. And it waited for them like a dark fog creeping up from the sewers every time they communicated with the ŻOB or passed food or medicine to them over the wall.

The ŻOB paid well, so Jan and his family never went hungry during those heady days hidden away in their apartment in a strange neighbourhood in Warsaw at number fifteen Panska Street.

Jan and Mama were polite to the neighbours they met along the way to the market. They'd nod or wish them good morning, but they never stopped for a prolonged conversation. It was best, Mama said, to be civil enough to be forgettable, but not friendly enough to be remembered. And so far the strategy had worked well. A few neighbours had dropped by to welcome them to the building in the first few weeks, but interest had quickly waned, and they no longer attempted a friendship.

Outside, the sun was shining, and the sky was blue. The street was busy with bicycles and carts. A few vehicles chugged by, and two cyclists crashed into each other, resulting in a shouting match between the men.

Mama and Jan spent the day at the market, trading for the things they knew would sell best to get the supplies they needed as a family and the items the ŻOB had requested. There were still around fifty thousand Jews living in the Warsaw ghetto, although whenever Jan snuck into the ghetto, it didn't seem that way.

The neighbourhoods were barren wastelands, the buildings run down, bombed or burned to the ground. Piles of rubbish were everywhere. Bodies showed up randomly in the streets as families dragged them out of buildings to be carried away by horse and cart to be burned or buried in one of the many mass graves dug all over Poland.

After containing as many as four hundred and sixty thousand residents at the peak of its population growth, to have only a fraction of that number remaining made the ghetto feel abandoned. Especially since so many of those remaining stayed hidden for much of the day, as though aware that their time was short.

Before midday, they'd traded for a large bag of flour that Mama was particularly happy about. It'd been a while since they'd been able to find flour, and she had already planned what she and Nacha would make with it that evening when they got home. Since the Wierzbickas moved in, they'd celebrated Shabbat every Friday evening. Jan's family was still Catholic, but he liked taking on the new tradition, and it seemed to mean a lot to Antoni.

Imagining supper that evening, his mouth watering, Jan carried a bag of supplies to the pre-arranged location beside the wall close to the market. He retrieved a ladder from a nearby stall, giving a nod to the stall owner, and set it up against the wall. The trick, he'd discovered, was to be confident and quick. If he stumbled or glanced about furtively, he'd invite attention.

At the top of the ladder, he held out the bag, and a pair of hands took it.

His eyes widened. "Walter?"

Walter grinned at him, his red hair blazing under the sun's glaring rays. "Hi, Jan."

Jan gripped his hand and shook it, not wanting to let him go. "I couldn't find you. I thought you were on this side of the wall."

"I decided to stay over here. We're fighting back. I can't stay hidden forever while my people suffer."

Jan knew what he meant. "If you need it, we have space for you now. We've found an apartment. You're always welcome."

"Thank you. I'll keep that in mind."

"Any word of your family?"

Walter's jaw tightened. "They were sent to Treblinka."

He didn't need to say more. They both knew what that meant. "I'm sorry."

Walter nodded. "I pray they didn't suffer."

As he walked away from the wall with the ladder tucked beneath his arm, Jan couldn't help feeling guilty. It wasn't his fault—he knew that. But he should've done more. Should've worked harder somehow to save Walter's family and the rest of the Wierzbickas.

If only he'd found two apartments, five or ten. They could've brought more families out of the ghetto and to safety. But he couldn't have known what would come—no one could believe what the Germans had done. It'd taken them all by surprise. They hadn't been prepared. They should all have fought back harder, should never have complied. But they didn't know, couldn't know.

When he returned to their stall inside the market, he kicked hard into a pile of bricks that were waiting for the purchaser to pick them up and take them away. Then he sat on the ground, back against the bricks, with a grunt.

"What's wrong, Janek?"

"We should've done more. Why didn't we fight harder? We could've saved them," he growled.

Mama rested a hand on top of his head, then leaned over to kiss his cheek. "You can't think that way. It will drive you crazy. We did what we could. We do it still. No one can do more than that. Be grateful we are here and that the sun is shining today. Tomorrow could look very different."

LATER AT HOME, JAN HOVERED IN THE KITCHEN, WAITING for a chance to grab something to eat when his mother or Nacha had their back turned. So far Mama had slapped his hand twice and chased him out of the kitchen with a dish towel once.

"I don't know what is going on with this gravy," Mama said, frustration deepening her voice. "It won't thicken the way it usually does."

Nacha leaned over and studied the pan. "Hmmm...it does look a bit strange."

Jan poked a finger into the gravy and then shoved it into his mouth even as Mama slapped at his hand. "Janek Kostanski!"

He frowned. "That doesn't taste like gravy." He spat the offending mixture back into his hand.

Mama gasped. "It must be bad if you're spitting it out."

She turned off the stove and wiped her hands on her apron. "I wonder..." She marched to the pantry and tugged the heavy bag of flour out into the kitchen. Then she opened the top of the sack and pushed the flour back with one hand. "Well, I never."

Jan peered into the sack. "What is that?"

"I believe it's cement mix."

Jan rushed to the kitchen tap, poured a glass of water, and rinsed his mouth, spitting into the sink. "Ugh. No wonder it tasted bad. I can't believe they fooled us like that."

Mama closed the top of the sack again. "Never mind. We'll take it back to the market tomorrow and trade it on."

"Mama!" he said, his brow furrowed. "We can't do that."

"We don't have a choice. We have a lot of mouths to feed. Come on—you can help me by carrying it to the front door ready for the morning."

He picked up the sack and set it on his shoulder, then marched to the front door, hot with anger. He understood why they'd done it—people were desperate. The war had made criminals out of many of them. Things they'd never dream of doing had become commonplace. But it was frustrating when it happened to his family. And tomorrow, they'd do the same to another family.

With the sack leaning against the front door, he returned to the kitchen and took a seat at the table as Mama and Nacha served the meal onto plates. There weren't enough seats at the table for everyone, so Nathan, Danuta and Jadzia sat on the floor in the living room to eat.

"You know," began Antoni as Mama spooned potatoes onto his plate. "When I was a boy, we often sat on the floor to eat. We were poor, and there were so many of us in my family—cousins, aunts and uncles. Everyone would get together after synagogue for Shabbat. The adults would drink a sweet wine, and then my grandfather would pray.

Blessed are you, Lord our God, King of the universe, who brings forth bread from the earth.

"And then we'd eat challah. It makes my mouth water just to think about it now." He laughed as Mama sat beside him in her chair and held out a hand to him. He squeezed her hand, then raised it to his lips to kiss it. The red of Mama's cheeks deepened as she drank him in. Then she released his hand, and they both cleared their throats.

"I'm so grateful we all get to be here together," Mama said. "Nacha wanted to make challah for us all, but unfortunately the flour we bought was no good. Never mind. We will manage without."

"And we will be grateful for everything we have, rather than what we don't," Antoni added with a wide smile. "Let us pray."

27

18TH APRIL 1943

I t was the first time Jan had ever celebrated the Seder. He'd seen Antoni, Nathan and Nacha's family prepare for the celebration in years past, but he'd never participated before. Mama wasn't sure they should, saying it was a sacred ritual. But Antoni insisted—he told her that it meant so much to him that they be part of it this year.

The rest of the family was gone. They were all each other had. And there was a significance to the tradition this time that none of them could've predicted. They were part of an exodus of their own. Jews were leaving a persecution all over again, although this time most were doing so unwillingly.

There was something in the atmosphere all over Warsaw —a quiet, a waiting, a tension mounting. Tomorrow was Hitler's birthday, and the Nazis had announced various celebrations and festivities to mark the occasion. It didn't escape Jan's notice that the *Fuhrer's* birthday would land on the first day of Passover.

It was like an omen of some kind, although Jan had never

believed in omens before. This seemed too prescient to be ignored. It gave him a feeling of foreboding, which when coupled with the city's mood, made him agitated and grouchy.

He'd already been kicked out of the kitchen several times by Mama and Nacha, who were preparing the Seder meal. But he'd grumbled and complained and then lashed out at Danuta, who teased him about having a tapeworm. Jadzia sat quietly in the corner, looking out the window.

The day was grey and chilly for spring. It made sense that the whole earth would mourn such a day, with its foreboding echoed in the low-hung clouds and the grey sky. When the time came for the Seder, Antoni prayed over a glass of wine. He called it a *Qiddush*.

They all took turns washing their hands in a large porcelain bowl. Then Antoni handed around various things to eat from a plate in the centre of the table. A raw vegetable dipped in vinegar, some kind of meat on a bone, and a hard-boiled egg. Jan wished he could eat the entire thing. It'd been so long since he'd seen an egg.

Mama had worked hard to trade for all the things they'd need at the market. She'd apologised that the wine was a home brew made from potatoes and some kind of dark wild-berry, and the herbs were a mixture of whatever she'd managed to pluck from the small communal garden in the courtyard.

Then Antoni poured another glass of wine, and Danuta asked the group a series of questions in her solemn, sweet voice.

"Why does this night differ from all other nights? For on all other nights we eat either leavened or unleavened bread; why on this night only unleavened bread? On all other nights we eat all kinds of herbs; why on this night only bitter herbs? On all other nights we need not dip our herbs even once; why on this night must we dip them twice? On all other nights we eat either sitting up or reclining; why on this night do we all recline?" She faltered on the last question, but managed to get through it.

Antoni acknowledged her success with a smile as he inclined his head.

Then the entire group spoke as one in response. Jan had practiced the answers that morning. Nacha helped him prepare by running through the questions and answers that morning while she folded laundry and he mended a hole in the toe of his right shoe.

Afterwards, they all washed their hands in the bowl again. And it was time to eat the *matza* and bitter herbs dipped in crushed fruits (berries discovered on a bush by a friend at the market) and wine. This was the part Jan had been looking forward to. The *matza* had smelled delicious when Nacha baked it.

He took the piece offered him and dipped it in the mixture, then bit into it. It was far more bitter than he'd realised it would be, and he did his best not to grimace. Nacha watched him and fought back a smile. Her expression almost made him laugh.

He had to focus on something serious or he'd burst out laughing and choke on the matza and spoil the whole thing. He breathed slowly and deeply, looking out the living room window and away from Nacha's mischievously glinting eyes.

Something in the distance caught his attention. A column of black smoke rose, curling over the ghetto. He rushed to the window, swallowing the last of the matza.

"What is it? What's wrong?" Antoni called from the table.

"Nothing. I'm going out for a little while. I'll be back soon." Jan slipped on his shoes by the door. With the freshly mended toe, they were far too small and his feet cramped if he wore them too long, but they were all he had, so they'd have to do for now.

As he shut the door behind him, he could hear Mama and Antoni calling after him in frustration. They weren't happy, but he had to go and find out what was happening at the ghetto.

The last time he met in private with the ŻOB in a sewer pipe beneath the city streets, they'd told him they intended to fight any further attempts at deportation. Perhaps the deportations had begun again. If that happened, there would be a fight.

If the battle had already begun, the ŻOB would need help. He worried about Walter as well. If only his friend would agree to leave the ghetto and come stay with them, he'd feel a lot better.

He jogged in the direction of the ghetto. The streets were eerily quiet. Very few people were out and about. There was a chill in the air. Overhead, the clouds whirled and churned in the sky. Leaves scattered across the street. A bicycle rushed by and almost clipped Jan when he stepped from the curb.

He ducked down an alley and climbed into the sewer system. He'd grown used to the myriad tunnels beneath the city that led into the ghetto and out of it again.

The Polish Underground used the network to smuggle goods and people into and out of the ghetto and between city districts within Warsaw, particularly the Zoliborz district and Warsaw's Old Town, where the ghetto was located.

It was the best way to move large amounts of supplies or weapons, as well as groups of people, without being seen. The Germans suspected the resistance of using the sewer system, and occasionally lobbed grenades under the manhole covers. They lowered listening devices into the sewer wells and waited for any noise to indicate their enemy's movements.

In general, though, they seemed wary of going near the

sewers since the Polish Underground put them to use, and the resistance fighters took advantage of their fear.

Jan heard voices up ahead and slowed his pace, keeping to the side of the pipe to avoid splashing that could be heard a long way off. He snuck up on a group of three resistance fighters having a quiet but heated conversation near a manhole.

The light from the manhole shone down close by and illuminated the group. He was surprised because conversations in the sewer system were strictly forbidden, especially near manholes, in case the Germans might be listening.

"They call us rats. Let us be rats then!" one man, wearing a shabby cap and too-large pants held up by suspenders said. "We'll hide in bunkers and tunnels. We'll come out and strike when they're not ready. We won't ever comply again."

"I have five hundred men ready to fight," added another man. He scratched his head. "But we're not well armed, and not one of us has any training."

"I've had it with doing what we're told," agreed the last man. "The Germans have given seven thousand Jews orders to show up for deportation tomorrow morning. Something to do with the *Fuhrer's* birthday celebration. They want to kill as many of us as possible for his birthday, it seems." The man spat into the water by his feet.

It was then the three of them noticed Jan watching silently from a distance.

"Is that you, Janek?" Marek asked.

Jan stepped forward. "What's going on?"

"The Germans have commanded us to report for deportation tomorrow. But we're not going to comply."

"Will the people do it?" Jan asked.

"We're all agreed," replied Marek. "We'd rather go down fighting than do a single thing they ask us. We know their plans now. The people on the early deportations didn't understand. They thought if they complied, they might be okay. But we know better. No one returns. We've heard the reports from villagers about the trains and trucks they see passing by, full of bodies."

The other men nodded.

Anger burned in Jan's gut. "If there's anything I can do . . ."

"We'll use the sewers to escape if we can. There's nothing you can do now but pray." Adas was a tall, thin man with a rifle slung across his back.

"I will," Jan agreed.

"Tomorrow is the Passover. Walter asked if we saw you to invite you to share the Passover with him in the ghetto."

This could be Jan's last chance to get Walter out of the ghetto to safety. "Tell him I'll be there."

Marek smiled. "I will. He will be glad to know it. If they plan to use our own sacred tradition against us, thinking we'll fold, they will find themselves sorely mistaken. We won't sit idle. We will fight."

Jan shook hands with each of the men and wished them well. Then he watched as they silently made their way along the pipe. They walked like cats, on silent feet, one hand on the shoulder of the man ahead of them, the other hand brushing the side of the pipe so they could feel their way forward in the dark.

✺ 28 ✺

19TH APRIL 1943

I t was the first day of the Passover. Jan told Mama early that morning that he intended to go into the ghetto and bring Walter home with him. She wasn't happy about him taking the risk, but she understood. And by now she was accustomed to him putting himself in dangerous situations.

"I trust you to know when to leave," was all she said.

He'd agreed that he would do his best to keep himself and Walter safe, and get them out of the ghetto if anything happened. There was plenty of conversation buzzing around the deportations and whether any of the Jews who'd received notices would show up at the *Umschlagplatz* as instructed. According to the Polish Underground and the ŻOB, they wouldn't, but Jan knew you couldn't tell what people might do when they were afraid.

Still, his entire body vibrated with tension as he snuck over the wall into the ghetto that bright, clear morning. Walter was waiting for him by the remnants of the former soup kitchen where Nacha had attended school. The place was abandoned now, with empty pots and pans strewn about and the building an empty hollow of charred remains.

The two boys embraced quickly, and Walter led Jan to a nearby building. It was seven stories tall, and many of the street-facing windows were broken. Just then, several trucks rumbled through the ghetto gates and stopped.

German soldiers bundled out of the backs of the trucks armed with machine guns and rifles. They set up around the soup kitchen behind makeshift defences.

One man, dressed in the black uniform of the SS, stood tall and straight, pressed a bullhorn to his lips, and began shouting commands.

"I am SS *Brigadeführer* Jürgen Stroop, and I am ordering all Jews who received a summons to report immediately for deportation. Report or you will be shot. This is not an option. Gather your family and one bag and make your way to the *Umschlagplatz* to be sent east with your fellow Jews."

He repeated the mantra over while Jan and Walter watched.

"It's starting," Walter said.

Jan nodded. "We should get moving."

Inside, they jogged up several flights of stairs until Walter stopped at one of the apartment doors and gave a discreet knock. The door opened, and they were greeted by a man with a drooping moustache, wearing too-large clothing tied at the waist with a rope.

He didn't smile, but ushered the two of them inside. "*Chag Pesach Sameach.*"

"*Chag Sameach*," Walter replied. "This is my friend, Janek."

The man held out his hand, and Jan shook it. "You are welcome, Jan. We have heard a lot about you, and we thank you for what you've done for our people, and for Walter."

Jan caught sight of his own reflection in the broken shards

of a mirror that hung on the wall. His hair was mussed and his tie askew.

"Thank you for having me."

Jan wished now he'd spent more time on grooming before he left that morning. He smoothed his hair the best he could and straightened himself up. He and Walter followed the man along a hallway, then through another door.

They slipped down a hatch beneath a floor rug and crawled through a floor space, emerging from a hole in a wall behind a painting into another small, dark room.

A group of people was there, seated around a long table, and each welcomed them with the traditional greeting. They talked together in hushed tones and with gentle smiles. It was a celebration, but a subdued one with an undercurrent of tension.

Jan recognised several of the men as leaders in the ŻOB, but didn't know their names. The one who'd opened the door for them had smooth black hair parted in the middle of his head. He seemed to be in charge and gave orders for the Passover meal to begin once Jan and Walter were seated.

The men sat around the table. Several women stood behind them, and the children were seated around the edges of the room on the floor. All were dressed in their best clothes with their hair neatly combed. All were thin, with bones protruding along their collars, their legs spindly and their cheeks sunken and hollow, with eyes bulging.

The ritual of the meal followed the same procedure as the previous evening. And this time, Jan felt more comfortable with each of the steps involved. Walter explained in a whisper that the second Seder was an important part of the Passover tradition. When the time came for the Exodus story, Jan listened eagerly to the recitation.

After the Seder was over, the women and children left quickly. The men sat around the table a while longer, smoking and thinking. Jan remained with them, a feeling of agitation beginning in his gut. They would have to get out of there soon. He only hoped Walter would go with him.

He had a bad feeling about what was going on outside the building. If what he'd heard from the resistance fighters was true, the people had no intention of surrendering for deportation. He wasn't sure what the SS commander would do, but he knew it would be brutal.

The man with the drooping moustache spoke up. "The time has come for us to fight. The women and children have returned to the bunker. We will finish our cigarettes, and then we must gather our weapons and take the fight to the Germans. They won't be ready for our strike, and for this reason alone we will have a brief advantage. Remember what we discussed. Strike and retreat, strike and retreat."

"How long will this give us?" asked one of the younger men.

"There's no way of knowing. Last time, they retreated. This time, they will be better equipped."

"What happens if we can't hold them back?"

"We get as many out in the tunnels and sewers as we can. And we fight to the last man. We can't allow the Germans alone to pick the time and place of our deaths."

They all stood slowly and shook hands, clapped each other on the backs, and began to disperse.

Jan tapped Walter. "We've got to go, Walter."

Walter faced him, brow furrowed. "The fighting is about to start."

"But if we stay, we'll both die. We're unarmed. We're not prepared. And I promised Mama I would leave if fighting broke out."

Walter's countenance was stubborn. "I can't leave."

Jan nodded. "I understand. But I have to go now."

"I'll see you out."

The two of them hurried through the various trapdoors and hallways they'd followed to get into the dining room, then down the stairs and out through the front door. The scent of smoke hit them before they reached the doorway, and the air thickened the moment they were outside.

Jan coughed and tugged a scarf from his neck to tie around his mouth and nose. The air was thick with smoke. The building across the road crackled as fire leapt from one story to the next. A black cloud billowed out across the road.

From the top floors, people leaned from windows, coughing and crying out. Someone jumped and landed with a thud on the street in front of them.

Jewish resistance fighters lobbed hand grenades and Molotov cocktails at the German troops from windows, adding to the fire and chaos. The Germans fought back, firing indiscriminately into the buildings as they hid behind their temporary fortifications.

Jan's eyes widened in horror, and he took off at a run. As they barrelled through the ghetto, he saw German soldiers pulling women and children into the street from buildings and bunkers, beating and killing them, piling them up in big mounds of death. Every building was on fire. The stench of smoke made the air impossible to breathe.

An SS officer shouted at them to stop and fired a shotgun at their retreating backs. But Jan and Walter didn't stop. They sped up, dodging and ducking around buildings and behind the charred remains of wagons and trucks. When they reached the wall, Jan spun about to face Walter.

"Come with me," he beckoned.

With one last glance over his shoulder, Walter climbed the wall and leapt down to the other side with Jan.

"You can't do anything to help them now. You'll only get yourself killed," Jan said. "Come on. Let's go home."

They turned their back on the flames leaping from

building to building and took off at a run. By the time they reached home, Jan's heart was heavy. Before they stepped inside to climb the stairs to the apartment, he turned to look back in the direction of the ghetto as he heaved for breath in the acrid air. The sky over the ghetto was bright as scarlet, and soot fell from the sky like blackened rain.

"That's the end of it," Walter said beside him, puffing hard.

It was clear the Germans meant to raze the entire ghetto to the ground as a punishment for the residents ignoring orders.

Jan shook his head. "I never imagined this."

"I should've stayed."

"Then you'd have died with them."

Walter didn't respond, but Jan understood what he was thinking. He knew his friend well. Walter had already lost his entire extended family. What was one more loss?

"I'm glad you didn't stay," said Jan, patting Walter on the shoulder. "Now, come on. Let's get inside before anyone notices you."

❧ III ☙

Under the new flag's given symbol of glory
The ranked boots pummelled in unison
The uncomprehending soil. The physical acres
Mudded indifferently with the many heel
    prints.
He was one of many in the anonymous ranks
Turning the bright fragments of memory as he
    marched... Of the orator's promise electri-
    fying his spine,
The dream of heroes. Weight of rifle on his
    bruised shoulder.
Invented manhood to him. The forward action
    was glory.

> — "ON A PHOTOGRAPH OF A GERMAN
> SOLDIER DEAD IN POLAND" BY JOHN
> CIARDI

❦ 29 ❦

1ST FEBRUARY 1983

MELBOURNE, AUSTRALIA

They want to interview me for the ceremony. To get my story, they said. My story. It's something I haven't told anyone. I don't know where to start. How do you begin something like that? It's been hidden deep inside me so long, I'm not sure how to start pulling it out.

One piece at a time, my love. That's what Jan said when I told him how I felt about it all. *It's your award,* I replied, *I don't know why I have to be interviewed.*

They'll put the interview in a pamphlet to be handed out on the day. I don't have to go on the stage, which is a relief. But I'm nervous still. How to find the words?

In the end, I agreed to do it because it seemed to mean a lot to my boys. And I'm happy for Jan and Waltrina. They deserve the award. I want the world to know what we went through and how they fought for us even though it might've meant a horrible and humiliating death for them.

Righteous among the nations.

It has a nice ring to it. I've longed to see them recognised all this time for what they did. They rescued us. It's as simple as that. Jan wanted to stay in the ghetto and fight that day when it burned to the ground, but he came back to us instead. He told me later he knew that if he stayed, he'd die, and then who would look after me and my family?

"I had a responsibility," he said. "A responsibility to you. I knew I couldn't save them, as much as it pained me to admit. But I could save you. And so that's what I did."

Janek and Waltrina Kostanski saved my family from death more times than I can count. And they did it knowing it could mean their own demise in the most painful and degrading ways the German military could devise.

The Nazis certainly knew how to be cruel. Even then I didn't understand just how bad things could be, but I've learned a lot about it since. Those of us who lived it understood the fear, but we didn't see the camps. Jadzia did—she was there. She witnessed what they did, but she wouldn't talk about it. The rest of us could only guess.

We saw people crammed into trains and taken away, never to return. Deported to somewhere in the east, we were told. But by the time the ghetto burned, we'd learned the truth about the extermination camps. Or at least some elements of the truth, but not the whole. No one knew the whole of it until the Russians liberated Treblinka.

The things I've read, the stories I've heard since, haunt my dreams. Or they did when I was younger. These days, I dream more about grandchildren and sunny days and sunburnt skies that warm my head as I walk along golden shores. This adopted home of ours has brought us so much peace and joy.

It's hard to remember the fear of those days, but now as I drive to the studio where the television reporter waits to speak to me, that feeling returns like a premonition of the interview ahead.

The journalist is beautiful, like some kind of hauntingly serene doll. She won't stop smiling with those impossibly white teeth as she leads me through the studio, introducing me to everyone we pass. I smile and nod, shake hands and utter greetings, but can't remember a single name she's told me.

By the time I'm seated with the camera pointed at my face, there's a line of sweat trickling down the centre of my spine. It's hot beneath the lights, and I'm nervous about what I'll say. Will the words come out in a way that makes sense? I haven't spoken them before, so it's hard to know.

I've talked to Jan about those days, of course, but it's different when you're with someone who lived it with you. You don't have to explain. There are things unspoken that have no need for words. He knows what I'm describing without me having to draw him a picture. And so the explanations, the stories—they're stuck deep down in the recesses of my mind. Memories without words. Experiences I never wanted to exhume.

She asks about those days, and what Jan and Waltrina did for us. So I tell her. Then I talk about living in the apartment with the Kostankis in that small hidden room for two years.

Two whole years without the fresh air or sunshine on my face. Two years without seeing anyone but Tata, Nathan, and the Kostanskis. No friends to go out with, no boys to flirt with, no school days or trips to the country.

No picnics or parks, no walking beneath the moonlight. I spent the last years of my teens locked in a tiny, dank apartment in battle-scarred Warsaw, afraid that the SS might knock on the door at any moment. Scared that the neighbours could hear us if we spoke too loudly, or laughed too much, or if Tata's violin bothered them, and they'd turn us in.

And all that while, we listened to the sounds of death in the streets below. We saw the billowing smoke from the ghetto until the eighth day of May in 1943, when finally the last of the ghetto residents were gone and the ghetto was no more. We witnessed groups of people being rounded up and sent away.

We heard rumours that the Jews in the extermination camps learned of the ghetto's insurrection and formed their own resistance movements. That the Germans cracked down on the rebellion in early November, killing a record number of Jews over the space of two days. When they blew up the Great Synagogue, it was seen as a last act of defiance by the Germans in the aftermath of their ghetto victory.

Meanwhile, we played games of cards and bickered over the last *pierogi*. We sang songs and listened to Tata playing Beethoven. I danced with Jadzia and Danuta, baked with Waltrina, and snuck to the window seat to sit close with Jan and talk about books we'd read or movies we longed to see, or whatever it was he'd done at the market that day out in the big, wide world I longed so desperately to rejoin.

❧ 30 ❧

1ST AUGUST 1944

Nacha lay back in the hidden room and stared up at the ceiling overhead. The book in her hand was illuminated by a lantern on the floor beside her, but the words had blurred. She'd lost interest in its pages. It was hard to concentrate on anything at all these days.

They were in the middle of a war zone. The Poles were rebelling against their German invaders, attempting to push them out of Warsaw. But she was stuck in the small apartment with her father, brother and Jan's sisters, while Jan, Waltrina and Walter all went out into the world to fight the battles she longed to fight.

It wasn't fair. She should be out there in the streets of Warsaw fighting to take her own city back from the Germans. She was a Jew. She had every right to be angry, every right to take up arms against the evil army who'd occupied Warsaw for so many years now and had sent most of her family to extermination camps. But Tata wouldn't let her go. She had to stay in the small, dank apartment that stank like Nathan's enormous sweaty feet all the time and do absolutely nothing other than bake and sew and read. It was infuriating.

Give her a gun and she'd show the Nazis how she felt. But she had no choice, and she didn't know how to use a gun. So she was stuck.

The pages of the story in her hand blended together and she found herself re-reading the same paragraph over and over again before finally throwing it down on the sleeping mat in frustration and emerging from the secret room, her hair a beehive of tangled knots.

"Nice hairstyle," quipped Nathan.

He and Tata were playing a game of droughts by the window. Tata smiled at her just as the air raid siren sounded throughout the city. The high-pitched keening sent a chill through Nacha's thin frame, and she ran to the window to look out over Tata's shoulder.

☙❧

IT WAS AS THOUGH THEY'D DESCENDED INTO HELL. ALL around them, the city burned. Jan hunkered down behind a stack of sandbags in the foxhole and peered through the sights of his rifle.

"Can you see them?" Marek asked, squinting through a pair of cracked binoculars.

"They're behind the fruit and vegetable shop," Adas replied.

All three men were huddled in the same foxhole after running from the scattered remains of a German division. The city was falling. It'd been coming on for some time now, but the Polish Home Army had sent word via radio to the rebels on the ground—the Soviets were coming. Warsaw would change hands soon enough, and the exiled Polish government wanted the Home Army on the ground to take charge of the city before the Soviets got there.

The last thing the exiled government desired after so many years of war and occupation was another occupation. The Home Army had fifty thousand troops, and the German numbers were dwindling.

The Soviets hoped for the Home Army to oust the Germans and the Polish government didn't want the Red Army to occupy Warsaw and instate an alternative government. Everyone had their motives, but in the end, it boiled down to Jan and the other rebel troops fighting a street battle with a disabled Nazi force while the Red Army bombed German positions and pushed in from the northeast.

A bullet pinged into the sandbag beside Jan's head. He ducked low, then shot back in the direction of the produce shop. Successive rounds rang out and Jan fired back again. Suddenly the sky was full of the roar of an arial attack.

Planes raced by overhead, the noise of their engines deafening. A few blocks away, they dropped their loads, and explosions were followed by an enormous cloud of black smoke that filled the air and made Jan cough.

"Let's get out of here," Marek said as he covered his mouth with the neck of his shirt.

They ran for cover, escaping the *Wehrmacht* troops who could no longer see them through the smoke. Jan pressed his back to the wall of a building and surveyed the city around him. It was coming apart. How long could this go on? So many lives lost, so much destruction. And now another army was breathing down their necks.

The uprising in Warsaw, led by the Home Army, had become disjointed and disorganised. The insurgents had split into small groups forced into defensive positions by the much-stronger German forces.

With the Soviet troops surrounding Warsaw, Allied relief

had trickled to nothing. It seemed the Soviets would neither help the Poles fight off their invaders nor allow anyone else to help either. Jan anticipated that the Home Army troops would run out of supplies within a few months if things didn't improve.

"I'm heading home," Jan said.

The two men waved and headed off in the other direction. Jan set out at a jog for home. They were still living in the apartment his mother had rented for them almost two years earlier. It'd become more of a home to them than any other place they'd lived, since they were all together.

In that time, they'd experienced joy and laughter, bickering and sadness, and everything in between. But they were a family, and Jan couldn't remember feeling so content in his personal life even as all the world disintegrated around them.

People scurried by. Bicycles rushed past and vehicles honked, trapped by the rush. No one wandered anymore. They didn't go out onto the streets without some purpose. Many had already left the city and become refugees heading west.

Where they'd go, no one knew, but west seemed like the only option open to them. Away from the retreating *Wehrmacht* army and the advancing Red one. To the west was freedom and hope. The east held only death and destruction.

Jan and his family had chosen to remain. They had all the food they needed and a roof over their heads. If they left the city, it would be on foot.

Walking west was an unknown prospect—where would they go? How would they find food? Would anyone take them in, or would they sleep rough until they died of exposure? No, the known was preferable to the unknown. At least, that was what Antoni and Mama had decided. Now Jan wondered if they'd made the right choice.

The screech of an aerial assault filled the air. Jan picked up the pace, glancing back over his shoulder as a trio of planes descended towards him. He hid in the doorway of a stone chapel. He tested the doorknob and found the door was locked. The noise was overwhelming.

He squatted and covered his ears as they let bombs loose over the city. The Germans were coming down hard on the uprising. They were like a cornered dog, its teeth bared.

He took off at a run again and found Walter outside the apartment building staring up at the sky, watching the clouds of black billowing westward on the breeze.

"What's going on?" Jan asked.

Walter cupped a hand to one ear. "What?"

"Are you okay?" Jan shouted this time.

Walter nodded. "My ears are ringing."

"Come on. We have to get inside."

The two of them jogged up the stairs, taking them two at a time. They burst into the apartment and found everyone wide-eyed and peering out the windows.

"What's happening?" Nacha asked, her face white.

"The Germans want to squash the uprising. They're sending in the *Luftwaffe*. We should get to a bomb shelter." Jan set his gun down by the door and slipped off his backpack.

"But it's not safe. We'll be seen. The Germans will take us to an extermination camp," Antoni objected, rubbing both hands over his face. "We should stay here. It's safer than going outside."

The sound of approaching planes buzzed on the horizon. Jan rushed to the windows and looked out. A *Luftwaffe* squadron approached, hanging low over the city like buzzards.

"They're coming back," he said. "Everyone, find somewhere to take cover."

"In our room," Nathan suggested. "It doesn't have windows."

"Good idea," Mama said.

She ushered everyone into the room, then shut the small door behind them. It was cramped and dark in the room, not enough space for anyone to sit or lie down. So they all stood, pressed up close to one another.

Nacha was beside Jan. He could sense her presence, but couldn't see her face. Suddenly her hand was in his, her fingers sliding their way across his palm and winding through his fingers. His heart skipped a beat as he closed his hand around hers.

The warmth of her touch sent a thrill up his spine even as the scream of engines shot by their apartment. The entire building shuddered. Then the boom of bombs dropping to earth shook the air.

"That was close," Mama whispered.

Nacha began to hum.

Soon they were all singing the anthem "Poland Is Not Yet Lost." The words brought a lump to Jan's throat. He stood straight and tall, singing alongside his family and loved ones with Nacha's hand firmly in his own as bombs fell over Warsaw.

31

20TH NOVEMBER 1944

They were outnumbered. That much was obvious. They were also very close to running out of supplies and weapons. The Soviet blockade of Allied support around Warsaw had begun to take its effect on the Home Army, and the rebels were growing tired.

The only supplies getting through to the fatigued and scattered fighters came from nightly supply drops of munitions and goods by long-range planes from the British Royal Airforce and Polish Airforce. But since they had nowhere nearby they could land other than Italy, the impact of their supply runs was minimal, and very little got through to Warsaw itself.

The war underway in the city waged between the *Wehrmacht* and the Polish Home Army had become a desperate battle between two sides, each losing their tenuous grip on any chance of victory.

The Germans were under pressure on all sides from the Red Army and the Allies. The Poles were outclassed and overpowered by the Germans. And the Soviets sat outside the city, starving them of resources, having taken most of Poland into communist custody.

The Soviets seemed determined not to help and were also preoccupied with the four German Panzer divisions dug in around the city. According to Jan's rebel friends, Marek and Adas, Stalin wanted to colonise Poland and had no intention of assisting the Polish National Army, or Home Army, in securing a defeat of Germany that might give them the impression they could self-govern after the war was over.

They said he intended to let them beat themselves to death against the might of the *Wehrmacht* and waltz in to claim the city as soon as those who might challenge their authority were gone.

Jan hoped that wasn't true. He wanted to believe the Soviet Army might liberate them and leave them to go back to their lives in freedom and peace, but he knew it was probably a naïve hope. And he shouldn't cling to naïvete now that he was in his nineteenth year of life.

He was a man, and he had to think like a man, not a child who didn't know any better. Too many years of war had honed his perspective and left him bereft of a belief in the ultimate good of humanity or the hope for a free, prosperous life. All he needed was to survive this day. To waken tomorrow and begin all over again.

❧

THERE WAS NO WAY FOR THEM TO REMAIN IN THE apartment any longer. Nacha felt a mixture of fear and relief wash over her when Waltrina told them. They'd finally be allowed out of this small, dark prison. It was ungrateful to think that way—she knew that. Tata had told her so a hundred times over the past two years. She should be thankful they weren't buried in the ground or doing hard labour in Treblinka.

The apartment was their oasis, their refuge from evil. She knew that. He was right, but at the same time it felt like a prison. She hadn't been allowed to leave in over two whole years. She'd wished so many times over the years that she'd been born a bird instead of who she was. A girl with no freedom, a girl with no life. Nothing to call her own but the fear of capture and a painful death.

And now the time had come—they'd face their future of either freedom or death. Death was more likely, of course, given the fact that Warsaw was a conflict zone and no one escaped the wrath of the German war machine. But they'd survived this long and perhaps God was watching over them, although her faith had been shaken by the death and destruction she'd witnessed for the duration of her teen years.

She was an adult now, and it was a difficult thing for her to admit, since she'd longed for a normal teen life for much of their incarceration and now she'd never have it.

She'd never get those years back. Instead, she'd be expected to be an adult with responsibilities, a spouse, children, and a house to keep. To pretend that she'd lived life to the fullest. And shame washed over her as she realised she was being ungrateful all over again.

So many people would never get to see adulthood, never get to have freedom and a family. And perhaps she wouldn't either because she couldn't see how they'd get out of the mess they were in this time.

Waltrina wrung her hands together. "The Germans say everyone has to leave Warsaw. *Oberführer* Meisinger has ordered it—anyone who stays behind will be sent to the death camps or executed on the spot. He's announced that he'll personally see to it on Himmler's orders."

"Spineless rat that he is. Everyone must leave?" Tata's brow furrowed. He leaned forward in his armchair. "But..."

"They will spot you if you go. Meisinger's men will figure it out," Jan added with a nod. "If Jews join the exodus of Poles leaving Warsaw, they'll be picked off by the Germans. There's no doubt about that."

"You don't think we could get through?" Nathan asked.

Jan sighed. "They'll want to see your papers, and unfortunately, you have none. Things are rapidly disintegrating out there. People are being shot indiscriminately. There's raping, burning, mass transportations to the death camps...everyone's at risk. I don't trust them to let Poles safely through their ranks, especially Jews. No, we can't go. And I don't want to. I want to stay and fight for our freedom."

"But the Home Army has been destroyed," Tata said. "There's no one left to fight with you."

"Then we will simply fight for our own lives," Jan replied. "We will find somewhere to stay until the Red Army takes the city, which won't be long now. They've dug in on the eastern side of the Vistula River. It isn't far, and the Germans are weakened."

Jadzia ran her hands over her apron. She stood in the kitchen, rolling dough out on the bench. It was the last of their stale breadcrumbs.

Waltrina had no intention of wasting anything, so they were preparing a feast for their final meal together. "There are jobs in the city, paid work."

"Doing what?" Jan asked.

"The Germans are paying women and girls to go through abandoned homes, removing clothing and other valuables for them."

"It's too dangerous," Jan stated.

Waltrina raised her chin. "You are the last person to complain about doing something dangerous. Besides, it would give us some protection, and we'd be able to stay close by."

"I want to do it too," Danuta added. She was eleven years old and already as tall as Waltrina. Her dark brown hair was pulled into a bun at the nape of her neck, and she had a graceful elegance that made her seem older than her years.

"I suppose that settles it, then," Tata said. "Waltrina, Jadzia and Danuta will work for the Germans. The rest of us will find somewhere to hunker down until this war is over. And we'll all pray that we'll be together again soon."

Nacha opened her mouth to object to the Kostanskis risking their lives for her and her family all over again, then shut it when she saw the look of determination on Waltrina's face. There was no way she would win the argument, and besides, fleeing with thousands of other refugees would be arduous and dangerous.

She hated that the Kostanskis had to put themselves in danger for her family, but she was grateful at the same time. She'd found her point of gratitude, and the thought brought a smile to her face.

She was truly grateful so that her heart fairly ached to think about it. In the end, nothing else mattered besides family and the kind of friends who would give everything for the people they loved.

THE APARTMENT WAS EMPTY AND DARK. MAMA, JADZIA AND Danuta had already left for their new jobs in another part of the city. Jadzia had managed to get new papers after the Gestapo destroyed hers.

The three of them would bunk in a building under German occupation, something Jan wasn't happy about. But the Germans had ordered the city to be completely evacuated and threatened that anyone who failed to comply would be shot.

He peeked around the corner, rifle held carefully in both hands, then sidled around and indicated for the others to follow him. Antoni, Nacha and Nathan followed him, with Walter bringing up the rear and keeping an eye on the situation behind them.

It was time to move, to find a place to weather the rest of the war. They couldn't evacuate with a Jewish family in tow, and so they would have to hunker down somewhere in the city. Finding somewhere safe that wouldn't be discovered by the German army was a challenge.

They couldn't stay in the apartment. If the *Wehrmacht* went home to home checking that the evacuation order had been completed, they'd be sitting ducks. Even walking out the front door left them vulnerable.

Everywhere he looked, buildings were bombed out, with smoke rising in spirals into the putrid air. The streets were deserted, and the brickwork that stood was pockmarked with bullet holes.

They came across a few German troops looting and destroying shops and homes, but otherwise they made their way through the city unhindered. The occasional bomber passed overhead in a squeal of engines and rage.

When they reached 23 Panska Street, they found a tall office building still standing. Jan led the group inside, checking each room on the ground floor for occupants. There were none. They listened for a few minutes but the building was silent and dark. A quick check revealed that the kitchen in the back had running water and a small pantry with rows of food cans stacked on its shelves.

"Jackpot," Jan said.

Antoni grinned for the first time in a long time. "That is a good sign."

"Let's take a look at the cellar," Walter said.

Walter led the way down the staircase by the kitchen. The cellar was darker than the ground floor had been, and there was no way to light it. But they'd brought lanterns and torches with them, so they soon had illuminated the space enough to find their way. The cellar was divided into several rooms. Some were used as storage for chairs and tables and other business-related furniture. Others were empty.

Jan chose one of the empty rooms, and they barricaded it the best they could with the items of furniture they could find along with some sandbags pulled from outside. They needed to be able to hide themselves from prying eyes, but also defend themselves if it came to that.

"Our very own bunker," Nacha said, settling down into it and resting on a pile of cushions pulled from a sofa on the ground floor.

"Should be comfortable enough," Jan said, taking a seat beside her. He set his gun down against the sandbags and leaned back on a cushion. "I could sleep here."

Antoni lugged an armful of cans into the room and stacked them in a pile behind the bunker. "I think we should bring the food down here so we can access it without leaving the room. It's safer to stay hidden as much as possible."

"Good idea," Nathan said, jogging up the stairs to help.

"We've got the supplies from the apartment as well," reminded Nacha, hurrying to add her backpack to the pile of food.

"A veritable feast," Walter added.

The mood was jovial. They'd survived so far, and now in this place they had hope they might make it through until the Red Army arrived. Surely it couldn't be long until their liberation now.

The Red Army was another unknown. The entire populace was hesitant to embrace them completely. No one knew what they'd do or how they'd treat the people of Poland, but anything had to be better than the German occupation that'd decimated the country and killed so many of their fellow Poles.

And at least the war would be over. Those two things were worth celebrating even if the uncertainty of a Soviet victory, and what it would mean, hung like a pall over the country.

❧ 32 ❧

It would be Christmas in four days, and although Nacha had never celebrated the holiday, she knew how much it meant to Jan and his family. Yet there'd be no Christmas for him this year.

He saw his mother and sisters occasionally on outings in the city at night. They arranged times and places to meet and would bring him supplies when they could. Still, he'd spend Christmas with her and her family in the cellar of a cold, dark office building in the middle of a burned, bombed and evacuated city instead of celebrating with his own family.

It hurt her heart to think of him going without because of them again. Yet if it wasn't for him, she didn't know how her family would've survived all this time. They wouldn't have. They'd have been killed years earlier with Babcia, Papa and the rest of the people she loved.

"I'm sorry you'll miss Christmas," she whispered.

Several of their party had already fallen asleep. It wasn't late, but they'd taken to dozing on and off from evening through to the early morning hours since they had nothing else to do. It also ensured that there was always someone awake to keep guard. But so far, the Germans fighting desperately for Warsaw in the streets above their heads hadn't discovered their hiding place. Although they were almost out of food, so they'd have to venture further afield to find more before too much longer.

Jan went out every few nights to forage among the apartments and office buildings nearby for supplies. He usually brought back enough to keep them all satisfied for a little longer. But he was covering a greater distance each time, and Nacha couldn't help wondering how long the fighting could last. Surely the end must be in sight. The constant bombardment from both the Germans and the Soviets in surrounding streets had exhausted them all.

Jan shrugged. "It's okay. It wouldn't be much of a celebration this year anyway."

"But you could be with your mother and sisters."

"I'll miss them," he admitted. "But I'm here with you and that counts as family, doesn't it?"

She squeezed his shoulder in the dark, her throat smarting. "Yes, of course it does."

She leaned back against the sandbags and closed her eyes, but she couldn't drift to sleep with her stomach in knots from hunger. She was empty, and she shivered with the cold. She huddled into the blanket wrapped around her, but couldn't warm up. Her eyes blinked open, and she stared at the dark ceiling overhead.

Nacha couldn't recall the last time she'd had a bath. She did the best she could, washing with a cloth dampened under the tap in the bathroom upstairs. But there was no shower or bathtub. She was cold all the time, since the cellar didn't have a fire, and there was no way to warm themselves other than to crush their bodies together in the small shelter they'd built for themselves using sandbags and random pieces of furniture.

She was tired all the time, since she could never drift into a deep sleep with the threat of discovery and a gruesome death hanging constantly over her head, not to mention the never-ending noise of war only metres from where they hid.

"What's wrong?" Jan asked.

"I'm hungry."

"I think there's a can of beans..."

"No, we ate it earlier."

"I'll go out and find some food. We'll need some in the morning, and this is the best time to scavenge."

She sat up straight as reached for his gun.

"It's dangerous. Wait for Tata to wake. He'll go with you." She didn't suggest Walter, as he hadn't been sleeping well lately and mercifully seemed to have succumbed to his own exhaustion. He was fast asleep on the other side of their bunker with a blanket tucked beneath his chin.

Jan grunted. "I'll be faster without him."

"But what if they see you? You'll be on your own."

He laughed softly in the dark, and she felt the warmth of his hand cup her cheek. "You act like I've never done this before."

She blushed, grateful he couldn't see her colour rise. "I know you have, but I worry. That's all."

"I'm glad you worry about me. It would be a sad day if I had no one to worry." His voice took on a sombre tone. He was thinking about his mother and sisters. She could read his every mood these days. They spent so much time together, it was as if she heard his thoughts. His tone brightened. "But I have you, so I'm happy."

"Yes, me and Tata, Nathan and Walter. We all care about you."

"It's your caring that means the most to me," he said. His

voice was soft, and she wished she could see his face clearly. He wasn't much more than a shadowy outline. His eyes were black and he was so close to her she could feel his breath in her hair.

Her heart skipped and her cheeks warmed further still. "I do care. You know I do."

"As do I." He cupped her cheek again, caressing it with his thumb.

He leaned down and brushed his lips against hers. She jolted with the sweet pleasure of his surprising kiss. She'd never felt about anyone the way she did Jan, but she didn't know he felt the same way. She'd kept her thoughts and emotions to herself, secreting them away in a corner of her heart where no one else could see.

Her entire body warmed and she shivered with delight. "Jan…"

He kissed her again, and she thought she might explode with the joy of it all.

"I'll find you some food so you can get warm and sleep. I'll be back in a while. Don't fret—I know these streets well enough now. And I'm accustomed to fading into the shadows. I've been doing it since I was fifteen years old."

She watched him leave, her heart still racing. Then she settled back against the sandbags with a smile tugging at the corners of her mouth, her hands clasped to her chest.

❧

THE NEXT MORNING, THERE WERE CANS OF CURED HAM AND stew, as well as a few sprouting potatoes that they sliced up and ate raw. The entire time they ate, Jan couldn't stop looking at Nacha. They'd kissed the night before, and he could think of nothing else.

Her lips were so warm and soft and he wanted to do it

again, although with everyone else now awake, they had no time alone, no time to talk about what'd happened. They could only exchange secretive glances over the top of the feast he'd found in an apartment about a kilometre from where they hid.

He'd almost been discovered by a group of drunken Germans who were reeling down the centre of the street singing at the top of their lungs. But thankfully, their noise had alerted him to their presence long before they had the chance to spot him. Besides that, he always travelled in the darkness and they were lit up like Christmas trees wherever they went, so they had no night vision.

Just then, footsteps on the staircase leading down to their hiding hole caught Jan's ear. He leapt to his feet and grabbed up his gun. He pointed it towards the staircase even as he crept across the room.

When Jadzia's thin, beaming face appeared, he laughed with surprise. Then he ran to her and kissed her cheeks. She threw her arms around his neck and squeezed him tight. She was dressed as a boy in a shirt and pants. Her golden hair was cut short, and she wore a cap on her head.

"You're here," was all he could manage to say.

She ruffled his hair with one hand. "I came bearing gifts. Merry Christmas." Her eyes sparkled. "I thought you might all be starving to death, and I managed to find some food in one of the houses we were going through. I decided not to hand it in to the Germans after all. I got some work in Warsaw, so I skipped out to bring this to you while I had a chance."

Everyone crowded around her, kissing her, hugging her and peppering her with questions. She answered as best she could as they all walked back to the bunker and crowded inside.

"How did you get here?" Nacha asked.

"I have papers. They let me through, I work for them after all." Jadzia looked different to Jan. The sadness from her time in the extermination camp had faded. She had a spark of life again, the way she used to, but with a confidence that was new.

"Where are you staying?" Jan asked.

"We're outside of Warsaw, in Jelonka," she said. "We have a house there. It's nice enough. And plenty to eat. The Germans let us keep some of the things we find."

"But if they catch you bringing food to us..." Antoni said, his voice grave.

"They'll kill me, of course." Jadzia shrugged. "But I didn't let them catch me. I can't stay long, though, or they'll know something's up. So, tell me what you've been up to and how you're faring. I want to know everything. Mama will kill me if I don't bring back stories to tell."

She stayed only a few minutes, but after she was gone, it was as if she'd breathed life into the group. The melancholy that'd clung to them lifted. And there was a spark of hope that hadn't been there before.

Jan had begun keeping a diary since they were cloistered in the bunker. He'd found a notebook upstairs in one of the offices, along with several pens, and wrote down his thoughts and remembrances.

He sat off to one side from the rest of the group, who were still going through the supplies Jadzia had brought them, and contemplated her visit.

He chewed on the end of the pen as he watched his friends joking and laughing together, quietly congratulating each other on the food they'd get to eat that evening, and thought through everything that'd happened since that first day the Germans occupied Warsaw. Then he set his pen to paper and began to write.

33

17TH JANUARY 1945

Almost a month later, the Germans still hadn't capitulated to the immense force of the Red Army. Jan and his fellow basement dwellers were growing sick and tired of living in a hole beneath the ground.

They hadn't felt the sun on their faces in so long, it seemed like a previous lifetime. Lately, Jan had been venturing out of the basement every night to give himself something to do. He fairly itched with the need to move, to use his muscles, to run and to fight.

Give him someone to fight, anyone. He'd take it. It was the sitting around, the waiting, the nothingness that ate at him like a rat at a carcass. They'd found weapons on their nightly scavenger hunts and had taught themselves to fashion handmade grenades. Whenever they'd encountered a German patrol, they'd managed to fight them off so far.

"Are you going out tonight?" Walter asked, sidling up to him at the base of the staircase. Jan stood looking up, his gun slung over one shoulder, waiting for the last light of sunset to dim through the windows on the ground level.

"Yep," Jan replied.

"I'm coming too."

"Fine with me."

"We should find food and water. We're a little low, and the tap is only dripping. The bombing must've hit the pipes nearby."

"Agreed," said Jan. "I thought I might go a little deeper into the city tonight. See what's out there. The Germans haven't been close lately. The fighting seems to have shifted to the west."

"The light has gone. Let's get moving." Walter shifted the weight of the rifle over his shoulder.

The two men climbed the staircase with caution, listening for any sounds that might betray the presence of the enemy. But there was nothing—no footsteps, no buzz of engines, no rat-a-tat of machine guns. Other than the occasional shot in the distance, the world around them was unusually quiet.

It wasn't entirely dark yet, but the sun had drifted beyond the horizon, and orange streaks lit up the cold sky. Jan could see his breath in front of his face as he walked. The scarf around his neck was ragged and his coat was too small, but he was warm enough once they got moving more quickly.

They hadn't gone far when they had to circumnavigate a crater in the road. Debris had fallen over the crater, making it unstable to walk on, and Jan had skirted his way around it enough times to know where to step and how quickly to move. But this time he thought he heard something beneath the rubble.

"What was that?" he whispered.

Walter leapt to the edge of the crater and almost overbalanced, then righted himself. "What?"

"Shhhh...listen."

They stopped still and waited. The sound of voices drifted up to them. Whispering and a cough.

"...from today, we will have half a cup of barley a day because we don't know how long this will last, and we haven't much food left." The voice stopped.

Jan lifted a piece of debris with both hands and found himself staring into a large crater in the tarmac filled with around fifteen people. They stared up at him in fright, eyes wide. The Jewish families were all skin and bones, pale and gaunt.

"Hello," Jan said.

"Who are you?" one of the men asked.

"I'm Jan Kostanski. This is Walter Cykiert."

A woman reached towards Jan. "We're so hungry."

"And thirsty," added the man.

Jan and Walter exchanged a look. How long had these people lived under the rubble in the street without sustenance?

"One or two of you can come with us. We're going hunting for food now. We can help you get water as well."

"But the Germans are out there," said the woman.

"They won't see us if we're careful. You can't stay down there forever without food. Come on." Walter beckoned. Two of the men climbed out of the crater and followed Jan and Walter. They were dressed in rags, and their bones protruded from beneath their sallow flesh.

Jan and Walter showed them how to run quietly. To find refuge in shadows and doorframes. To stay away from the sounds of fighting. They led them into a building and took them from apartment to apartment, looking for one they could break into and fill their backpacks with food. They found water there too and filled jugs and containers, as many as they could carry.

Then they showed the men how to pick through the

wardrobes. Most had been cleaned out, but they found a couple of cupboards with clothes left in them. Jan updated his coat to something bigger, and the Jewish men chose several warm items to wear themselves and some to take back to their family, along with an old blanket.

On the way out of the apartment building, they almost walked directly into a German patrol. Four *Wehrmacht* officers strode in formation along the street, checking windows and doors for any sign of movement. Jan pushed the others back behind him, almost stumbling over the doorstep.

"Germans," he hissed.

They hurried through the ground floor of the building and out a back exit. Then crept through the remnants of a garden and over a fence, along an alley, keeping low as they went. Finally, they returned the Jewish men to their families beneath the rubble.

Jan wondered how they kept warm down there and offered to help them find a better place to stay. But they refused the help. They'd been safe there so far, they said. They didn't want to risk getting caught somewhere else.

Then he and Walter returned to the basement with their booty. Nacha was waiting for him, a smile on her face. Her brown eyes glinted at the sight of him, or perhaps it was the food. He didn't want to presume.

But he wished he could tell her all the things on his mind —how he thought of her constantly. How he longed to put his arms around her and hold her close. How her words meant everything to him, and how one day they would be married and raise a family together. But he couldn't. They were never alone. And so he treasured his plans and his memories of her touch in his heart as he settled down in the bunker and listened to the renewed boom of the Soviet artillery as it decimated his city.

IT WAS THE SILENCE THAT NACHA NOTICED FIRST. THE city was completely quiet. There was no staccato firing of a machine gun in the distance, no boom of artillery, no whine of bomber engines overhead. Everything was still.

"Hush," she said.

The rest of the crew in the bunker fell still. They listened, eyes narrowed.

"What is it?" Tata asked.

"Don't you hear it?"

"What?" Nathan said.

"The fighting has stopped."

They all stood slowly and made their way in a line up the staircase. Nacha peered out the front door of the office building. The street was empty. But still, the silence rang in her ears like the screech of crickets on a warm summer's night.

"There's nothing out here," she said.

Just then the crunch of a thousand feet on gravel and crushed concrete marched in the distance. It was quiet at first, grew louder by the second. Overhead, a crow descended to land on the remnants of a shattered wall. Bricks lay scattered in every direction. The buildings around theirs were like a shadowland of ancient ruins. Only their building and a few others remained whole.

They stayed hidden and out of sight, waiting to see what would come. When the Red Army marched into view, people began to emerge from buildings, ruins, sewers and holes in the ground. They crept, walked and skulked slowly over to meet the army. It marched, in glorious order, its strength on full display, through the rubble of Warsaw.

Jan turned to face Nacha. She offered him a smile. "Is it really over?"

He sighed. "It's over."

She leapt into his arms and buried her face in his chest. He wrapped her up and held her close. The scent of his skin was like an elixir. She wanted to caress his face and kiss him and tell him all her secrets in that single moment. But there was no time.

They all ran through the doorway and into the street to watch the armed men in their dark uniforms march by. And she wondered how life could ever go back to the way it was. The city was ruined. It was a wasteland. The people were dead or scattered.

But now there was hope.

With a cry of joy, she spun in place, her arms held out on either side of her. Tata laughed, tears wetting his cheeks, and reached over to kiss her on the cheek. Nathan embraced her, and she watched as Walter and Jan danced in a circle, hugging one another.

Then Jan was back. He put his hands on either side of her waist and lifted her into the air until her face hovered over his. He lowered her gently until her lips met his. Then she kissed him with all the passion that was in her heart as Tata and Nathan danced a jig in the middle of the street behind them.

❧ 34 ❧

8TH MAY 1945

The crowds jostled Nacha as she clung to Jan's hand. The streets were full of people who'd begun returning to Warsaw to look for their homes. Most found everything they had laying in ruins and looted or destroyed. But today no one was thinking about the past, of the lives lost or the homes burned to the ground.

Today was a celebration. It was VE Day. The Allies had finally won victory in Europe, the Germans had surrendered, and the people could breathe a sigh of relief after years of devastation were over.

Hitler had taken his own life a week earlier, and Poland was free of German occupation. The fact that they still lived under occupation, but this time with the Red Army troops stationed on every corner, hadn't escaped their attention. But it felt different to the blind terror of Nazi control. The most important improvement, of course, being that Nacha and her family could walk freely through the streets without having to worry about being shipped off to an extermination camp.

The Red Army had liberated Treblinka, Auschwitz and other camps on their way through Poland. Reports had trickled in of the horrors they found, although the Germans had hidden most of their crimes well. The few survivors who remained told stories of the Nazis rushing through thousands of exterminations in the camps' final weeks of operation when they realised their time was quickly coming to a close.

Rather than letting the prisoners go free, the SS guards worked harder to end their lives sooner. Then they burned all of the paperwork that had been meticulously kept over the years regarding the camps' operations, and buried all evidence of what they'd done.

She could hardly believe it was over. She'd spent much of her life in hiding. Now as she walked beside Jan, she couldn't help trembling and glancing around. As though the Germans might spring up from behind a pile of rubble or round the corner on the back of a group of Panzer tanks at any moment.

Whenever a Soviet soldier shot his pistol into the air in celebration, she wanted to dive for cover behind one of the vehicles or wagons that were parked along the street.

Tata and Nathan stood by a streetlamp. Tata was on tiptoe, straining to see over the heads of the crowd of people surging down the street, flags waving as streamers and confetti were shot into the air.

"Do you see them yet?" Nacha asked.

Jan shook his head. "They'll be here soon—don't worry. Mother told me to look for them today."

It was finally time for the family to be reunited. They'd seen Jan's mother and sisters a few times over recent months, but they'd always had to be separated again afterwards for some reason or other. Now, however, they could finally be together, and Antoni and Waltrina had promised that nothing would separate their families ever again.

Nacha's heart ached at the thought of them being together again. They'd lived in the apartment for years and grown so close. It was difficult to be separated for so long while the Russians and the Germans fought over Warsaw on the last gasping breaths of war.

"There they are!" Jan said, pointing.

Waltrina, Jadzia and Danuta were pushing their way through the crowd. The only faces in a sea of dark humanity that were working towards, rather than away, from Jan and Nacha.

When Waltrina reached Tata, she leapt into his arms and wove her own around his neck. Nacha's cheeks flushed as she watched Waltrina and Tata kiss passionately beneath the streetlamp. No one paid them any mind. Kissing in the street had become commonplace that day. Everyone was celebrating in their own ways—drinking, dancing, embracing, shouting. It was a street party like none she'd ever seen before.

And in the middle of it all stood Tata, holding Waltrina in a desperate embrace, their lips locked together and their cheeks wet with tears.

3RD MARCH 1946

There was nothing for them in Poland. Warsaw was razed to the ground in the final months of the war. The rest of Poland lay in ruins. So many of the Polish people had been killed and displaced. So, Jan and the rest of his family became refugees and caught a train to Germany.

Once they arrived in Germany, they'd lived in a tent in a large refugee encampment. They were waiting to billet with a German family. But from what Jan had seen so far, the German people had suffered immensely from the Nazi preoccupation with *Lebensraum,* a delusional geographical expansion of the territory held by the Third Reich.

Cities had been bombed and burned. Families torn apart. Food was scarce. So finding a place to stay for the many homeless who wandered the streets of the capital wouldn't find a quick solution.

The Allies intended on extracting a penance for the

destruction the Germans had wrought across the world and had shipped thousands of able-bodied men off for forced labour to help rebuild what they'd torn down. And the German people in Berlin appeared to have had their spirits crushed.

They shuffled around with bent backs and refused to make eye contact with the refugees who'd flooded into their country as soon as the war ended. The infrastructure had been decimated by the Allies. Bridges, factories, roads, rail lines and supply chains all lay in ruins.

Soldiers had returned from the front lines and now wandered the streets searching for loved ones, or food to eat, or shelter. Families who'd lost everything joined the melee, creating a surging mass of humanity that was homeless, without loved ones, paralysed by confusion and hopelessness.

Entire brick walls in the centre of the city were pasted with paper notices of people searching for the missing. In a population of seventy million people, around thirty million were looking for someone. It threw the country into gridlock, and chaos reigned in the city streets.

The Allies were divided over Germany's fate, and so they split the country down the middle. The Soviets would control Germany's eastern half, and the British and Americans would free the west. When Jan and his family arrived in Berlin, they found themselves constrained to the eastern portion of the city by a line of surly Soviet guards.

Their original plan had been to make it through to West Germany so they could apply for asylum in England, Canada or America. But they weren't able to get through the divided city to the other side, and so they were stuck in the refugee tent city instead. It wasn't the life they'd hoped to find.

After a while, they gave up on the idea of finding a way out of Europe through Berlin and returned to Warsaw. The city of Jan's youth was no more. The destruction now even more confronting, having been away for several months. It pained him to see his homeland brought so low.

Stalin had promised the other Allies that Poland would be free to elect a government of its choosing, but in the time since Jan and his family travelled to Germany and back again, all the Soviets had done was to crack down on any dissent in the provisional government to their communist rule in Poland.

They'd heard that many of the Nazis had been arrested and sentenced to death, including SS-*Oberführer* Josef Albert Meisinger, the Butcher of Warsaw. Jan received the news with a numb heart—justice was served, but it'd come too late.

Jan's priority now was the future. He wanted to marry Nacha and start their lives together somewhere new. He would leave his home behind for the hope of a better future.

They were camped in another refugee tent on the outskirts of Warsaw when Mama came to him one evening.

"Antoni are getting married," she said.

Jan smiled and kissed both her cheeks. "I'm happy for you, Mama."

Tears glistened in her eyes. "Will you walk me down the aisle?"

"Of course I will."

"We're going to have a baby," she said, gently patting her stomach.

Jan gaped. "Really? The family is growing."

She laughed. "I can hardly believe it. I'm too old for this."

He embraced her. "No, you're not, Mama. And we're all here to help you. There's something I must tell you as well. Nacha and I are getting married too."

Mama sobbed. "Oh, Janek, there is so much joy. I would never have imagined this might happen. I hoped it would, somewhere deep down in my heart. But it seemed so impossible. That we would survive the war at all, and now to be so happy."

Mama and Antoni were married at the government registry. There were no priests to be found in the vicinity, and besides, Mama said it was for the best anyway since it wouldn't be fair to have a priest marry them rather than a rabbi. And they were all sad for a few moments when she said that, since their rabbis and priests were all dead. But then they pushed those thoughts aside because there was a wedding to prepare for.

The rest of the family went with them to the registry, which was held in a tent on the edge of the refugee encampment. They cheered when Antoni kissed Mama and dipped her in his arms, then pulled her close and held her tight.

After that, Jan and Nacha stood before the registrant and said their own vows. Jan swallowed back tears as he promised to spend his life loving, serving and protecting Nacha. Hadn't he done that for years already? He couldn't imagine living any other way.

Mama sobbed in the background as Jan took Nacha in his arms and kissed her on the lips. Her kiss pushed every worry, every thought of the future, every fear from his mind. There was nothing but Nacha and their love for one another.

A man without legs sat on a cushioned chair on one side of the tent. A barrel organ was perched on a small wooden wagon in front of him. He spun the handle and played a melody Jan didn't recognise as they walked back down the makeshift aisle as husband and wife. Jan tossed the man a coin, and he bobbed his head in thanks.

Then the newly joined family walked out of the tent together. Mama with her arm linked through Antoni's. Nacha with her hand in Jan's. Nathan, Jadzia and Danuta talking and laughing together behind them. Whatever the future held for them, no matter the hardships, pain, adventures or joy, they would face them together. And for the first time in a long time, Jan had hope that perhaps life could be good.

❧ 36 ❧

MELBOURNE, AUSTRALIA

Nacha smoothed the tablecloth over the white Formica table and smiled. She set a fresh vase of cut flowers in the centre of the table, then carried the plates of scrambled eggs, pancakes and toast to the table.

They were having an English breakfast to celebrate life in their new home, an apartment above the fruit shop that Jan had established a few months earlier when they first arrived in Melbourne, Australia, as new immigrant refugees.

"Breakfast is ready," she called.

Four-year-old Andrew and two-year-old George came barreling down the short hallway from their bedroom into the kitchen. Andrew climbed into a chair at the table while George fell short and landed on the laminate floor.

When he cried, Nacha went to him, scooped him up her

arms and set him on the chair with a kiss to his chubby cheek.

"No need to cry, my love. You're not hurt."

She spooned eggs onto their plates, along with pancakes with butter and honey.

Jan came jogging up the stairs from the fruit shop, his apron wrapped around his waist and a smile on his face. At thirty-three years of age, he was more handsome than ever. He had a golden tan, was strong and fit, and his generally happy demeanour had a chance to shine every day now that their lives were free from danger and tragedy.

His missing teeth had been replaced by dentures soon after they arrived in Australia, and his smile was wide and full of genuine joy. They both had scars, invisible to most, but they were healing, moving on and building a new life together as a family. He loved it here—they both did. She hadn't felt as safe and happy in a long time as she did now.

"It's close to opening. I have time to eat, then I have to go."

She kissed him, then he rushed to wash his hands at the sink.

"It smells delicious."

Nacha served food onto a plate for Jan and set it in front of him at the table. "Will Mama and Tata be coming over soon? We're going to the market, and it's already late."

"They should be here any moment."

"I wish you could come with us."

"I've got to work. Sorry, honey." He winked at her as he chewed a bite of eggs.

She laughed. "I know. I hate being away from you, that's all."

They'd been married thirteen years and had finally made it to a safe haven. Somewhere they could start their lives again. A fresh beginning without any reminders of the past to get in their way. Europe was still struggling to its feet, but Australia was almost untouched.

The country had lost many sons and fathers in the war, but only the northern tip had experienced conflict. The rest of the land was as it had been before the entire world was thrown into years-long battles twice in the space of only a few short decades.

It would take Nacha a while to get used to her new home. Winter in Melbourne was cold and rainy, but could also be hot. It seemed to fluctuate day to day. There was no snow on the ground, and the locals shivered under thick coats in the cool wind that she thought of as nothing more than bracing. She hadn't weathered a summer yet, but she'd heard it could get insufferably hot.

They lived in the suburbs of the second-largest city in Australia, and they'd only driven their used car outside the city a few times. The countryside was wild and mostly empty, with stretching green fields and long, jagged coastlines that nibbled at an ocean so brightly blue, she couldn't look at it without squinting.

She sat at the table with the rest of her family just as Mama and Tata burst through the back door. The door stood at the top of a staircase that ran down the back of the building to a parking lot behind the fruit shop. Tata had used the key she bought for him and couldn't get it back out of the lock again. He struggled with it, swearing beneath his breath as Mama carried an armload of food and groceries into the kitchen.

"Good morning, my loves," Mama said, bending to kiss both boys on the cheeks. They were eating and didn't stop chewing, preferring instead to slap egg-y kisses on her face, making her laugh as she wiped her face clean with a dish towel from the kitchen.

"How was the traffic?" Jan asked.

Nacha knew he meant, how did you find the drive? Tata and Mama were new to Australia as well and Tata had decided to embrace the entire culture and way of life by purchasing a second-hand Holden station wagon and driving every day even though he'd never driven much back in Poland, and it'd been on the other side of the road.

Jan worried about them, but Nacha didn't let it bother her. They'd been through so much already, there was no way anything could hurt them now.

"Antoni always forgets about staying on the left when we get to an intersection," Mama said with a chuckle. "I have to remind him 'Stay to the left, left, left' as we turn."

Tata shut the back door finally with a sigh, then settled into a seat at the table. "You can imagine how much I enjoy that."

They all laughed. Nacha handed Mama and Tata plates and began spooning eggs and pancakes onto them.

"I think it helps," Mama said with a wink at the boys.

Nacha had taken to calling her "Mama", just as Jan did, after she and Jan were married, at Waltrina's insistence. It was second nature now. And she'd realised that all along she'd thought of Waltrina as her mother for a long time. She was so grateful to have her as a mother-in-law.

They ate together, regaling each other with tales of their new lives. Where Mama had gone for a walk. How Tata wanted to get a dog. The fact that Jan still struggled to use English phrases when dealing with customers. Nacha suggested he join some social groups and clubs to hone his language skills. She'd found picking up the language much easier than he had, although she was still fairly limited in what she could say.

"I'm not joining a club. I'm too busy," he replied.

And she had to admit he was right. He had the fruit shop to run, as well as a business he'd established with Walter, who now lived in Austria. They imported and exported items into and out of the Soviet Union through Austria. Jan would fly to Austria later in the year for one of their cross-border trips.

Nacha referred to it as their smuggling operation, since it was done in secret, and Jan would wink at her and tell her he'd never stop carrying supplies over heavily guarded walls to the people who needed them—it was in his blood. The Iron Curtain was just another fence he could scale, and the thrill of not getting caught still brought a smile to his face.

It was a profitable enterprise, and one that ate up all his spare time. Not to mention the family commitments—he was an involved father and loved spending time with her and the boys.

When breakfast was over, Nacha carried a handful of plates into the kitchen and set them on the sink. She stopped still for a moment and looked around their unit. It was small, but bright. They'd been gifted a number of items of used furniture through the local refugee centre. And they had managed to find clothes, toys and other goods cheaply at charity stores throughout the surrounding suburbs.

Andrew was enrolled at the local preschool and attended two days per week. He loved it there and was already speaking English with a thick accent, enough that the preschool staff could understand him and he them. Life was good—far better than she could ever have imagined a little over a decade earlier.

Tata and Mama had taken the boys out to the backyard to play with a new soccer ball they'd brought with them. She returned to the table to get the rest of the plates and Jan grabbed her from behind, then pulled her into his lap.

She pretended to struggle, and fell against his strong chest. He kissed her, his eyes gleaming.

"You get more beautiful every day."

She blushed. "You always say that."

"It's true. How did I get so lucky to find you when I was only a boy?"

She shrugged. "It's hard to believe."

"We made it," he whispered, kissing the tip of her nose. "We have a new life for ourselves and our boys. They'll never know the struggles we've endured."

She looked out the back door at the small yard beyond the stairs and car park. Tata kicked the ball gently to Andrew while Mama pushed George around on a tricycle. "They're very blessed."

His arms were her safe place. She nestled into his warmth and let her head rest against his chest. There was no other place she'd rather be. Imagining a future with him here was something she could finally do again.

She'd given up dreaming and hoping for so many years. The struggle for survival was all consuming. But now she could dream again. And her dream was of him and their family living in this land for as long as they had breath in their lungs.

❦ 37 ❦

10TH FEBRUARY 1983

MELBOURNE, AUSTRALIA

I step out of the car and open the back door to help Mama from her seat. I'm fifty-seven years old and Mama is on the cusp of turning eighty. Both of us have grey in our hair, although I still have a lot less than she does. But we feel the aches and pains of ageing, and sometimes I wonder how Mama stays as young as she does, given all she's been through. She's wearing her best burgundy dress with the sash around her waist.

When Tata died, she seemed to shrink a little bit. But she forged on, determined to keep living for her grandchildren, for us. She missed Jadzia and Danuta at first. They stayed behind in Poland, and we'd only see them once every few years. Nathan arrived here before we did and has been a source of great comfort for Mama since his father's death.

Since then, Jadzia and her family made the journey down

under as well, but we still long to see Danuta's face more frequently. Mama does too. I can tell by the way she lingers over phone conversations with her or gazes out the window at the horizon whenever the sun turns pink in the afternoon.

I still think of Danuta often myself and wonder how our lives might've been if we'd stayed behind in the Warsaw I used to love.

So much time has passed since those days when I sprinted through the ghetto carrying a backpack full of supplies to the people who needed them. But I'm thinking of those times now, since we're finally here at the ceremony.

Nerves flutter in the pit of my stomach as Nacha takes my arm. I walk with both Nacha and Mama through the crowds and into the conference centre. The auditorium is full, and I wonder what else people have come to see because surely they couldn't all be here for me and Mama.

Andrew, Mark and George came in a separate car, and they hurry through the crowd now to where Mama, Nacha and I have found reserved seating in the front row with our names on them. Mark is my half brother, but only a few years older than my own children. He acts more like a cousin to them than an uncle. He wears the solemn eyes of a war refugee combined with the larrikin spirit of an Australian in a way I never will.

He is too young to know any of the troubles we faced then, and we bear the blame of not telling him more about his past. Sometimes the pain is better left behind. But there's a healing in the telling, something I'm only learning now.

Jadzia, her husband and family are there already there. Her children are grown. They, along with Nathan and his wife and family, take up an entire row. A band plays soft, lilting music on the stage. Bright lights illuminate the auditorium, and people chatter loudly as they find their place in the stadium seating that faces the stage.

Journalists stand with microphones held at their sides on either end of the stage. Cameras with camera operators focus their large lenses on the journalists, who fix their hair or speak to their producer with one finger to an earpiece.

Everything is in place, and I can feel the sweat streaming down the centre of my spine. Facing off with the Gestapo didn't bother me as much as this does.

A speaker strides onto the stage. He has a brown moustache and brown wavy hair brushed back from his face. It touches his collar. A thick blue tie is tight around his neck, and a pale blue shirt is tucked into tartan pants.

The ceremony begins when he clears his throat and steps up to the microphone.

"Welcome, ladies and gentlemen, to this special celebration. Today Yad Vashem recognises Waltrina Wierzbicka-Kostanska and her son Janek Kostanski as Righteous Among the Nations for their inspiring work smuggling food and supplies into the Warsaw ghetto over many years during the Second World War."

He continues speaking, eyes firmly fixed on me and Mama, with a smile plastered to his face beneath that twitching moustache. It's as though he's talking about someone else.

I've tried to push many of the memories of that time from my mind, to bury them beneath far happier ones—our wedding, the day each of the boys was born, their first steps, the morning we got the letter about our refugee visas to Australia.

Innumerable happy times now bully the trauma into submission and keep it well below the surface of my conscious thoughts. But this ceremony is dragging every single recollection back to the surface like fingernails on a blackboard.

Every now and then, the man pauses for effect in the

narrative, and the audience applauds and cheers. Mama and I aren't used to this kind of recognition. We've had none for so long, and we never thought we deserved any. I feel tears pricking the corners of my eyes. Mama reaches for my hand and squeezes it. We exchange a look that says, *Can you believe this?*

Nacha holds tight to my other hand. I'm infinitely glad they're both here. I'm not sure how I would've managed to get through the ceremony if they weren't here to ground me in the reality of this moment rather than diving headlong into the past.

Andrew and George are adults now. They sit beside me, straight backed, as they listen to the strange retelling of my own life story while I yet live and breathe. I watch them both for a moment. They're transfixed. They haven't heard many of these stories. Only a few. And even then, they didn't pay much attention, since it was Dad doing the telling. They couldn't take it in, couldn't understand what it must've been like. We're so far removed from that now and their lives are so different to what mine was in an infinite number of ways.

After his speech, it's time for me and Mama to go up onto the stage. We climb the stairs together, her hand in mine as I steady her ascent. We walk together to the microphone. The man is smiling at us both, urging us forward. We face the audience, and I feel a lump fill my throat.

If only you knew, I think as I stare out at them. If only they knew what it felt like to reach into my soul and pull out the truest form of love a person can find—the love of one person willing to risk it all for the sake of another.

The greatest love of all is when someone will lay down their life for their friend. And I was ready to do it day after day because love is what drives me, and love is the one thing worth dying for.

I carry that love still, in the memories that line the

deepest recesses of my heart, in the twinkle of my wife's eye, and the sincerity in my sons' smiles. It was worth it, I want to say. And I would do it all over again for a love like that.

But I can't find the words. They don't roll off my tongue in this language the way I'd like them to. So instead, my speech is brief, stilted, as the English words tangle in my throat.

Mama says a few words as well, and her voice is clear and strong. But she finds the language as hard as I do. So we wave and smile with tears in our eyes as the entire auditorium stands to their feet in one sudden movement and cheers. I'm overwhelmed.

How can it be that so much hate existed in the same world as this love?

People are capable of both—I know that better than most. I've seen it with my own eyes. Good and evil, love and hate, side by side in the world. And no explanation makes sense except an otherworldly one.

But it's soon over, and we're ushered from the stage. Dozens of people want to meet us, shake our hands, take photographs with their fancy little cameras. I remember a camera carried by a friend in the ghetto. The pictures were never found of the bodies in the grave. His pictures died with him.

And now cameras are everywhere, carried in little soft cases and no need of a tripod. The world is truly a marvellous place, the way it rebuilds and grows back into the cracks and crevices that destruction left in its wake, turning them into something beautiful and good.

I sit after a while, fatigued but content. Andrew is beside me, staring at his hands. He turns to me, eyes glistening.

"I don't know how you did it, Dad." He chokes on the words.

I put a hand on his shoulder, tears forming in my eyes. "What do you mean?"

"I've really thought about it a lot. I don't know if I could've done those things. I want to believe I could, but I'm just not sure."

I tell him, "No one knows until they're in that situation. I did it because it was the natural thing for me to do. All my friends who went against their own instincts died. I never went against my instincts. My instincts were to protect the people I loved, to run when the time came, to hide when it made sense and to fight when it was necessary. I followed my instincts, and I lived."

THE END

READY FOR MORE?

Don't miss out on the bestselling historical fiction, *Beyond the Crushing Waves*, by USA Today Bestselling Author, Lilly Mirren.

An emotional story of forced child migration, inspired by true events.

Beyond the Crushing Waves

LILLY MIRREN

Two generations face heartbreak and injustice in this poignant and emotional novel inspired by true events.

Mary Roberts is a poor gutter child living in a council flat in 1950's London. When she and her sister are left at an orphanage by their mother, they don't think their lives can get any worse.

Harry Evans is an orphan who finds himself, with Mary and her sister, on board a ship bound for Australia. They're sent to a farm school for children, where abuse and neglect are rife. A journey that will change their lives forever, and from which they'll never return.

Married to her dream man, and with a baby on the way, Dr Mia Sato's life is in perfect order. When her beloved grandmother has a fall, the photograph clutched in her hand prompts Mia to ask questions her grandmother isn't willing to answer. When she cries out a confession that rocks Mia to her core, it leads to a shocking discovery of a past filled with lies, broken families and forced child migration.

Based on one of Britain's most secret and shameful real-life scandals in which over 100,000 British children were forcibly deported to Canada, South Africa, and Australia over several decades. Lilly Mirren's heartbreaking, captivating and ultimately uplifting tale reminds us that no matter where the journey leads us, our heart will always find its way home to those we love.

For readers of *Before We Were Yours* and *Where the Crawdad Sings*.

Buy Now

ALSO BY LILLY MIRREN

HISTORICAL FICTION

Beyond the Crushing Waves

An emotional standalone historical saga. Two children plucked from poverty & forcibly deported from the UK to Australia. Inspired by true events. An unforgettable tale of loss, love, redemption & new beginnings.

Under a Sunburnt Sky

Inspired by a true story. Jan Kostanski is a normal Catholic boy in Warsaw when the nazis invade. He's separated from his neighbours, a Jewish family who he considers kin, by the ghetto wall. Jan and his mother decide that they will do whatever it takes to save their Jewish friends from certain death. The unforgettable tale of an everyday family's fight against evil, and the unbreakable bonds of their love.

ALSO BY LILLY MIRREN

WOMEN'S FICTION

THE WARATAH INN SERIES

The Waratah Inn

Wrested back to Cabarita Beach by her grandmother's sudden death, Kate Summer discovers a mystery buried in the past that changes everything.

One Summer in Italy

Reeda leaves the Waratah Inn and returns to Sydney, her husband, and her thriving interior design business, only to find her marriage in tatters. She's lost sight of what she wants in life and can't recognise the person she's become.

The Summer Sisters

Set against the golden sands and crystal clear waters of Cabarita Beach three sisters inherit an inn and discover a mystery about their grandmother's past that changes everything they thought they knew about their family...

Christmas at The Waratah Inn

Liz Cranwell is divorced and alone at Christmas. When her friends convince her to holiday at The Waratah Inn, she's dreading her first Christmas on her own. Instead she discovers that strangers can be the balm to heal the wounds of a lonely heart in this heartwarming Christmas story.

EMERALD COVE SERIES

Cottage on Oceanview Lane

When a renowned book editor returns to her roots, she

rediscovers her strength & her passion in this heartwarming novel.

Seaside Manor Bed & Breakfast

The Seaside Manor Bed and Breakfast has been an institution in Emerald Cove for as long as anyone can remember. But things are changing and Diana is nervous about what the future might hold for her and her husband, not to mention the historic business.

Bungalow on Pelican Way

Moving to the Cove gave Rebecca De Vries a place to hide from her abusive ex. Now that he's in jail, she can get back to living her life as a police officer in her adopted hometown working alongside her intractable but very attractive boss, Franklin.

Chalet on Cliffside Drive

At forty-four years of age, Ben Silver thought he'd never find love. When he moves to Emerald Cove, he does it to support his birth mother, Diana, after her husband's sudden death. But then he meets Vicky.

Christmas in Emerald Cove

The Flannigan family has been through a lot together. They've grown and changed over the years and now have a blended and extended family that doesn't always see eye to eye. But this Christmas they'll learn that love can overcome all of the pain and differences of the past in this inspiring Christmas tale.

HOME SWEET HOME SERIES

Home Sweet Home

Trina is starting over after a painful separation from her husband of almost twenty years. Grief and loss force her to return to her hometown where she has to deal with all of the things she left behind to rebuild her life, piece by piece; a hometown she hasn't visited since high school graduation.

No Place Like Home

Lisa never thought she'd leave her high-profile finance job in the city to work in a small-town bakery. She also never expected to still be single in her forties.

MYSTERIES

White Picket Lies

Fighting the demons of her past Toni finds herself in the midst of a second marriage breakdown at forty seven years of age. She struggles to keep depression at bay while doing her best to raise a wayward teenaged son and uncover the identity of the killer.

In this small town investigation, it's only a matter of time until friends and neighbours turn on each other.

AUTHOR'S NOTE

I first read about Janek Kostanski in an old newspaper article, listed in the Sydney Morning Herald, titled "Heroic saviour of the Warsaw ghetto". I'm not sure how I stumbled across it, but as I read it, tears fell down my cheeks. It was clear to me that Janek, and his family, had lived a story that needed to be told, and I was astounded that no one had done so yet.

Due to the death of all of the characters in this tale by the time I learned of it, I have relied in places on constructing scenes and dialogue based solely on my imagination. Some interactions are informed by my research but most have only a few lines of description available in the collective texts that can be found in English language resources.

In certain parts of the story I have also compressed characters. For example, Josef Albert Meisinger, the Butcher of Warsaw, who I've commingled with the story of Oskar Dirlewanger. Dirlewanger's role and personality was not much different to Meisinger's.

I have used poetic licence surrounding such characters and where they might've been, or what they might've done in various situations for the sake of narrative cohesion. I have also dramatised events that primary sources outlined with much more compacted descriptions.

As a result, the story you have read is not a narrative nonfiction piece, but an historical fiction novel that skews as closely to what has been described by the people involved, or recorded in historical depictions, as I could manage to make it.

The essentials of this storyline are true. The dramatisation is from my imagination. Janek Kostanski was at least as heroic as my descriptions have allowed him to be. It is certain there are many details missing as these are the highlights as described by him in interviews and letters.

His mother is as heroic as Janek, perhaps more so when you consider that she went against every instinct to protect her own children, by continually helping another family in the face of egregious danger. However, Włodzisława (who I have called Waltrina for ease of pronunciation), unfortunately did not write letters or give interviews, that I could find. And so I have depicted her through Janek's eyes.

The truth includes the fact that Janek did smuggle supplies and food to his Jewish *family* whose home was separated from his by a wall through their courtyard. He did take Nacha to the movies, risking both their lives for a bit of fun in a dark world. He was arrested by the Gestapo with fifty Jewish boys who were all killed, while he was beaten and had his teeth knocked out before being rescued by his mother.

Also, Jadzia *was* interred in an extermination camp and only escaped death due to her mother's bargaining skills. And Antoni (Ajzyk), Nathan and Nacha *were* all bound for Treblinka on a train when they managed to escape through the window and back to Aunt Irka's. These facts, and many others related in the story, are all true and are more dramatic than anything an imagination could conjure.

The heinous crimes listed in this book, done by the Nazi

invaders, are also unfortunately true, though dramatised for the purposes of the narrative.

I hope you enjoyed reading Janek's story and that he brings you hope, as he did me, that there are good people in the world, willing to risk their lives to save another.

Warmest regards,

Lilly Mirren

DISCUSSION GUIDE

BOOK CLUB QUESTIONS

1. Can you identify some of the themes running through the book?

2. Who was your favourite character, and why?

3. What would you have done when it came time to smuggle the family out of the ghetto?

4. How did beliefs about the inherent goodness of people impact the decisions characters made throughout the story?

5. Discuss how it would feel to be rejected by your community.

6. Can you identify with the reactions of any of the characters?

7. How did the main characters change and grow?

8. What motivated Janek?

9. How do you think you would have reacted to the Nazi rule in Warsaw?

10. Describe your thoughts about Waltrina and Antoni, and how they led their families through the war.

ABOUT THE AUTHOR

Lilly Mirren is a USA Today Bestselling author who has sold over one million copies of her books worldwide. She lives in Brisbane, Australia with her husband and three children.

She always dreamed of being a writer and is now living that dream. When she's not writing, she's chasing her children or spending time with friends.

Her books combine heartwarming storylines with realistic characters readers can't get enough of. Her debut series, The Waratah Inn, set in the delightful Cabarita Beach, hit the USA Today Bestseller list and since then, has touched the hearts of hundreds of thousands of readers across the globe.